Fantasy on Parade

THE WALT DISNEY PARADE
OF FUN, FACT, FANTASY AND FICTION

WITH ILLUSTRATIONS BY THE WALT DISNEY STUDIO

Purnell

Contents

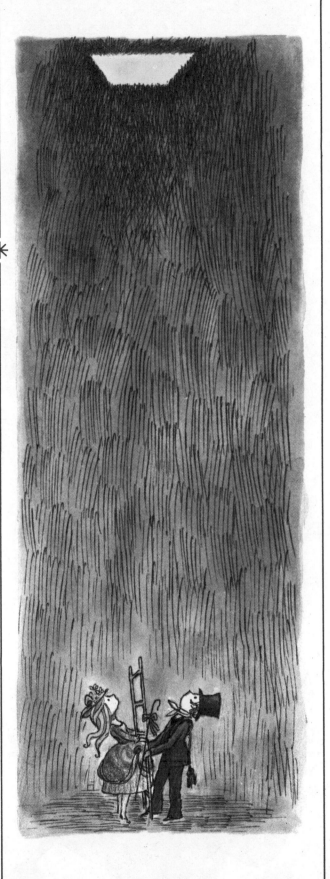

Pecos Bill

Great Cowboy

Down Texas way a river flows. Where it comes from no one knows. Where it is going to no one cares, so long as it runs away from there! It is the Pecos River. It was down in the valley of that river that Pecos Bill made his home.

The story of Pecos Bill began this way: A covered wagon was crossing the Texas plains. Lots of wagons were in those days. Everyone was looking for more room out in the wide West.

The family in this wagon really needed elbow room. The wagon was filled to the top with big boys and small ones, little girls and tall ones. There were pots and pans and jars and crocks and churns. That wagon was full! It was noisy, too, what with children talking and laughing and crying, all at the same time. So perhaps it isn't surprising that no one noticed when the smallest boy of all, a baby named Bill, rolled off the back of the wagon and went bouncing away. . . .

The wagon rolled on, and there sat the baby, baby Bill, all alone on the Texas plain. Well, he wasn't really alone. There were animals aplenty. When one coyote pup came sniffing along, Bill followed that pup, and by nightfall they reached a coyote den.

When the mother coyote came home, it was quite a surprise for her to find that a strange little critter had joined her litter! She could soon see he was tough, though, a match for any pup. He could out-scrap and out-howl all the rest right off, so the mother coyote made him feel at home. And that's where Bill grew up.

Soon he knew every trick the coyotes knew, and he learned a thing or two from other animals as well. He had hardly cut his baby teeth before he could out-hiss any snake. By the time he was three he could out-jump a jack rabbit. Before he was four he could outrun a deer.

7

When Bill was seven or nine or thereabouts—no one was keeping much track—a stranger appeared in Pecos Land. It was a baby horse. That little colt was all alone and about tuckered out. A pack of vultures was wheeling around, circling lower and lower overhead, just waiting for the end.

Then Bill appeared, young Pecos Bill. He sailed into those vultures and set their feathers flying. He found the poor colt some water. He took him home and gave him some food.

From that time on, if you saw Pecos Bill you were sure to see the horse. Those two were always together, close as warts on a toad. Not that they always agreed. When the time came for the horse to be broken to saddle, they had one big disagreement. Seemed the horse plumb didn't want a saddle on his back. He didn't want to be ridden. Matter of fact, he was tough about it. Only thing was, Pecos Bill was tougher, as that bronco soon discovered. Pecos was soon in the saddle to stay.

When word got around of the great bronco-buster, some cowboys there in the Texas country figured they were as tough as anyone around, and they could ride that mustang, too. So they tried. Kept a crew busy for quite a spell picking those cowboys up and carting them away after they'd taken their turns. That's when Pecos Bill's horse got his name—Widowmaker.

And that's how Pecos Bill got his career—cowboy. He was the roughest, toughest cowboy

west of the Alamo. Bill and his horse Widow-maker were known through all the West. That is to say, Bill and his horse—and his rope! For Bill could rope with his lariat anything he could see.

Bill said, "I could rope the lightning, or a drop of falling rain."

No one doubted him, least of all after the day the cyclone came. That day the Texas sky was dark. A howling, twisting cyclone was blowing out of nowhere down on the Texas plains. It was knocking the legs out from under horses. It was blowing away cows and barns. That cyclone was bad, all right, but what could anybody do to stop it? Somebody thought of Bill.

Pecos Bill was ready to try. He jumped right onto that swift black cloud, and settled down. While the cyclone heaved and bucked and blew, Pecos harnessed it with his rope. He tamed it to a breeze!

By this time Bill had got himself a herd of cattle. He was mighty proud of those cows. But a band of cow thieves came whooping down the Pecos Valley. They were rounding up prize beef. When Bill came down from that cyclone trip, he found that the thieves had made off with his whole herd.

Bill didn't like that. He didn't like it one bit. He and Widowmaker started out after the thieves, and caught up with them in the hills. What a beating Bill gave those fellows! He roped them and he shook them and he slapped them around. All the gold flew out of the bad men's teeth, folks say. That is why there is gold in those hills to this day.

Bill and Widowmaker started for home, driving Bill's whole herd. They had a mighty wide desert to cross, mile after mile of burning sand. First they ran out of grass for the cattle. Then Bill ran out of food. That was bad enough; but even worse, they all needed water. Even Bill's canteen was dry.

Bill knew he and his herd would never make it home if he couldn't find some water. He was really burned dry, and so were the poor cows. So Bill took a stick and he dug in the sand. He scraped till he dug the whole Rio Grande!

There is another time folks tell about. Some Indians were on the warpath. They got out their war paint, and they painted themselves up for battle from head to toe. They looked mighty wild and rough, and they felt it!

They built a big campfire and got out their drums, and they started up a wild war dance. "We heap big warriors, hoo hoo hoo!" they chanted as they danced. What a hullabaloo! "Ugh!" they cried. "We tough guys! Each one tougher than two."

But they had forgotten Pecos Bill!

Bill heard about the Indians' plans. "I'll fix those Injuns," he said. And those who heard him saw his eyes begin to glow.

Bill and Widowmaker started out by night on the Indians' trail. They raised a blazing cloud of stardust behind them on the plain.

"Smoke signals!" cried the Indians. "Big trouble heading this way!" And they started to run.

Closer came the dust cloud under Widowmaker's pounding hoofs. Faster and faster the Indians ran. They ran right out of their war paint! Yessirree! Left it in bright streaks behind them on the desert's rocky walls. You can see it in Arizona to this day, there in the Painted Desert.

To celebrate, Pecos Bill threw a leg over a cloud and started shooting stars out of the sky. Bang, bang, bang! Down went star after star, till there was just one big bright one left in the sky.

Bill blew on his gun and put it back in his holster.

"I'll leave that star for Texas," he said.

And that is why Texas is known still as the Lone Star State.

Seemed there was nothing Bill couldn't handle, until along came Sluefoot Sue. She came riding down the river on a giant fish. Fresh as the dew on a prairie rose was Sue. She was also the first woman Pecos Bill had seen.

When he looked at her, he felt a pounding in his ears and a churning in his chest. His blood was a-boiling and his stomach did flip-flops, so he knew this must be love.

This was agreeable to Sue, and they set a wedding day. But there was a price Bill had to pay.

"First," said Sue, "I want a bouncy bustle. It's the latest style these days."

That was fine with Bill. He made her one from a bunch of wire springs.

"Second," said Sue, batting her eyes of blue, "I want to ride Widowmaker."

Ride Widowmaker? That was not so easy. Bill was willing, but how about Widowmaker? He was a tough old one-man horse. Nothing had ever come between him and Bill. Would the first thing be sweet Sue?

Widowmaker tossed his head and he whinnied and snorted. But at last Pecos Bill sweet-talked him into letting Sue jump into the saddle on his back.

Sue was pleased—but then, she didn't see the mean look in old Widowmaker's eye.

Well, away they went, Widowmaker and Sue. Everyone in the Pecos land was there to watch. And Widowmaker really gave them a show. He put on a one-horse rodeo. He kicked and he galloped. He snorted and he bucked. He rolled his mean old fiery eyes. But Sue stuck on.

She hung on as tight as a saddle bur—until her bustle began to bounce! *Sproing!* went those wire springs. Up went Sue! Down she came into the saddle again. *Sproing!* went the springs, and up again she flew.

Higher and higher and *higher* bounced Sue, up, up into the sky. There was just one chance to save her. That was Pecos Bill's lariat. He'd roped bears and flying buzzards, he had roped a railroad train. He had roped a whirling cyclone and a drop of falling rain. Surely he could lasso Sluefoot Sue!

Bill coiled his lariat. He swung the loop of rope. Sue bounced once more, and as she flew, he let the coil of rope fly, too.

No one spoke, no one breathed as the rope snaked upward after the soaring figure of Sue. Then the loop of the lariat quivered in the air. Down it came. Pecos Bill had missed.

The crowd could not believe it. They were plumb baffled. But they hadn't looked at Widowmaker. They hadn't seen the mean look in his flashing old eye as he stepped on the end of Bill's rope!

Sue sailed on up into the sky, out of sight behind a cloud. And she was never seen again.

That broke Bill's heart. He rode away across the plains and he never returned. Some say he went back to the coyotes. They say that when the coyotes howl at the moon when it is full, you can hear Pecos Bill howling with them. He is lonesome, they say, for Sluefoot Sue, still bouncing somewhere among the clouds.

That's not real certain, but one thing is sure: Ask who the greatest cowboy is and still everyone in Texas land will tell you, "Pecos Bill!"

Paul Bunyan

Giant of the Forest

In the great Northland the rivers run swift, and trees grow tall enough to blot out the sun. It takes big men to tame that timber and float the logs down through white water to the lumber mills.

Yes, lumbering men are a big, proud lot. But they take off their caps at the name of Paul Bunyan, the greatest logger of them all.

Where Paul was born is not quite clear. Some say he's a Downeaster from the State of Maine. They say his cradle was so big it was anchored in the ocean off the shore. It rocked up waves that tumbled in to make the highest tides ever seen.

When Paul learned to walk, he once tumbled down and flattened all the trees on the hill above his town—which may or may not have been Wiscasset, Maine.

It took the whole town to raise that child. In one meal he drank all the milk a herd of cows could give in a week. And making his clothes kept the women sewing from dawn to dark.

The folks of that village kept on feeding and clothing and loving the boy until he became a fine, hungry giant of a man, sixty-three axe handles high. Then he saw that he was eating them out of house and home, so Paul went out West, where there was lots of room.

Paul had no more than reached the Middle West when the Winter of the Blue Snow came howling down. Yessir, the snow was blue with cold that year.

One day as Paul was snowshoeing over the countryside, he saw a big blue drift shiver and shake. Well, he shoved away the drift, and discovered a calf, turned blue from the cold.

13

That calf was no more than six feet high, so Paul thawed him out and named him Babe and took him home for a pet. But Babe grew two feet every time anyone looked at him! Soon he was quite some size—as big for an ox as Paul was for a man. That was going some! And he stayed bright blue.

When spring came, Paul and Babe wandered around the countryside, looking for a job their size. Babe's hoofs sank into the soft spring ground as they went. The spring rains filled the hoof-prints and made the lakes you see to this day out in Wisconsin and Minnesota.

Paul took another look around the country-side. "Trees!" he said to Babe. "That's what grows biggest in this ground. Trees are the crop for you and me. We'll set us up a lumber camp, Babe my friend!"

So they did. They set up a camp deep in the north woods. Paul melted down seventy-seven ax blades to make him one fifteen-foot, two-bladed ax. In one swing he could flatten all the trees on a four-acre plot. If he happened to miss a few on a swing, he'd pick them off as he pulled the ax back.

Paul moved around the country a lot, looking over timberland. It was rough country for travel in those days, but that was no trouble to Paul. He could cross big Lake Superior in three good jumps. The Mississippi he could jump across and back without touching.

When Paul needed a meal, he could always do some hunting. There were plenty of bear, deer, moose, and wolves around in those days—though even Paul would admit that wolf meat doesn't make much of a meal. When Paul was hunting,

14

just for fun he liked to straighten out twisting animal trails. He'd fasten Babe's harness to one end and just pull away in a good straight line. You could hear the crunching back in the trees as that old trail straightened out. One of those trails makes the boundary line between the Dakotas today.

Babe was handy in other ways too. When Paul and his crew got their first forest lumbered off, they found they had forgotten something. There was no river to float the logs down. They were a good long distance from a sawmill and there were no roads between.

That didn't stop Paul for long. He hitched Babe to a plow and they dug them a river, right over to the Mississippi, and the logs went floating down. The Missouri, folks call that stream Babe and Paul Bunyan dug.

The lumbermen got a great kick out of watching Paul and Babe at work. That was one reason loggers from east and west came looking for a chance to work in his camp. But there were other reasons why they liked Paul Bunyan's camp best of all.

Take Paul's cook shack; it was really big. He had horse-drawn teams to carry loads of food down the long rows of tables and get it to the men good and hot. There were boys on roller skates to pass salt and pepper and bread and butter in a hurry.

Out in the kitchen was the famous pancake griddle, bigger than a school gymnasium. Paul hired boys whose whole job was to keep that griddle greased. They skated all day on its red-hot top, wearing slabs of bacon strapped to their feet. The wise ones strapped extra slabs to the seat of their pants in case of a fall.

Once, for a treat, the cook popped popcorn on the griddle. Well, the corn popped up in such a blizzard that the cook boys were lost, twenty of them. It took them eight days to eat their way out of the great drifts of popcorn.

Some great meals were stirred up in Paul Bunyan's cook shack, all right. But they took a lot of planning, too. Paul logged off all the trees in North and South Dakota. Then with a shovel he flattened all the mountain tops, and he laid out farms to grow vegetables.

Of course there were some stumps left, but Paul pounded them down into the ground with a mallet, one blow to a stump. Soon the ground was as level as a table, all set for seeds. When the garden plots got dry, Paul would roll up some clouds wherever he found them and bring them back to give his fields a good soaking rain.

There were times, though, when even that garden didn't keep the camp in food. For example, there was the Year of the Two Winters. Summer never did come. As soon as one winter was over, the next one began. It snowed and snowed.

The trees were covered with snow, so the men couldn't work. They hung around in the bunkhouses, singing and roughhousing. When they decided to get some shut-eye, they found the flames in the lanterns had frozen! Couldn't sleep with all those lantern lights, so they threw the flames out into the snow. Forgot all about 'em until spring came when those flames melted down and set the woods on fire. But that's another story. Back in the dead of winter the men still had to eat, and the camp ran out of food in that Year of Two Winters.

Paul set out with Babe the Blue Ox to see what he could find. All he found was a load of dried peas. Well, that was better than nothing. So Paul started to haul it back to camp.

He was nearly home when, as he crossed a frozen lake, the ice broke. In went the load of peas, wagon and all!

That was bad, but it wasn't enough to stop Paul. He called his men from the camp nearby. They shoveled away the snow and cut down all the trees around the shore of that lake. They heaped up the logs and set them afire. Well, sir, they turned that whole lake into one big soup pot. They had a lake full of green pea soup.

They froze some on sticks, like lollipops, and took them to the woods for lunch as the snow began to melt. But by the end of the week they were sick of pea soup. By the time the snow was gone, that lumber crew never wanted to hear the words p-- s--- again.

It was the following spring when a strange thing happened. Paul set up camp on a river bank, and his men soon filled the river with logs. When the time came for the big drive, crews started downriver with the rafts of logs. Day after day they floated down, with nothing but forests on the banks. After some days they spotted a lumber camp on the river bank. That was a welcome sight. They waved and shouted greetings. Then they rubbed their eyes and looked again.

It was their own camp they were drifting by! That river ran around in a circle; they were back where they had started from. You can hear men tell even today of that Round River drive.

They tell, too, of the dry spell in the Big Onion River country. That year no rain fell. First the leaves dried up on all the trees. By the time Paul's crew got the timber cut and stacked for the drive, the river had dried up, too. Now that was bad. Just one spark could burn up their whole winter's work. And they couldn't sell timber stacked up in the woods.

So Paul and Babe set off again. This time they bought up the whole onion crop of Kansas, Nebraska, and Iowa. When they came back, Paul fed the men raw onions until every man was weeping a steady stream of tears right into the river bed. Soon that river was racing along again, and Paul and his men drove their logs down a river of onion tears.

Oh, those were the days, when the West was

young and the logging camps were in full swing. But it didn't take long for crews like Paul's to slash through the forests. Farms began to grow up where towering trees had stood. Towns grew up among the farms. Soon the country was plumb settled; there wasn't room for Paul Bunyan.

Paul and Babe had worked their way west clear to the Pacific Coast. Now when the great Northwest went civilized too, with power saws buzzing in the woods, Paul and Babe turned their backs on it all and headed north.

Some say Paul has a camp near Hudson Bay. Some say he is logging Alaskan trees. Men who wander in the forests and listen to the breeze say that now and then they hear a deep voice singing far away:

Oh, everybody's heard of me,
The logging man, Paul Bunyan,
How me and Babe the Big Blue Ox
Made camp on the old Big Onion.

We cut trees on a mountain
That stood upon its head.
We straightened crooked rivers
To find out where they led. . . .

If you wander in the forest, just listen to the breeze. You may hear a deep voice far away, singing through the trees. See Northern Lights a-glimmering in curtains, fans, and wheels? That's Babe and old Paul Bunyan just kicking up their heels!

17

Windwagon Smith

Prairie Sailor

Bᴀᴄᴋ in the days when the West was young, there were scouts and explorers and fighting men who blazed trails into the wilds. Close behind them came the pioneers with their families, rolling by the wagonload out to the free lands to make themselves new homes.

No sooner did a pioneer get up the walls and roofs of a new home than his wife began thinking of things she wanted. She wanted salt for the salt box and flour for the flour barrel and a nice piece of side pork for the stew kettle. She also hankered for turkey red curtains and fancy oil lamps, hair ribbons for the girls and knee patches for the boys, and a new bonnet for herself to wear to the nearest town.

So pretty soon there were traders on the trails, hauling goods to sell to the pioneers. The Oregon Trail and the Santa Fe Trail were the two that were known the best. It was on the trail to old Santa Fe down in Mexican Territory that this tale was spun.

Its proper beginning was up in Kansas in a

little prairie town. That little town, Old Westport, mostly just drowsed in the dust under the Kansas sun. It only woke up when a wagon train was gathering for the long haul, nearly a thousand miles, down to Santa Fe. Then every man jack dreamed a dream of the riches to be made hauling freight to Santa Fe.

One day things were so quiet you could hear two little dust motes colliding in a sunbeam, if you opened your eyes to listen. The city fathers were sitting in a row on the porch of the Star of the West. This café was, so to speak, the social center of the town; and there sat the city fathers with their chairs tilted back and their feet on the porch rail, with their eyes shut, thinking deep thoughts.

"Ahoy there!" a voice bellowed, and every eye snapped open at once to gaze on a wondrous sight.

Drawn up in front of the Star of the West was a covered Conestoga wagon—but such a cov-

ered wagon as they'd never seen before. Like the usual ones, it was high as a house, with wheels as tall as a man. But this one had no teams of dusty oxen out in front. Instead, on top of the wagon a deck ran from stem to stern, for all the world like a ship at sea. Aloft was a mast rigged with a tattered sail to catch the prairie wind. And at the rear—beg your pardon, the stern—a tiller swung a rudder.

"A gen-u-ine prairie schooner!" gasped one of the city fathers.

With a clang an anchor dropped over the side, landing neat as a horseshoe around a hitching post. And from the deck a voice like a foghorn called again, "Avast, me hearties!"

Down rattled every foot from the porch rail as the city fathers sprang to attention. Mayor Crum stepped forward.

"Howdy!" said the Mayor, after clearing his throat. "Stranger, where are you from?"

"Avast there, lubbers!" said the stranger. "My

name is Captain Smith, and I come from the seven seas. Now I've built me this tidy schooner and cruised to the West to sail the lone prairies."

"Hmm," said the Mayor, thinking deep, "no oxen to feed, I see. As for your sails, we know there's wind enough in Kansas. Tell me, sir, can your craft haul freight?"

"You can bet your last blinking barnacle," cried Cap'n Smith. "Freight is ballast, you know. Her hold will take a full cargo. She'll sail the prairie as if it were the sea."

As he spoke, he slid down a rope to the street, and in less than the time it takes to say "Windwagon Smith's Conestoga Schooner," Cap'n Smith and the city fathers were gathered around a table in the Star of the West, deep in palaver.

"Now look at the course charted here on the map, the trail that leads down to old Santa Fe," Cap'n Smith said to the Kansas folk. "Oxen and wagons take almost two months. I'll sail it in fourteen days."

The storekeeper was a sharp one for figuring things out, so he took pencil in hand with a pad. He scratched down some figures and added them.

"That's a quarter of the time," he said. He wrote some more figures and pushed them about. "Why, that's four times the profit! Land sakes!"

"With a whole fleet of windwagons," the Mayor said dreamily, "look at the money we'd make!"

Captain Smith pulled out a thick wad of papers. The men gathered around. "Just so happens," smiled Smith, "that I have charts here with me for a super windwagon you might like to see."

Well, before that meeting disbanded they had settled a thing or two.

"We'll name her the *Prairie Clipper!*" Mayor Crum soon decreed.

He and the others dipped into their wallets

for money to pay for the keel. And they settled the bargain with handshakes over bowls of buffalo stew.

Now the waitress at the Star of the West was Molly, the Mayor's daughter. A beautiful girl was she, with hair like a Zanzibar sunset and eyes like the deep-blue sea. While the town leaders were busy adding up their profits in their heads, Captain Smith kept his eyes on Molly, adding up this and that, too.

There was no drowsing in Old Westport on sunny days from then on. Everyone was busy working on the clipper. They laid out the keel, with ribs of the stoutest hickory and white oak. They chose the sturdiest birch for the wheels. They sawed and they hammered and planed.

But every night after work was done, Captain Smith and Molly climbed to the craft's highest perch. There they'd sit beneath the same moon that shines down on the seven seas, with buffalo grass billowing all around. And Captain Smith would tell her tales of life on the ocean deep.

Well, the keel was laid, the hull was caulked, the deck was holystoned, the mast was raised. The Ladies Sewing Circle marched down Main Street to present the sail. And the *Prairie Clipper* was ready for launching.

What a sight for everyone's eyes! Her twelve-foot wheels rose from the grass tops. Her mast seemed to scrape the skies!

Up the gangplank marched all the investors. No one noticed that in the excitement sweet Molly had stowed away. Then the brass band played. Captain Smith raised the sail. He grabbed the long tiller as the sail billowed out in the Kansas breeze. And the windwagon started to roll!

What a cheer went up from the watching crowd as the *Prairie Clipper* headed down the Santa Fe trail, picking up speed like a song. The city fathers lined the rail, waving their hats with pride.

Out into the sea of buffalo grass the windship pointed her prow. The Captain hauled on the tiller pole to steer her this way around a hill where coyotes sang, that way around an Indian camp.

Faster and faster the windwagon rolled. She swayed and she rattled and bumped. One by one the city fathers left the rail and staggered down into the hold, where they groaned and they moaned as they were thumped about.

"Let us out!" cried the Mayor. "Put us ashore. Stop this contraption or we'll sue!"

"Right you are!" said the Captain. "Hold on tight and I'll bring her about."

He pushed on the tiller. The axles groaned. The windwagon laid over hard, tumbling the men in the hold. Then she swung in a halfcircle, turning back toward town, with the sail angling out from the mast.

Captain Smith took a deep breath and pulled on the tiller to straighten her out on course. Doggone it, the wheels stuck fast!

Smith pulled and he tugged with all his might, but those wheels would not unjam! They cut a swath through the buffalo grass in a circle two miles wide.

Now each time the wagon circled near the town, a man or two would jump out. The townsfolk gathered to watch their neighbors return and to pick them up and dust them off.

When the men were all ashore, the wagon still sailed. The townsfolk could see Captain Smith on the deck. They could hear him cry as the wagon sailed by, "Farewell! I'll go down with the wreck!"

But what was this? Next time the wagon hove into sight, there was sweet Molly at the Captain's side. She had climbed from her hiding place in the hold to join Windwagon Smith at his lonely post.

"You'd better get off!" cried the Captain. "We're in for a blow from a hurricane. I'm afraid her seams will rip."

Sure enough, across the prairie loomed a mean-looking black cloud.

"We can ride it out, Captain!" sang Molly.

But just then the twister hit! As the windwagon sunfished and tilted and bucked, the tiller wrenched itself free.

"We *will* ride out the gale!" cried the Captain. "I can steer her again!"

He got a firm grip on the tiller, and away they sailed, straight as a string. But that twister spun down and picked up the windwagon. The last the townsfolk saw of it, the *Prairie Clipper* was sailing off on the top of the storm as the twister departed, due west.

That old windwagon was never seen again. But in tales the oldtimers told they spoke of a ship they saw in the clouds when the sunset had turned to gold. She'd be sailing across the painted sky, with Windwagon Smith at the tiller, and sweet Molly standing close by his side. They said you could hear Cap'n Smith a-singing high above:

Yippy-ay, we're sailing,
A-sailing are we,
Just Molly and I
On the lone prairie
In our wagon way up in the sky, the sky,
In our windwagon up in the sky.

John Henry

Down on the Chesapeake and Ohio Railroad line, work on the Big Bend Tunnel was coming along just fine. There was a crew of rough, tough workmen the likes of which you seldom see. And the men who set the beat for the others to compete with was a fellow named John Henry.

John Henry was a big man. "And hollow!" said his Ma. "He was born hungry, that child, hungriest youngun I ever saw! Day he was born, he ate hog jowls and turnip greens, three whole kettles full—biggest meal I've ever seen. Then he asked for a mess of black-eyed peas, and he chewed on a ham bone to cut him some teeth."

On meals like that, John Henry grew and grew. He had muscles like tree trunks. His height was seven feet two.

He liked to play and sing; and as he grew to be a man, he married him a pretty wife, name of Polly Ann.

Came the time to find his life work, John Henry looked around. No farming for him; he wanted something hard to pound! He tried working in a factory, tried cutting down trees, tried being a mill hand; he was content with none of these. Then someone happened by and put a hammer in his hand.

"I have found my work!" John Henry cried. "I'll hammer to beat the band."

John Henry and his hammer went to work, building a railroad track. He'd hammer steel ten hours straight, eat a meal and hurry right back.

Wham went his hammer! Loud he sang,
"I will live and die with my hammer in my hand."
Wham went his hammer! *Bang* went the beat.
To watch him lead that crew was a powerful treat.
Wham went his hammer! It flashed like gold.
John Henry pounded steel like butter, we are told.
Wham went his hammer! Rock split in two.
The Big Bend Tunnel was three quarters through!

One day John Henry was sick, and his pretty Polly Ann took his place and worked with his hammer like a man. But the boss man off in the city wanted speed. He saw a picture in a book.

"This is what we need!" the boss man cried, and he bought a steam drill. "This will speed our work up if anything will!"

The steam drill arrived, manned by a sawed-off fellow. My, you should have heard John Henry bellow!

"It's the devil's own contraption!" John Henry cried. "What's more, I could outwork it, any day I tried."

"Fine!" said the boss man. "Let's have a race."
They picked the rocky tunnel mouth for the place.

"Thirty-five minutes," the boss man said.

"I'll beat that drill," John Henry cried, "or drop down dead!"

Wham went his hammer. *Buzz* went the drill.

Wham flashed the hammer, faster until the clock ticked around toward the race's end.

John Henry's back was wet with sweat, his knees began to bend.

Polly Ann was standing by with a mess of black-eyed peas. *Wham* went his hammer!

"Stop, John Henry, please! Your heart is going to burst!" cried his pretty Polly Ann.

"I'll win this race," John Henry gasped, "and die with my hammer in my hand."

Bang went the gun. The race was done. No need to measure. John Henry had won. But there lay the winner, by the weeping Polly Ann. His great heart burst, John Henry died with his hammer in his hand.

Many a year has passed since then; many a crew has worked. But wherever this song rises up to the skies, never a man will shirk:

John Henry had a hammer.
It flashed like gold.
John Henry and his hammer
Is a tale that's often told.

He could shiver solid rock,
Or shake a mountain down.
His hammer flashed like silver;
How that man could pound!

John Henry and his hammer
Helped to build this land.
And in his pride John Henry died
With his hammer in his hand.

The Reluctant Dragon

Long ago—might have been hundreds of years ago—in a cottage half-way between this village and yonder shoulder of the Downs up there, a shepherd lived with his wife and their little son. Now the shepherd spent his days—and at certain times of the year his nights too—up on the wide ocean-bosom of the Downs, with only the sun and the stars and the sheep for company, and the friendly chattering world of men and women far out of sight and hearing. But his little son, when he wasn't helping his father, and often when he was as well, spent much of his time buried in big volumes that he borrowed from the affable gentry and interested parsons of the country round about.

One day the Boy was reading out loud.

BOY: "Then up rode Sir Hubert on his milky-white steed. 'Fear you not, Fair Maiden,' quoth he,—"

Just at that point his father, the shepherd, came rushing up all out of breath.

FATHER: It's 'orrible, son—'orrible! I seen it! 'Arfway out of 'is 'ole 'e was—covered with scales and such like—an' a tail with sort of an 'ook on it!

BOY: It's only a dragon, Father.

FATHER: Ooh—only a—only a dragon!! Oooh— I must warn the village—now don't get excited. 'Elp! Everybody lock yer doors! 'Elp! A dragon's comin'!!

As he ran down toward the village, the Boy called after him calmly.

BOY: Don't worry, Father. I'll have a look at him—soon as I've finished this chapter.

After he'd had his tea, the Boy strolled up the chalky track that led to the summit of the Downs; and there, sure enough, he found the Dragon . . .

The Dragon was taking a bath and singing happily to himself.

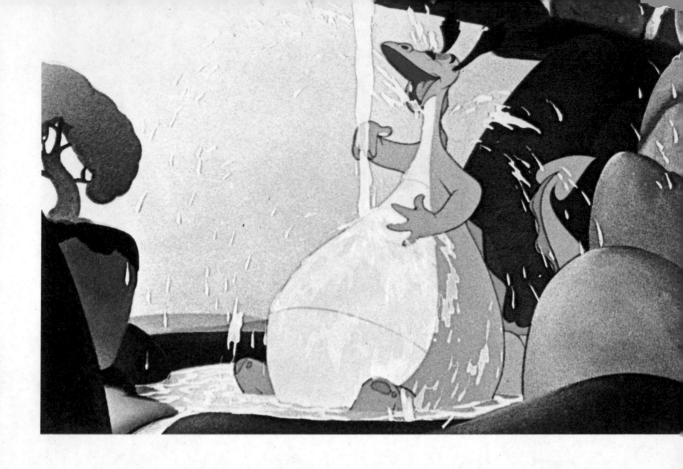

DRAGON: Mi-mi-mi-mi—! La-la la-la la-la-la-la-
la—

> The Boy stepped a little closer.

BOY: Ahem—hello—*hello,* Dragon!

DRAGON: Hello! Now, Boy—don't bung stones
at me or squirt water or anything. I
won't have it!

BOY: Oh, I just came up for a friendly chat—but
if I'm not wanted—

> Just in time, the Dragon remembered
> his manners.

DRAGON: Oh—well! Do be seated.

BOY: Thank you.

DRAGON: But if you don't mind—the other way,
please. I'll only be a minute.

> So the Boy looked the other way
> as the Dragon finished his bath.
> Then he began:

BOY: Have you had any *nice* battles lately?

DRAGON: *Battles?* No—no battles.

BOY: Oh! Too busy scourging the countryside
and devouring Fair Damsels, eh?

> The Dragon was disgusted.

DRAGON: Scourging? Devouring? Good Heavens,
no!!

BOY: But—but don't you ever do *anything*
desperate?

DRAGON: Well—*yes!* I *do* make up poetry.

> The Boy was disappointed.

BOY: Poetry?

DRAGON: Verses, you know. Care to hear my
latest sonnet?

> The Boy didn't care to, but he
> didn't want to be rude and say
> so right out.

BOY: Well, I—uh—

> The Dragon didn't wait for him to
> finish.

DRAGON: You'll love this—I call it, "Just a-Drift-
ing."
"Just a-drifting o'er the lea,
Like a dewdrop, fancy free.
Playing with the gentle breezes
Romping with the bumble beezes
Oh what fun—joy never ceases
Just a-drifting—"

The Boy felt he should get down to business immediately.

BOY: Very nice—but you're in for trouble, you know.

DRAGON: Trouble?

BOY: You see, you're a pest and a baneful monster and—

DRAGON: Not a word of truth in it! My character will bear the strictest investigation—
"Prancing, dancing to and fro—
Not too fast—not too slow,
Where the early birds are seeking,
Early worms who slyly peeking,
Hear the night owls softly shrieking,
Just a-drifting."

BOY: But you don't understand. My father's arousing the village, and they'll be here with spears and things to exterminate you! You're an enemy of the human race.

But the Dragon was so entranced with his poetry that he didn't become the least bit aroused. He simply kept on reciting happily, swaying back and forth in time to the rhythm of the words.

DRAGON: Ho-o-oh—I haven't an enemy in the world—too lazy to make 'em.
"Skipping, tripping here and there,
Hither, thither, everywhere,
Topsy-turvy, willy-nilly,
Like a silly daffydilly,
Just a-drifting."

"Oh, if you won't be sensible," cried the Boy, getting up, "I'm going off home. . . . I'll look you up tomorrow, sometime or other, and do for goodness' sake try and realize that you're a pestilential scourge, or you'll find yourself in a most awful fix. Goodnight!"

What the Boy had feared, however, soon came to pass. The most modest and retiring Dragon

in the world, if he's as big as four cart-horses and covered with blue scales, cannot keep altogether out of the public view. And so in the village tavern of nights the fact that a real live dragon sat brooding in the cave on the Downs was naturally a subject for talk. Though the villagers were extremely frightened, they were rather proud as well. It was a distinction to have a dragon of your own, and it was felt to be a feather in the cap of the village. Still, all were

agreed that this sort of thing couldn't be allowed to go on. The dreadful beast must be exterminated, the countryside must be freed from this pest, this terror, this destroying scourge. The fact that not even a hen-roost was the worse for the Dragon's arrival wasn't allowed to have anything to do with it. He was a dragon, and he couldn't deny it, and if he didn't choose to behave as such, that was his own look-out. But in spite of such valiant talk, no hero was found willing to take sword and spear and free the suffering village and win deathless fame; and each night's heated discussion always ended in nothing. Meanwhile the Dragon lolled on the turf, enjoying the sunsets, told antediluvian anecdotes to the Boy, and polished his old verses while meditating on fresh ones.

One day the Boy, on walking into the village, found everything wearing a festal appearance which was not to be accounted for in the calendar. Carpets and gay-colored stuffs were hung out of the windows, the church-bells clamored noisily, the little street was flower-strewn, and the whole population jostled each other along either side of it, chattering, shoving, and ordering each other to stand back.

As the Boy scurried along the street the people began to shout:

"Here he comes now!"

"Oh, ain't 'e 'andsome!"

"Ain't 'e grand!"

"Blimey—'e's a spectacle, 'e is!"

The Boy saw some friends in the crowd and ran over to them.

BOY: Hey! What's all the excitement?

    "It's Sir Giles, stupid!" they cried.

BOY: Sir Giles?

    "Hooray! Hooray for Sir Giles!" shouted the villagers.

BOY: Hooray for Sir Giles!

    "Hooray for the Dragon-Killer!" cried someone.

BOY: Hooray for—Sir Giles? The Dragon-Killer! Ooooooh!

    Gosh!

Presently from the far-away end of the line came the sound of more cheering. Next, the measured tramp of a great war-horse made the Boy's heart beat quicker, and then he found himself cheering with the rest, as, amidst welcoming shouts, shrill cries of women, uplifting of babies, and waving of handkerchiefs, Sir Giles paced slowly up the street. The Boy's heart stood still and he breathed with sobs, the beauty and the grace of the hero were so far beyond anything he had yet seen. His fluted armour was inlaid with gold, his

plumed helmet hung at his saddle-bow, and his thick fair hair framed a face gracious and gentle beyond expression till you caught the sternness in his eyes. He drew rein in front of the little inn, and the villagers crowded around with greetings and thanks and voluble statements of their wrongs and grievances and oppressions. The Boy heard the grave gentle voice of the Knight assuring them that all would be well now, and that he would stand by them and see them righted and free them from their foe; then he dismounted and passed through the doorway and the crowd poured in after him. But the Boy made off up the hill as fast as he could lay his legs to the ground.

As soon as he was within sight of the Dragon, the Boy shouted.

BOY: It's all up, Dragon! he's coming—he's here now!

    The Dragon remained calm as usual and spoke in cool tones.

DRAGON: Now, Boy—it's impolite to interrupt a person! Who's coming?

BOY: Sir Giles—on a big horse—with a long sword and a spear, and you'll have to fight him—

DRAGON: I never fight—never did—doesn't agree with me.

BOY: But—but—but—

DRAGON: Now, Boy, just run along. Tell Sir Giles to go away—I'm sure you can arrange it—toodle-oo.

The Boy made his way back to the village in a state of great despondency. First of all, there wasn't going to be any fight; next, his dear and honored friend the Dragon hadn't shown up in quite such a heroic light as he would have liked; and lastly, whether the Dragon was a hero at heart or not, it made no difference, for Sir Giles would most undoubtedly cut his head off. "Arrange things indeed!" he said bitterly to himself. "The Dragon treats the whole affair as if it was an invitation to tea and croquet."

The Boy decided he really must see Sir Giles. The villagers were straggling homewards as he passed up the street, all of them in the highest

spirits, and gleefully discussing the splendid fight *that was in store. The Boy pursued his way to* *the inn, and passed into the principal chamber.*

The Boy went to Sir Giles' room and paused at the door. The Knight was busily engaged with a scrubbing brush.

BOY: Excuse me, Sir. You are Sir Giles, I presume?

The Knight looked up and spoke in a kindly voice.

KNIGHT: Come, come, lad—stop mumbling.

BOY: I came to talk about the Dragon.

KNIGHT: Ah, ya-as—another tale of woe and misery. Devoured your flocks, no doubt?

BOY: Oh, no sir! He—

KNIGHT: Aha! Made off with your loving parents, has he? They shall be avenged!

BOY: You don't understand—

KNIGHT: What! Don't tell me he's kidnapped some Fair Damsel with flaxen hair, ruby lips, ivory skin—why, he can't do that to her! He shall pay dearly on the field of battle!

BOY: But that's just it—he won't fight.

KNIGHT: Ya-as, he—what! He won't fight? Preposterous! Fellow must be an infernal cad! Bit of a rotter, what?

The Boy rushed to his friend's defense.

BOY: He is not. He's a nice old Dragon who likes to write poetry.

KNIGHT: Poetry?

BOY: Yes—verses, you know.

KNIGHT: Bah Jove—how jolly! I'm a bit of a bard myself, you know.

The Boy was astonished.

BOY: *You* a poet, *too?*

KNIGHT: Ya-as—no doubt you've heard of my "Ode to a Fleecy Cloud"—
"Oh fleecy cloud
Oh cloud of fleece
Up in the sky so high
oh—
Oh my—"

But come—let's not dillydally. We must meet this fine fellow at once!

BOY: Then you'll explain to the Dragon about the fight?

KNIGHT: Ya-as—quite right. Quite so, quite so. *"You're taking a lot of trouble on your friend's* *account,"* he added good-naturedly, *as they* *passed out through the door together. "But cheer* *up! Perhaps there won't have to be any fight* *after all."*

That wasn't exactly what the Boy wanted but he said nothing. When they arrived at the cave, he greeted the Dragon first.

BOY: Hello, Dragon.

DRAGON: Oh, hello Boy. I'm having a picnic. Won't you join me?

BOY: Well—I brought a friend to explain—
The Dragon interrupted happily.

DRAGON: Well, splendid! The more the merrier! Now Boy—you sit here, and your friend can sit there.

KNIGHT: Thank you.

DRAGON: Let's see now—pickles—jam—muffins —tea. Ah, yes—here—do have a jam sandwich, Sir—ah—Sir—ah—

KNIGHT: Thank you—this is jolly!

> The Dragon whispered to the Boy.

DRAGON: What did you say your friend's name was?

BOY: Oh, that's Sir Giles.

DRAGON: Sir Giles—well!

> The Boy continued in a loud whisper.

BOY: Yes, the Dragon Killer. Pssst, Sir Giles, you'd better tell the Dragon quick!

KNIGHT: Ah, ya-as—you know, I've been looking forward to meeting you. The Boy here tells me you're quite an accomplished poet.

> The Dragon was very pleased to hear this.

DRAGON: Oh—he *did?* Really!

KNIGHT: Ya-as—and if it's not too much bother —I'd be pleased to hear you recite.

DRAGON: Oh, my dear fellow, no bother—no bother at all. Would you care for a sandwich?

KNIGHT: Bah Jove—jam!

DRAGON: Here—do have another sandwich, and a piece of cake. How about a crumpet —an olive—and a spot of tea?

KNIGHT: Thank you.

> The Knight spoke through a mouth full of food.

DRAGON: This is called, "To an Upside-Down Cake." Ahem!
"Sweet little Upside-Down Cake,
Cares and woes, you've gottem
Poor little Upside-Down Cake,
Your top is on your bottom.
Alas, little Upside-Down Cake,
Your troubles never stop,
Because, little Upside-Down Cake,
Your bottom's on your top."

KNIGHT: Bravo—how int'restin'—strawd'n'ry!

> The Boy was getting uneasy. He thought they should get to the point.

BOY: *Now,* Sir Giles—tell the Dragon *now!*

KNIGHT: Ah, ya-as—you know—I'm a bit of a bard myself.

DRAGON: Well—not really? How nice!

KNIGHT: Ya-as, ya-as quite—ahem!
"Radish so red,
"Radish so red,
Plucked from the heart
Of your warm little bed.
Sprinkled with salt
On the top of your head—
Delicious!"

DRAGON: Oh, that's *exquisite!—Simply* exquisite!

KNIGHT: Oh ya-as—quite right.
    The Boy didn't like the way things were going at all. He decided to take things into his own hands.

BOY: Do you mind if I recite a poem?

DRAGON: You? Oh, why not at all.

KNIGHT: Of course—raw-ther!
    The Boy cleared his throat.

BOY: " 'Tis evening—
From the stars above
A soft, mysterious light
Brings thoughts of friendship,
Joy, and love—
Now *how about that fight??!*

KNIGHT: Splendid! Splendid, quite!

DRAGON: Fight? Fight? There's nothing to fight about. Besides, I don't believe in it!

BOY: But Dragons and Knights always fight. You can't disappoint the whole village!

KNIGHT: Lad's right—not cricket, y'know.
    But the Dragon was firm.

DRAGON: Please—I do not wish to discuss it further. I absolutely will not fight—I refuse to listen—I won't hear of it! Good night!
    The Boy sighed and the Knight shook his head sadly.

KNIGHT: Y'know, it's a shame—it doesn't seem right. This is really a beautiful spot—

34

BOY: For a fight!

KNIGHT: Ya-as—quite right.

BOY: Why, I almost can see it—flags are a-waving—

KNIGHT: People cheering—

BOY: Bands a-playing—

KNIGHT: The Dragon appears.
What a beautiful sight!
With his scales all a-gleam
In the dawn's early light!

DRAGON: You're just flattering me.

KNIGHT: No, old fellow—it's true!—that beautiful damsel throws flowers at you.

DRAGON: At who?

KNIGHT: At *you!* Hoo-hoo!—

BOY: Look! Here comes Sir Giles on his milky-white horse!

DRAGON: His brave battle cry he's yelling, of course?

KNIGHT: SIC SEMPER TYRANNUS
TALLY-HO AND PRO TEM.
YOICKS, TEMPUS FUGIT,
AND CHERCHEZ LA FEMME!

DRAGON: As I ramp and I roar,
I cut quite a figger.

BOY: Sir Giles has a spear—
Like a sword—only bigger!

DRAGON: I get set for the charge, and—did you say "spear"?

KNIGHT: Ya-as—*spear.*

DRAGON: Oh—oh dear! No, I'll get hurt.
I won't do it! Good day!

KNIGHT: Just a second, old chap—
We might fix it this way.

DRAGON: You mean—psst-psst-psst

KNIGHT: Psst-psst-psst   Psst-psst-psst?

DRAGON: Psst-psst-psst   Psst-psst-psst

KNIGHT: Psst-psst-psst   Psst-psst-psst
Psst-psst-psst   Psst-psst-psst
Psst-psst-psst   Psst-psst-psst
The Dragon winked at the Knight.

DRAGON: OH!—
The Knight winked at the Dragon.

KNIGHT: Quite so!

DRAGON: But are you sure it's quite honest?

KNIGHT: Just a second—we'll look.

DRAGON: Nothing against it here in the book.

BOY: If it looks like a battle, I'm *sure* it's all right.

KNIGHT: Very well—then it's settled.
Tomorrow we fight. Good night.

BOY: Good night.

DRAGON: Good night.

KNIGHT: Good night.
Sir Giles and the Boy started back toward the village. The Dragon chuckled to himself.

DRAGON: There's going to be a fight—
There's going to be—
A fight? But Boy! Sir Giles! Just a minute—
Wait! Oh, why don't I keep my big mouth shut!

Next morning the people began streaming up to the Downs at quite an early hour, in their Sunday clothes and carrying baskets with bottlenecks sticking out of them, everyone intent on securing good places for the combat.

But things were in a terrible state inside the Dragon's cave. The Dragon was disconsolate and the Boy didn't know what to do to help the situation.

DRAGON: It's no use—you might as well tell the people to go away. I can't do it—

BOY: Aw, but try again.

DRAGON: You've got to be mad to breathe fire. And I'm not mad at anybody.

BOY: But try real hard—*concentrate!*

The Dragon, with a terrific effort, managed to cough out a tiny puff of smoke and a small weak flame. He looked at the Boy apologetically.

DRAGON: Not very good, is it?

BOY: Terrible! Too bad you're not a real dragon, instead of a punk poet.

The Dragon pricked up his ears.

DRAGON: *Punk poet!* Say that again!

BOY: *Punk poet!*

Then lo and behold, clouds of black smoke and long tongues of flame began to issue from the Dragon's throat.

DRAGON: Say it again!

BOY: PUNK POET!

DRAGON: Again!

BOY: PUNK POET!

DRAGON: WHOO-WHOO! I'M MAD!

BOY: PUNK POET, PUNK POET, PUNK POET

The Dragon became a fearsome sight as the insulting words lashed at him. The Boy was delighted!

The higher portions of the ground were now black with sightseers, and presently a sound of cheering and a waving of handkerchiefs told that something was visible to them. . . . A minute more and Sir Giles' red plumes topped the hill, as the Knight rode slowly forth on the great level space which stretched up to the grim mouth of the cave. Very gallant and beautiful he looked on his tall war-horse, his golden armor glancing in the sun, his great spear held erect, the little white pennon, crimson-crossed, fluttering at its point. He drew rein and remained motionless. The lines of spectators began to give back a little, nervously; and even the boys in front stopped pulling hair and cuffing each other, and leaned forward expectantly. . . .

A low muttering, mingled with snorts, now made

itself heard; rising to a bellowing roar that seemed to fill the plain. Then a cloud of smoke obscured the mouth of the cave, and out of the midst of it the Dragon himself, shining, sea-blue, magnificent, pranced splendidly forth; and everybody said, "Oo-oo-oo!" as if he had been a mighty rocket! His scales were glittering, his long spiky tail lashed his sides, his claws tore up the turf and sent it flying high over his back, and smoke and fire incessantly jetted from his angry nostrils.

The Knight was amazed.

KNIGHT: Bah Jove!

The Dragon was playing his part with all the fire at his command. He roared at the crowd.

DRAGON: Boo!

He emitted great smoke rings—
Boo boo! Boo boo boo!!
Then he disappeared behind a rock.

KNIGHT: Dragon! I say, Dragon!
    'Strawdinary—blighter's disappeared!
      The Dragon peeked out playfully.

DRAGON: Yoo-hoo! Here I am!

KNIGHT: Oh—so you are.
    The Dragon was pleased with himself.

DRAGON: How'm I doing?

KNIGHT: I say, old boy—stop acting so silly, will you? I mean this is serious business, y'know.
    So the Dragon accommodatingly changed his mood. He began screaming as though he were terribly afraid of Sir Giles.

DRAGON: Help! Help! Oh! Help!

Sir Giles pretended to pursue the Dragon into the cave. The delighted crowd heard what seemed to be a violent battle going on. Groans and shouts and cries for help issued from the cave. But inside, the Boy was seeing something very different from a fight to the death. The Dragon was serving tea for the benefit of Sir Giles, while both of them screamed and yelled for the benefit of the crowd outside.

DRAGON: One lump or two?—Ouch!

KNIGHT: Don't mind if I do—You bounder!

DRAGON: HELP! HELP! HELP!

They finished their tea, giving great howls of pain between sips.

KNIGHT: Now—I'll chase you.

The Dragon obligingly ran out of the cave with the enthusiastic Knight at his heels, the Boy running after them. Then out on the Downs in a cloud of smoke, the finish of the fight took place. The Knight gave the word.

KNIGHT: Sorry, old chap—the time has come, y'know.

DRAGON: You mean I die now?

KNIGHT: Ah ya-as indeed—as per agreed
We'll seal our pact, old thing,
With just a dash of catsup.

DRAGON: Oh Death, where is thy sting?

With a last yell, the Dragon rolled over on the ground and the Knight

triumphantly placed his foot on his foe's neck. It was all so realistic that the Boy ran to them breathlessly.

BOY: Dragon! Dragon, speak to me—are you all right?

As he approached, the Dragon lifted one large eyelid, winked solemnly, and collapsed again. He was held fast to earth by the neck, but the Knight had hit him in the exact place agreed upon, and it didn't even seem to tickle.

"Ain't you goin' to cut 'is 'ead orf, master?" asked one of the applauding crowd. . . .

"Well, not today, I think," replied Sir Giles pleasantly. "You see, that can be done at any time. There's no hurry at all. . . . I'll give him a good talking-to, and you'll find he'll be a very different dragon!"

Then Sir Giles began to talk very earnestly to the Dragon in private, and as it seemed a good time to eat, everyone got out their baskets and started to picnic.

After refreshment, Sir Giles made a speech, in which he informed his audience that he had removed their direful scourge, at a great deal of trouble and inconvenience to himself, and now they weren't to go about grumbling and fancying they'd got grievances, because they hadn't. . . . Then he told them that the Dragon had been thinking over things, and saw that there were two sides to every question, and he wasn't going to do it any more, and if they were good perhaps he'd stay and settle down there. So they must make friends, and not be prejudiced, and go about fancying they knew everything there was to be known, because they didn't, not by a long way.

Whereupon the Dragon felt called upon to make a speech too.

DRAGON: Cross my heart and hope to die,
      I'm a reformed Dragon, aren't I?
      I promise not to rant and roar
      And scourge the countryside, any more.
        Everyone cheered and then the
        Knight rose again.

KNIGHT: I propose a toast to the Dragon!

    "Hear hear!" cried the crowd.

BOY: I propose a toast to the Knight!

    "Hear hear!" shouted the crowd.

DRAGON: I propose a toast to the Boy!

    "Hear hear!" yelled the crowd.

KNIGHT: I propose a toast to *every* member of the crowd—separately, of course!

    "Hear hear!" screamed the crowd. That took a very long time indeed and it was begining to grow late when the villagers started packing their baskets to go home. The Knight and the Dragon and the Boy, however, started back to the cave. The lights in the little village began to go out, but there were stars and a late moon. As they climbed the Downs together, the poetic spell of the night took hold of them.

DRAGON: Oh moon of cheese—

KNIGHT: Oh cheesy moon—

DRAGON: Up in the sky so clear—

KNIGHT: Oh—oh dear—

DRAGON: S'beautiful—simply beautiful!

And, as they turned the last corner and disappeared from view, snatches of an old song were borne back on the night breeze. I can't be certain which of them was singing, but I think it was the Dragon!

Tales of Zorro

Zorro Outwits Death

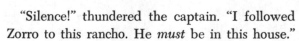

THE rancho of Alejandro de la Vega was usually quiet and peaceful, but this evening there was much activity. The commandante of the pueblo of Los Angeles had tracked the night-rider Zorro to a point near the Vega property. The soldiers' horses were hobbled in the Vega corral, and lancers stood watch around the Vega home. In the living room, or *sala*, the commandante strode back and forth. Standing by a sideboard, helping himself to the fresh fruit and washing it down with vintage wine, was fat, unshaven Sergeant Garcia.

Don Alejandro stood by the huge, tiled fireplace. He was angry that his home should be taken over by the soldiers who were unjustly persecuting and imprisoning his neighbors.

His son, Don Diego, seemed unconcerned. He sat straight and handsome in a ruffled shirt and delicately embroidered silk dressing gown. He played on the heavy oak piano, which had been brought around Cape Horn to Los Angeles all the way from Spain. Don Diego appeared to concentrate on an old Castilian song he was playing, but actually he was listening carefully to every word the commandante spoke.

For Don Diego was more than a young dandy returned from the university of Spain. He was also the masked man Zorro, who rode by night to right the wrongs done the citizens of Los Angeles by the greedy commandante and magistrate.

"I'm sure Zorro is in this house," stormed the commandante.

"That would seem hard to believe," said Diego, smiling.

"He is *not* in this house," stated Sergeant Garcia, who waddled like an overfed duck to the commandante.

"Silence!" thundered the captain. "I followed Zorro to this rancho. He *must* be in this house."

"But I have ordered the entire building searched," protested Garcia, "and I personally inspected the lower portions."

"You searched the wine cellar, you mean," corrected the captain.

"I can swear he is not hiding in any of the wine casks," boasted Garcia proudly, "and my loyal troops report he is nowhere else in the building."

"Then he is hiding on the grounds. He must know them well, for I believe Zorro to be none other than Don Alejandro's head vaquero, Benito."

"But captain," pleaded Garcia, spitting grape seeds past Don Alejandro into the fireplace, "you have already captured Benito twice and let him go. You said the lovesick Indian vaquero could not possibly be Zorro."

"Well, *now* I say he is. When he is brought to me, we shall have a trial, then a public execution. We will be rid of this bandit Zorro."

Diego coughed slightly and patted his mouth with a handkerchief. "All this talk of executions gives me indigestion," he said, standing up at the piano. "With your kind permission, I will retire to my room."

"Diego, stay where you are," commanded his father. "You will soon be the master of this rancho, and you must stand up for your men, especially those as valuable as Benito."

"Father, I try. I really do," said Don Diego, "but I cannot stomach all this talk of violence. I think I shall go upstairs and read poetry." So saying, he walked from the room, coughing again into his handkerchief.

Don Alejandro watched his son with sadness. He did not know his son was Zorro. Nor did anybody know, except Don Diego's faithful servant, Bernardo. But Bernardo was a mute and could not speak, so the secret was safe.

"There is work for Zorro tonight," said Diego to Bernardo as he closed his bedroom door. "The captain is determined to seek out Benito and hang him. Get me the mask and cloak, and we must find Benito before the lancers bring him in. Quickly, there is no time to lose." He pressed a hidden button, and a secret panel slid open. Both Diego and Bernardo stepped behind it.

A secret passageway led downstairs from Diego's bedroom, past the library, and underground for nearly a quarter of a mile to the cavern where Diego kept his sleek, black horse, Tornado. Only Diego and Bernardo knew of the passageway. Even Diego's father, Don Alejandro, did not know of its existence.

Don Diego pulled off the ruffles and silk and donned the black clothing, mask and cloak that made him Zorro, the champion of the people. Stationing Bernardo in the bedroom, he stealthily made his way down the secret stairway and out the hidden passage until he reached the cavern where Tornado was corralled.

Working with sureness and speed, Zorro saddled his black horse and led him through the thick brush concealing the narrow opening of the cave. Once outside, Zorro mounted Tornado and spurred him on. "We must hurry and find Benito," he whispered to the horse. "I think I know where he is hiding."

Gracefully Tornado galloped through the canyon. The horse knew the trail well, and he expertly dodged between boulders and rocks that would slow any other horse. When they neared a thick wood, Zorro reined his horse and slowed him to a walk.

At the edge of the trees Zorro called softly, "Benito."

There was no answer, but Zorro could hear rustling in the grove. "Benito, it is Zorro. Where are you?"

From the darkness a voice replied, "Oh, Zorro! I thought it might have been the commandante."

Zorro dismounted and walked forward to speak with Benito.

"How did you find this place?" asked Benito. "Only Don Diego and a few of my close friends know of this grove."

"I know many things, Benito. I know you are running away, but that you have no plan for escape. And without a plan, you will surely be caught by the lancers."

"But if I stay," said Benito earnestly, "I will be hanged because they think I am you!"

"Here is what you must do," instructed Zorro. "Take a horse and ride to Monterey. See the governor, who is now aware of the injustice and suffering caused by the commandante. Tell him your story, and I am sure he will offer you protection. Soon we will be rid of this evil commandante, and you will return to your job as vaquero."

"I will do that, senor," replied Benito. "And I am thankful."

"Where is your horse?" asked the masked man.

"Under the cover of night, my close friends are bringing it to me. I am hoping the lancers will not see them taking the horse from the stables."

"What!" exclaimed Zorro. "Bringing the horse

here? The commandante will certainly follow them. There is not time to lose. We must set a trap."

Running to a nearby tree, Zorro tied one end of his lariat to the trunk. He stretched the rope across the trail and hid himself in the bushes. Then he settled down to wait.

Soon two vaqueros, leading Benito's horse by the halter, trotted down the path. They went directly to Benito's hiding place, and in the dim light Zorro could see Benito tying his pack to the saddle. But before he was through the commandante and his lancers came riding through the brush.

"Aha, Zorro, we have you now," called the commandante to Benito.

The captain was in the lead, and Zorro let him ride beyond the lariat before he pulled it tight across the trail. He had sprung his trap.

Sergeant Garcia and his horse plowed into the rope. The horse stumbled, but Sergeant Garcia continued sailing straight ahead and bashed his head against a walnut tree. He hit the ground and when he tried to get up and help his captain, he slipped on loose walnuts and fell again into the tree trunk. Using sound judgement gained from his many years as a soldier of the king, he decided to lie back and nurse the lump on his head rather than help to fight Zorro.

Other lancers were falling over each other as their horses tripped on the taut rope. In the confusion the horses milled aimlessly about. The troops could not locate their mounts in the darkness, and confusion mounted.

In the meantime, Zorro ran forward to help the vaquero Benito.

The commandante had pulled his sword and faced the terrified Benito, who had no weapon. The captain snarled, "And you, bandit, had best begin saying your prayers."

Zorro, his sword already drawn, called, "If it is Zorro you seek, captain, here I am!"

The commandante wheeled and faced Zorro. The two touched blades and the duel began. The commandante was good, but Zorro was better. With parries and thrusts Zorro forced the captain away from Benito. The captain gave way little by little, retreating over ground covered with roots and vines. The masked man slashed and cut, swinging his blade faster than the eye could see.

The commandante tried to call his men, but the lancers staggered blindly amid the loose horses.

Zorro yelled at Benito, "Mount your horse, and ride. Go now. Quickly!" Benito rode out of the woods to safety, and Zorro pressed forward, the clashing blades singing of danger.

The commandante, backing up, slipped on a stone and fell to his knees. As Zorro prepared to disarm his foe, he saw Sergeant Garcia, who was charging like a nearsighted buffalo. The lancers, following the sergeant, approached with pistols drawn.

Zorro darted into the thick brush and ran to Tornado, who was standing quietly in the woods. He leaped on his mount and galloped from the trees as pistol shots sounded from the clearing.

"To horse! To horse!" shouted Garcia, who could not find his own mount. The commandante, recovered from his fall, located his horse and led his lancers in chasing the black-cloaked Zorro.

The wind felt cool on Zorro's face as he and Tornado galloped swiftly across the land Zorro knew from his childhood. Using familiar trails, he kept barely ahead of the pursuing commandante and the lancers. His black clothing blended with the dark woods and made it impossible for the lancers to see their target.

Zorro pulled Tornado to the left and down a gravel path into an arroyo. When he had reached the bed of the shallow canyon, he rode his horse to a large rock. Rider and horse poised silently behind the boulder, where they could not be seen, and watched the pursuers.

The lancers, with the commandante in the lead, thundered down the gravel pathway and continued galloping down the arroyo. Zorro watched them until they were out of sight. Then he urged Tornado up the path and along the arroyo edge.

In the still night Zorro heard the captain call his men and command them to return to the Vega house for regrouping. Zorro knew he had to act with haste. Using a little-known path through the rocks, he returned to the secret canyon and the hidden cavern.

Tying Tornado in the corral, Zorro quickly made his way up the passage to his room. With Bernardo's help he slipped on a dressing gown and walked down the staircase as the commandante stormed in the front door.

"I heard noises, and they disturbed me so much I could not read my poetry," Don Diego complained.

"You think about poetry when Zorro has escaped with the prisoner!" roared the commandante.

"But you said the prisoner *was* Zorro. Are there two of them?" asked Diego in all innocence.

Garcia followed the captain into the *sala* and went directly to the fruit bowl.

Don Diego ran his fingers idly over the piano keys. "You know, father," he said, "I do believe the piano needs tuning."

His father looked at him in exasperation. The commandante glared. Garcia, dropping a peach pit on the floor and taking another big gulp of wine, paid no attention to Diego's complaint. Nobody seemed to hear him . . . nobody except Bernardo, who winked and held up his hand, forming a circle with his thumb and finger to indicate a job well done.

The Fire in the Night

Diego de la Vega stood inside the balcony doorway of his Monterey hotel room and stretched. He was tall—so tall his fingers almost touched the white-washed ceiling of the room. He could feel the brisk sea air from Monterey Bay, and the breeze was refreshing.

Diego had arrived yesterday in Monterey, the capital of California, accompanied by his trusted servant, Bernardo, and Sergeant Garcia. Diego and Bernardo could have made the trip from Los Angeles by themselves, but Garcia went along for added protection. Protection? Twice Garcia had fallen off his horse; once he had gotten them lost in the reeds on the wrong side of the Salinas River; and that time with the bee-hive while gathering firewood was best forgotten. It was so painful Garcia still wouldn't put honey on his bread without a grimace.

The business had been taken care of, and now Diego was ready to relax a few days before returning home. He had taken a room in the hotel on the plaza. The second floor of the hotel had a balcony running the length of the building, and the rooms opened off the long, narrow platform. It was on this balcony that Diego now stretched and gazed at the bustling scene below him. Numerous peons had small stands in the town plaza, and they sold everything from fresh fish (caught in quantities in the bay) to pottery, corn, leather goods and fresh vegetables, which seemed to thrive in the inland valley.

Suddenly a piercing scream broke the peaceful scene. It was Theresa, who owned a tamale stand. In a voice that on a clear day could be heard halfway to Santa Cruz, she was yelling at two men near her stand.

"Go away," she bellowed like a wounded tigress, "I work hard here. Why should I pay you? What could happen to my stand? I hate you. Go away. Pronto!"

The men looked around furtively. They tried to quiet her, but it was useless. As one of the men placed a restraining hand on her shoulder, she smacked him with a cornstalk. A crowd began to gather, and the men hurried away. Sergeant Garcia, attracted by the noise, came waddling up. Half out of respect and half out of self-preservation, the crowd parted as Garcia approached.

Theresa turned on the hapless sergeant. "Fine lot of good *you* do," she screeched. "Why didn't you help?"

"How could I?" asked Garcia. "I only got here."

Theresa fumed. Diego could almost see the sparks coming out her eyes, she was that angry.

"You and your lancers are useless," she stormed. "Where are you when these two bandits try to hold me up? They demand I pay them money so they can 'protect' me. I can protect myself, thank you!"

Diego nodded in silent agreement.

"If you will give me their names, I will catch them," Garcia suggested.

"Names! If I knew their names I would catch them myself, fat one."

Garcia was getting no place and seemed defeated. "I wish I could help you, senorita," he said.

"Sergeant, you can help me only if you stop eating. You arrived yesterday, and today for the first time I run out of beans by mid-morning."

"It is well that you get so much business," said Garcia with pride.

"Si, except that *you* buy on credit," retorted Theresa.

Diego had heard enough, so he retired to his room. He forgot about the patter between Theresa and Garcia, but if he thought he had heard the end of it, he was quite wrong.

Diego was a light sleeper. Since he assumed his dual identity as Zorro his reflexes had become sharp as a barber's razor. A word, a sound, a lonely call in the night—all would awaken him. It was a clap of a leather heel against brick and a muffled whisper that woke Diego that night. He sat up in bed and pushed aside the blankets. He tiptoed to the balcony and looked across the plaza. Two figures in dark clothes were visible in the gloom and wisps of fog that swirled in from the bay. They were standing whispering by Theresa's tamale stand. Remembering the incident of that morning, Diego rushed into action. He donned the black mask and cloak which transformed him from the book-loving, soft-speaking Diego into the hard-fighting, sword-swinging Zorro.

Looking about cautiously to make sure he was not seen, Zorro stepped over the railing of the hotel balcony, caught hold of the bannister and dropped to the ground. Stealthily he picked his way across the deserted square. He walked quickly, but he had to circle the plaza, keeping always in the shadows. The sound of a single footstep would give him away. As he crept forward he could see one of the intruders stuffing dry hay and straw under Theresa's stand. As he got closer he saw with horror that the second man

carried a torch, which he attempted to hide by shielding it with his coat.

Just as Zorro drew close to the stand, the men jammed the torch into the tinder. The structure burst into flames as Zorro called, "Hoa . . . If you value your lives, do not move!"

The men turned, and Zorro saw their faces in the orange glare of the burning stand. Each man pulled a long, wicked knife and prepared to lunge at Zorro, whose swiftly flicking sword kept them at a safe distance. The three circled, each waiting for an opening, in the light of the fire.

The flames attracted spectators, and soon peons were rushing into the square. They saw the masked Zorro and yelled, "The man with the mask. He must have started the fire!" They ran toward him.

In Los Angeles Zorro would have been recognized as the champion of the people, but way up in Monterey he was not known. He had to retreat before the mob rushed him. His two opponents realized this, and they inched forward, ready to spring.

Slowly giving ground but still keeping his sword dancing in front of him, Zorro spied a wooden bench against a building. At that moment the two henchmen rushed forward. With his free hand Zorro toppled the bench and the men stumbled in a tangle of arms and legs. Zorro fled down a side street and through the unknown alleyways of Monterey.

He turned a corner and stopped by the entrance to a livery stable. He inched inside the door and waited. His pursuers came running down the street and fanned out in all directions. A stranger stuck his head inside the doorway. Zorro was close enough to shave the man with his sword, but he dared not move. The stranger could see nothing, so he ran on.

Hours later Zorro slid out of the stable and worked his way slowly back to the hotel. Again the plaza was bare, but he could see the still-smoldering ruins of the tamale stand. He listened carefully, but not a footstep did he hear. He ran across the square and leaped toward the balcony, catching hold of a support and pulling himself

up. A few minutes more and he was Diego de la Vega, back in bed as the first pink of dawn appeared over the Monterey hills.

There was much commotion in the plaza next morning when Theresa discovered her stand burned to ashes. Garcia tried to calm her, but to no avail.

She repeated her tale of woe to Diego, and as she was talking a stranger walked up. He was Senor Jaime Ropa.

"I have come to offer my condolences to Senorita Theresa," said Ropa.

"A lot you care," sputtered Theresa. "I don't see you offering to rebuild my stand."

"Ah, senorita, that is exactly why I am here." He smiled an oily smile.

At this Theresa simmered down. Garcia and Diego looked with surprise at Senor Ropa.

"Are you really going to help me?" she asked.

"I have known difficult times myself," he explained in a soothing voice. "And I want to help you repair your stand. How much will it take?"

Without hesitation Theresa replied, "Five hundred pesos."

"I can arrange such a loan," said Ropa. "When would you want to pay me back?"

Theresa had to think a moment on that one. "With good luck, in a year, perhaps, maybe two," she said thoughtfully.

"Then it is agreed," said Ropa. "I will loan you five hundred pesos. If you pay me back in a year, you will repay only seven hundred and fifty. In two years it will be one thousand pesos."

"One thousand! That is robbery!" screamed Theresa.

"Senor Ropa is surely joking," said Garcia, chuckling at the obvious jest.

"No," said Ropa, looking amazed and hurt that his offer was not appreciated. "I am entitled to interest for the loan."

"Fifty percent interest each year is robbery!" snorted Theresa. "Get out."

Ropa's soothing voice rasped as he said, "I am sure you will want to reconsider my offer. I will be back."

"I never want to see you again," spat Theresa. "You are as bad as those pigs who burned down my stand because I wouldn't pay them protection money. Get out. Pig!" She started to batter her clenched fists against his back, but Garcia and Diego pulled her off, still fighting and kicking.

Diego told Theresa, "Senorita, I will loan you

the five hundred pesos. You may pay me back when you are able. And there will be no interest."

Theresa threw her arms around Diego's neck and gave him a big kiss. Diego, shocked by her impulsive action, stood there, slightly embarrassed.

Winking slyly at Bernardo, Garcia moved toward Theresa, hoping she would give him a big kiss, too. But as he stood there with his lips puckered, Theresa turned on the big sergeant and began peppering him with her fists. "Why didn't you look out for my stand?" she demanded between breaths. "Where were you when the fire started?"

Diego smiled. "There's no telling about women," he murmured to Bernardo as the two walked away, leaving Garcia to take care of himself. Diego suggested that he pay his respects to the governor, perhaps mentioning the outrage against Theresa. Bernardo agreed, and they headed for the governor's office.

They were walking down a narrow street leading to the Presidio when Diego stopped short. Ahead of him, coming out of a dingy tavern, were the two men he had seen last night. He would never forget those evil faces, lighted by the dancing orange flames. Keeping out of sight, Diego and Bernardo trailed the two and crept forward until they could overhear the conversation. They heard only the words "ten tonight at Pine Point" before the two men moved out of earshot. Motioning for Bernardo to follow the pair, Diego went ahead to see the governor. But his thoughts were not on talking to the governor of California. Instead, he was thinking about the sinister men, and Pine Point and . . . Zorro.

He rented a horse at the livery stable where he had hidden the previous night and tied the animal to a hitching post behind the hotel. Then Diego retired to his room to wait for Bernardo's report. But Bernardo did not appear, and as ten o'clock drew near, Diego donned the clothes of Zorro, stole quietly downstairs and rode out of Monterey toward Pine Point.

The point was a cliff overlooking the Pacific Ocean, where the surf beat and whipped against big, ugly boulders. Diego carefully scouted the point. Thick stands of pine trees grew fifty feet back from the cliff edge. There was a small beach far below, and Zorro could barely see a rugged path leading upwards from the beach to the point. It was an ideal place for a meeting, he thought. If a man were trailed on horseback, he could escape from his pursuer by sea. If he were followed as he rowed in from the ocean, he could escape through the woods.

Once Diego made certain nobody else had arrived at the point, he peered toward the ocean. He saw two dim figures in a boat rowing toward shore. Obviously he was in the right location at the right time. He stood far back from the point near the edge of the trees for concealment but close to the cliff edge so he could see the boat when it beached.

He stepped closer to the edge to get a better look at the boat.

Suddenly a voice called out, "What do you want, senor?"

Zorro spun around to see a dark figure walking from the pines. But as he stepped toward the stranger the ground crumbled beneath him. The soft earth was giving way, and clods of dirt rumbled down the cliffside. Zorro lurched to regain his balance, but he clutched vainly at thin air. He was falling toward the frothing, boiling sea two hundred feet below.

As Zorro fell toward the churning ocean, he pawed desperately for a hand-hold on the cliff face. He landed on a narrow ledge, and miraculously his hands grasped a scrubby bush. He grabbed hold as the rocks and stones and dirt rained down on him. Never had his hands and arms ached so much, and never had his body been so bruised from the shower of stones that cascaded on him as he clung to the cliff.

Zorro had landed on an old trail leading from the bluff to the beach. The two men in the boat were coming up a newer trail, farther down the coast. When they reached the top, they joined the dark figure from the woods, and all three peered over the cliff edge. In the darkness they could not see the black figure of Zorro perched

on his narrow ledge—all they could see were the waves crashing far below.

The three men conducted their business quickly. They exchanged necessary information and agreed to meet the following night at "the camp." Zorro could not hear the voices distinctly. Nor could he hear any of the words . . . except the single phrase, "the camp."

In due time the meeting broke up, the single figure leaving through the forest and the two henchmen picking their way down the dangerous path to the ocean. When they arrived at the beach they looked again at the cliff, as if searching for some clue to Zorro's fate. They could not see Zorro, and they pushed their boat through the breakers and returned to Monterey.

When he was certain they had left and couldn't see him, Zorro began the tortuous job of climbing up the cliff. For a few feet the going was easy—he was on the old path. But the trail vanished—

a landslide many years ago had wiped out an entire section of ledge, and now there was no place to go. Here and there an occasional bush grew from a crack in the cliff. Reaching first for one and then for another, Zorro pulled himself up. Slowly and painfully, hand over hand, he scaled the cliff wall. His foot slipped, and a shower of dirt fell the long way down to the ocean. As he hung flat against the cliff Zorro could hear the rumbling surf. The thought of falling into the white froth spurred him on, and he continued the ordeal of climbing the cliff.

It seemed hours before he finally pulled himself over the edge, and he lay face down on the damp ground panting from exhaustion. When he recovered his strength, he crawled across the open area on his hands and knees—he didn't dare walk upright for fear of being seen. Zorro found the horse still standing quietly where he had tied him, so he mounted and rode to town.

Arriving in Monterey, he tethered the horse at the edge of town and, keeping in the darkest corners, made his way to the hotel. Only after he made doubly sure there was nobody in the plaza did Zorro cross the square and vault the balcony railing to his hotel room. As he opened the door he realized—too late—there was somebody in the room!

He stepped inside, hand on his sword, and breathed a heavy sigh of relief to see that the "intruder" was his servant, Bernardo. While Zorro was peeling off his torn clothing and bathing his throbbing muscles in warm water, the servant used his hands and gestures to tell his story:

Bernardo had followed the two men down to the wharf, where they had boarded a boat and headed up the coast, north, toward the sand dunes. Bernardo had chosen to follow them on horseback along the coast rather than in a skiff, so he had rented a horse and set out along the dunes. He had always managed to keep them in sight, and several miles up the coast they had put into shore. Bernardo had hidden himself near "the camp," as they had called it, while the men dozed, ate dinner and then set off for their "ap-

pointment." Bernardo had marked a hill so it could be seen by land or sea, and then he had ridden back into Monterey.

Zorro and Bernardo now decided the best move would be to see Sergeant Garcia. If they could get him to visit "the camp," he could collect enough evidence to arrest the culprits.

But next morning Sergeant Garcia was not too keen on sailing north along the sand dunes.

"Sergeant," argued Diego, "you look peaked. Are you sick? You have lost weight."

"Have I?" asked Garcia, eyeing his stomach, which stretched like a mighty desert from his chest to his legs.

"Certainly. You must be down to a mere 350 pounds. Now, what you need is a good sea voyage. Spend a day out in a boat. Do you good."

"Do not mention boats to me, Don Diego," wailed Garcia. "Since my trip to California from Spain, I have avoided them. Most of my time was spent near the rail."

"Enjoying the fresh sea breeze?" ventured Diego.

"No, my friend. Being sick."

"Oh," said Diego, disappointed. But he quickly tried a new approach: "As a soldier of the king, you should inspect the coastline north of here. Look for pirates."

"Don Diego, we have a navy for that."

"The scenery is wonderful this time of year."

"Don Diego, I am a soldier, not an artist. Besides," he looked at a pretty girl walking past the barracks, "the scenery is nice in town, too."

Diego tried another tack. Moving closer to Garcia and speaking in low tones, he said, "Sergeant, listen carefully. Many years ago, when the Indians threatened a raid, the men of Monterey moved their supply of wine to the hills north of town. My servant and I found out about it yesterday."

"Yes?" said Garcia, brightening.

"These are the finest wines in all California," continued Diego.

"Go on. Wines, you say?" bellowed Garcia.

"Shhh, sergeant. We must keep this very quiet.

Bernardo and I know exactly where they are hidden. If you will come with us, we will take you there."

Garcia did not hesitate an instant. Turning to his corporal, he announced, "I am going to locate extra rations for the men. I'll be back later." And Garcia, Diego and Bernardo walked toward the waterfront.

When all three were settled in the boat, they pushed away from the dock. At that moment Garcia decided to change seats, and he stood up. The great bulk of Garcia moving was too much for the small craft, and it pitched sharply. Garcia spun off his feet and fell outward. His fingers touched the wooden ties of the pier, and for a moment Garcia hung, halfway between the land and the sea. He held onto the wharf with his hands, but his feet were still in the boat. He rolled from side to side as Diego tried to bring the boat closer in.

Suddenly Garcia fell with a mighty roar. Water geysered up, drenching Diego and Bernardo. Garcia floundered helplessly in the water. A friendly seal swam up and, sticking his nose in Garcia's face, barked. Garcia panicked at the sight of the be-whiskered seal and thrashed even more. With the help of a few dockhands, Diego and Bernardo pulled Garcia to the beach, where he lay like a huge marooned whale. Dripping wet and soaked clear through, he began removing his boots. He poured water out of one, and from the second came more water and a fish. Garcia looked at his prize ruefully, picked it up and began squishing back to the barracks.

"Looks like our plan was all wet," said Diego, laughing.

Bernardo made a face at Diego's bad pun.

Back in the hotel room Diego and Bernardo made other plans. It was now necessary for Zorro to do the job by himself.

Late that afternoon hardly anybody paid attention to Diego de la Vega and his servant riding north out of town. The two went in silence, and they rode slowly to save their horses. When they neared "the camp" Diego rode behind a low hill, and when he emerged he was dressed as Zorro.

It was agreed Bernardo would stay out of sight unless absolutely needed. So he rode to a safe distance and waited to be called.

Zorro tied his horse and crept forward until he reached the rim of the bowl-like valley called "the camp." It was completely in shadows, but from the glare of the campfire Zorro could make out the two toughs—they looked much as they had the night of Theresa's fire. Zorro leaped forward, and the battle was brief. Taken completely by surprise, the men were defenseless. Zorro had knocked one out before the second attacked. The masked man side-stepped and neatly tripped the second, who went sprawling in the sand. Before he could rise, Zorro had tied his hands; and while he struggled in vain to free himself, Zorro tied the other.

The two men, bound and gagged, sat by the campfire. In the dim light they looked exactly as they had before Zorro's quick attack. Unable to say a word, they waited silently for the arrival of their leader. And off in the shadows, also waiting, was Zorro.

Inside of an hour Zorro heard motion in the dunes. He tensed. The men at the fire still struggled with their bonds. The leader reined up and

dismounted. As he walked toward the men, Zorro stepped from the shadows, his sword drawn and ready for action.

"Wait where you are," he commanded.

The leader stopped stark still. Zorro could see the color drain from his face.

"This cannot be. We—I saw you die last night, falling from the cliff. You must be a ghost."

The leader was, of course, Senor Ropa, the supposed "friend" who offered to loan Theresa the money.

"I see your game now," said Zorro. "The Ropa fortunes have vanished. You probably gambled them away. So you became a leech, sucking the hard-earned money from the peons. If you couldn't get it by threats, you burned their stands, as you did Theresa's, and then offered to loan money at high interest rates. Either way, you got your blood money. How low you have fallen, Ropa. You are worse than the dirtiest scum on a prison ship."

Ropa waited for an opportunity and moved swiftly. As Zorro finished speaking, Ropa feinted and drew his sword. Zorro's blade darted forward, but with a sharp rap the thrust was parried.

The two men backed away and once again touched blades. If Zorro believed he might easily overcome the older man, he was wrong. The steel blades flashed in the firelight and rang over the deserted sand dunes as Zorro strived to disarm his foe. He slashed and cut, the blade flicking in and out. But he never seemed to gain an advantage. With a supreme effort he pressed forward and Ropa, stepping back, fell over a stone. As Zorro rushed forward the older man leaped up and pitched a handful of sand straight at Zorro's eyes.

Zorro reached for his face, trying to stop the stinging, burning sensation in his eyes. Ropa, rather than continue the fight he knew he could not win, raced for his horse. He jumped on his mount and galloped over the empty dunes.

His eyes watering so he could hardly see, Zorro ran toward his horse. By the time he was in the saddle Ropa had a good start. Zorro pursued the other man, but it was slow going. His horse could not run fast in the soft sand, and he seemed to be tiring after a few yards. Oh, if Zorro only had Tornado to ride, the chase would be over by now.

He spurred his horse. Ropa was still ahead, and Zorro could easily follow hoofmarks in the sand. A short way ahead he could see the sand whipped up by Ropa's horse. Little by little, Zorro seemed to be gaining. He got closer . . . closer . . . closer.

Zorro reached for his lariat and spun a loop. Swinging it over his head, he waited for the right moment and let fly.

The noose sailed through the air and fell over Ropa's shoulders. Ropa fell from his mount into the sand. He was finally in Zorro's power.

Zorro tied Ropa securely before returning to locate his other prisoners. Then he tied one to the other around the waist and, with their hands still bound with cord behind their backs, they began the long slow trip into town.

The next morning the story was all over Monterey. In jail were Ropa and his two henchmen. Everybody knew about Zorro's close call, but still nobody knew who Zorro really was. He had vanished from Monterey as mysteriously as he had come.

Diego de la Vega and his servant joined those in the plaza who talked about the strange comings and goings of Zorro. But Diego was more interested in getting Theresa's stand re-built. He loaned her the money, and she quickly made a deal for some lumber. By noon the stand was partly completed.

In charge of the whole operation, but doing little of the actual work, was Sergeant Garcia.

He had no sooner taken over than Theresa screamed at him to get out of the way. He turned to reply and she kicked him in the shins. Then she tried to bite him and before long, he was running back and forth (mostly back) trying to defend himself.

Yes, Diego thought to himself, laughing inwardly, everything in Monterey is back to normal again.

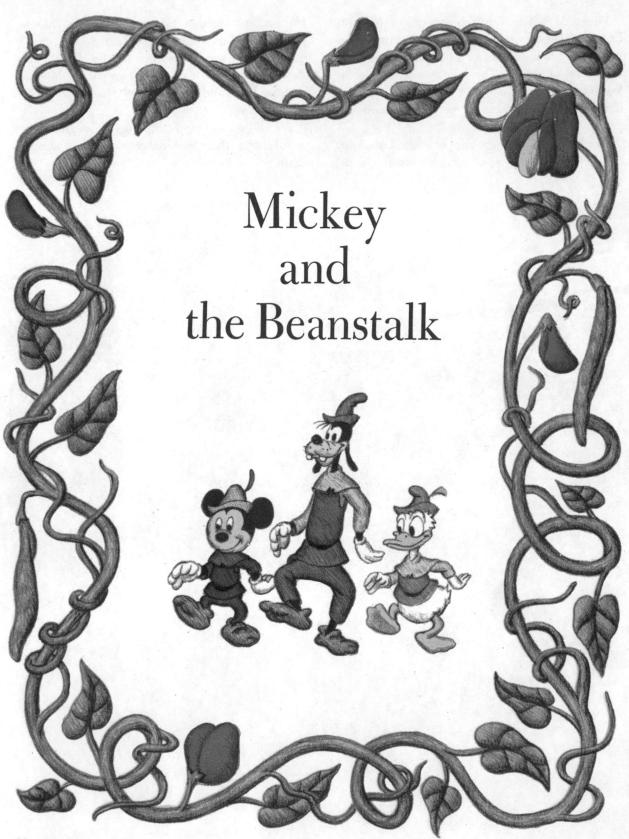

Mickey
and
the Beanstalk

THERE WAS ONCE a most beautiful valley. Rolling hills stretched all around it, and a broad river flowed peacefully through it. There were green trees, quiet roads, and pleasant farms. And best of all, the air was always filled with laughter, so that far and wide this enchanted spot was known as Happy Valley.

Now the secret of the valley's enchantment was a magic singing harp. It was her songs, ringing out from a castle which stood in the center of the valley, that cast the magic spell of happiness over the land.

But one day a giant shadow fell over the castle. And when the shadow lifted, the magic harp was gone.

With her went all the happiness of the valley. The crops withered away. The trees died. The river dried up and disappeared. And the people grew sadder and hungrier day by day.

In one little home in the valley lived three friends—Mickey, Donald, and Goofy by name. Once they had been happy and prosperous farmers, with plenty of good food on their tables. Now they were down to their last crust of bread and their one last bean!

What could they do, they asked themselves over and over again, to keep from starving? To be sure, they still owned one cow, but she was such an old and faithful friend, they knew they could never eat her.

"We could sell the cow," suggested Mickey.

"It is the only way," the others agreed.

So off to market trudged Mickey with the faithful cow.

At home, while they waited, Goofy and Donald prepared for a great feast. They got out their biggest roasting pans and platters, their spices and seasonings and recipe books.

Then back came Mickey from market. In a little box he carried the payment he had received for the cow—not steaks or roasts or chops, not even a soupbone, but beans!

"Beans!" screamed Donald.

"Beans!" groaned Goofy.

"But, fellows," Mickey tried to explain. "these are magic beans. If you plant them by the light of a full moon, you get—"

"More beans!" Donald broke in, and he hurled the beans to the floor, where they rolled through a knothole and disappeared.

That was a black moment for the three friends. They trudged gloomily off to bed, supperless and sad.

But as the three friends slept, and just when everything looked darkest, in through the window came a ray of light. It was moonlight—the light of a full moon! And a silvery beam shone down through the knothole where the magic beans had fallen.

It was just as Mickey had promised. Under the spell of the moonlight those magic beans sprouted and grew. First up through the knothole curled a slender sprout. But it did not stop there. Higher and higher it climbed, while the three friends slept on.

Thicker and stronger and taller grew the magic beanstalk until it began to lift that little house up from the desolate valley—up, up, up to a magic land above the clouds.

So it happened that when morning dawned, the three friends looked out, not upon the dismal, dried-up ruin of Happy Valley, but upon the strange and wonderful landscape of this land in the sky.

In the distance gleamed a huge castle.

"Hey, fellows!" cried Goofy, who woke first and was the first to look out the window. "See what I found. A castle—a castle in the sky!"

"Gee!" cried Donald, scrambling up beside him for a look. "Maybe there's food there!"

"Let's go and see!" said Mickey.

So off trudged the three friends. The castle was farther away than it looked. They walked and walked through a giant land. Giant grasses and flowers towered above their heads. Giant

caterpillars humped along the forest paths. There were giant footprints, too, but our friends did not stop to worry about those.

At last only a wide moat separated them from the castle. Mickey found a giant pea pod which made them a splendid boat, and away they rowed, straight up to the castle's forbidding walls.

Then up a long stairway of stone they clambered, until at last they found themselves in the castle itself. And there before them was the answer to their dreams—a huge table loaded down with wonderful things to eat!

It was a truly giant-sized table, as tall as a young mountain. But that could not stop those

hungry searchers now. Up the towering legs they scrambled and then, without a moment wasted, they began to feast upon the huge cheeses, the mounds of great, green peas, the bowlfuls and jarfuls and platefuls of all sorts and flavors of food!

But wait. What was this? Through an open doorway they heard the thud of giant footsteps. And they heard a big voice singing—

> *"Fee-fi-fo-fum!*
> *He-hi-ho-hum!*
> *I'm a most amazing guy,*
> *A most amazing guy am I!"*

The next moment, there in the doorway stood the owner of the castle, Willie the giant. What made him an amazing guy, they learned from the rest of his song, was that he could change himself into any shape he chose.

Donald and Goofy trembled as they listened to the giant's song. They did not care to see the giant's other shapes; they raced away to hide. But Mickey was watching the giant's shadow. It was the same huge shadow that had fallen over Happy Valley the day the magic harp disappeared!

Mickey had just time to scuttle under a folded napkin as Willie pulled his big chair up to the big table and sat down to eat.

"Yum, yum," said Willie happily. "Pot roast—chocolate pot roast, with green gravy!"

He picked up his napkin—and there was Mickey! Mickey ran for shelter, but Willie had seen him. A giant hand pounced, and Mickey was trapped.

"Ho, ho!" laughed the giant, holding up his small prisoner. "Where do you think you're going?"

Mickey thought fast.

"Is it really true," he said admiringly, "that you can change yourself into anything?"

"Sure." Willie gave a giant giggle. "Go on, suggest something."

"Anything?" said Mickey, eyeing a huge fly swatter.

"Sure, anything," said Willie.

"Well," said Mickey, thinking hard, "could you change into a—well, a fly?"

Willie was disappointed. "Aw, you don't want a fly!" he said. "How about a bunny with long pink ears?"

"Of course, if you can't do a fly—" Mickey suggested.

"Oh, all right!" said Willie sulkily. "A teeny-eeny fly, with pink wings!"

Then, while Willie muttered his magic words, out came Goofy and Donald, and with Mickey they seized the handle of the big fly swatter, ready for one big swat!

But Willie fooled them. He turned into a huge bunny with pink ears. And when he saw them waiting there with the fly swatter, he saw through their trick.

"Hey!" he roared. "Are you trying to fool Willie? I'll fix you!"

And he snatched them all up in his great big fist.

"I'll fix you," he muttered again, "but first I want my dinner and some music."

And Willie unlocked a box on a high shelf and pulled out the missing magic harp of Happy Valley!

"Miss Harp!" cried Goofy. But before he had time to say any more, he found himself being tossed, with his friends, down into that same dark box, and he heard the clank of the key as the giant locked it up.

Then Willie dropped the key into his breast pocket and went back to his dinner, feeling well satisfied with himself. He did not guess that Mickey had dropped down, by accident, behind the box, and was hiding there, waiting for a chance to rescue his friends.

Mickey waited and waited. At last his chance came—when the giant had finished his dinner and the magic harp had sung him to sleep.

Then Mickey went to work. First he anchored a spool of stout thread to the shelf with a big needle. Then, as the thread unwound, Mickey dropped with it, down, down, down, toward the giant's chest, until he landed with a small thud.

On tiptoe Mickey padded across to the pocket where he had seen the giant put the key. Yes, there it was! But as Mickey lifted the key, the giant's snuffbox flew open, and Mickey breathed in a great gulp of the nose-tickling stuff!

"Ka-ka-tchoo!" The whole pocket shivered under Mickey's sneeze.

Willie roused up at the sound and sniffed about. Then the snuff caught up with him, too.

"KA-KA-TCHOO!" he roared, while Mickey trembled.

But Willie only looked drowsily around the room, stretched once, and went back to sleep.

Mickey breathed a sigh of relief. Then up the thread he went again, hand over hand, carrying the heavy key. It took every bit of his strength to pull himself and the key over the edge of the shelf, and then to lift the key to the lock—and turn it!

It worked! Up flew the box lid, and out scrambled Goofy and Donald.

There was not a moment to lose. Down the thread they slid; then up to the table to rescue the harp and down again to the floor they raced.

Now they were really on their way, but Mickey had one last inspiration. He stopped to tie the giant's shoelaces together, to keep Willie from chasing them.

He was just in time, too, for Willie woke up as the three friends were running across the castle's great stone floor.

With a roar he lurched to his feet, swinging his club. But the shoelaces tripped him up, and he tumbled across the table.

With another roar he flung his club at Mickey.

"Whew!" cried Mickey, as he dodged the flying weapon. "That was too close for comfort!"

On they raced, and in another moment they had squeezed under the big outer door of the castle, while behind them Willie fumbled at his shoelaces.

Before they reached the top of the magic beanstalk, they could hear Willie's footsteps thudding behind them. He was on the trail again!

They practically fell down that beanstalk! Down, down, down—and at last the parched earth of their home valley was under their feet once more.

Then Mickey snatched up an old saw and zizz, zizz, zizz, they sawed through that thick beanstalk as fast as they could work. At last it cracked, it wavered, it swayed. Then, with a tremendous thud, it crashed down into the valley!

And high, high above, where the stalk had pierced the clouds, they could see Willie's angry, puzzled face peering down.

" 'Bye, Willie!" shouted Mickey.

Then away they raced, to return the magic singing harp to the castle on the hill.

Soon the sweet notes of the harp's magic song rang out over the sad valley again. And the old enchantment was reborn. First a rain cloud came racing over the hills, and a warm shower fell upon the parched earth, and set the dry river to bubbling once more. Then the sun shone, and the trees and grass sent out new little shoots of green. And soon the lovely sound of laughter filled the air once more in Happy Valley.

"Gosh," said Goofy, as the three friends stood in the doorway of their new home that evening, "it sure is fun to be happy!"

Little Hiawatha

Indian Brave

Mᴀɴʏ ʏᴇᴀʀꜱ ago, when the forests were young, there lived a boy and his name was Hiawatha. He lived with his grandmother, whose name was Nokomis. His home was a tepee and it stood on the shore of a big, shining lake.

Nokomis was wise in the secrets of the forest, wise in the stories and legends the Indians told nightly around their campfires. She often told her grandson about them as he sat watching her weaving their warm woolen blankets, or grinding kernels of corn to use for their evening meal.

The small boy felt a thrill of pride at the stories. How he yearned to become a mighty hunter.

"You must learn the life of the forest," said Nokomis, and she explained a thousand and one things that were a question in the little lad's mind. What made the rainbow? What did the owls say when they hooted during the night? Why did the dogs bay at the moon? Why and where did the bears disappear during the cold winter months? Why? Why?

Each day the boy Hiawatha grew wiser in the

71

secrets of the forest. He learned the language of the birds, how and where they built their nests. They were all friendly. He learned about the four-footed animals, the busy beavers, the squirrels, the soft-eyed deer, the rabbits. They were trusting friends, too.

One day the old arrow-maker fashioned a bow and arrow for Hiawatha and gave it to him as a gift. It was a small bow and a small arrow, for he was only a small boy. But Hiawatha felt as big and grown-up as any of the big and grown-up hunters.

"Now that I have a bow and arrow, I'll be a hunter today," he said to his friends the birds and animals.

"Are you going to hunt us?" they asked.

"Oh, no indeed," replied Hiawatha.

There was a green island across the lake.

"That is where I will go hunting," said Hiawatha. He carried his birch-bark canoe down to the water's edge. He stepped in. The obliging animals gave it a little push and the morning breeze and rippling waves gently carried him over to the island.

The canoe touched the shore. Hiawatha stood up to take a look. The canoe tipped. He lost his balance. Oops! Hiawatha fell in with a splash!

The water was not deep because he was so close to the land. He only got a good wetting. Hiawatha waded ashore and pulled his canoe up onto the beach.

Many bright little eyes watched the boy. Many little animals were laughing to themselves as they saw Hiawatha shake the water off himself. Surely this newcomer was not to be feared. Especially if he didn't know enough to get out of a canoe without falling into the lake.

But Hiawatha thought differently. Today was the day he was going to start being a mighty hunter. In fact, right now! He looked around sharply and there, within easy reach of his arrow, were many animals. They were all staring at him

in friendly curiosity. There were squirrels, birds of many feathers, flat-tailed beavers, a deer, chipmunks, and rabbits with twinkly noses. And they did not look one bit scared. That would never do! At least they should look afraid of a mighty hunter. Hiawatha decided to teach them a lesson, to make them respect and fear a hunter who had the name of Hiawatha.

The little Indian boy raised his bow. He pulled back on the bowstring to shoot the arrow. He pointed it at them. Before he could send that arrow whizzing through the air, it slipped from his hand and it fell to the ground. The animals were all amused and watched from safe places as he picked it up and set it in place again. Hiawatha would not give up easily.

Because grandmother Nokomis had taught her grandson so well about the forest folk, Hiawatha knew they were surely laughing at him, the would-be hunter. He did not like that one bit!

"I didn't practice enough with my bow and arrow," said Hiawatha. "But they should be scared of a hunter, anyway."

For a minute Hiawatha was unhappy. And then —he saw strange tracks on the ground. Never had he seen anything like them. Not a sign of the soft pads of a paw and none of claw marks, either.

"Grandmother, what animal makes tracks like these?" Hiawatha asked, forgetting his grandmother was at home and he was on his first hunting trip, all by himself.

"This is funnier and funnier," laughed the delighted animals. "We know whose prints those are, but we won't tell. Let him find out for himself."

The excited Indian boy studied the odd tracks again. "I will stalk this strange animal as a mighty hunter should do."

He put his ear to the ground, but he heard no thumping sound. On his hands and knees he followed the winding trail until suddenly he heard a sharp, whirring noise. And there before him, in the middle of the path, stood a giant cricket, rubbing its wings together to make the sound the boy had heard.

Hiawatha stared into the big cricket's eyes, that stared back into his own. He forgot all about using his trusty bow. All he wanted to do was get away as fast as he could. He turned and fled.

The little forest animals thought it was the funniest thing they had ever seen. They popped out in the open and chirped and chattered and chuckled and chortled gleefully.

"Imagine! Afraid of a cricket!"

"And him with a bow and arrow, too!"

Hiawatha heard the taunts and teasing remarks and he knew they were poking fun at him again. Instead of being brave, it looked as if he was a coward.

"Even we cottontails are not afraid of a cricket," said the littlest rabbit. He laughed so hard he could hardly sit up.

That brought Hiawatha to his senses in a hurry. He was angry at himself for running. He was embarrassed by their teasing, because he knew they were right. He was not acting like a brave hunter; he was acting like a scared boy. But he did not enjoy being laughed at—especially by anything so little as this little rabbit.

"I'll teach you not to laugh at me," cried Hiawatha. He grabbed his bow and arrow and pointed it straight at the heart of the littlest rabbit, who had laughed so hard at him.

The little rabbit took one look at Hiawatha's grim face. This was serious. He hopped, skipped and jumped off as fast as he could. Around the

bushes, between the trees, over the rocks, this frightened rabbit ran.

Panting, out of breath, the little rabbit at last had to give up. He could run no more. Hiawatha had cornered him and there was no escape.

The other animals all watched in horror as the Indian boy chased their friend. They gasped in dismay when the little rabbit reached the end of the trail and could go no more. They saw how the rabbit trembled in terror when Hiawatha pulled the bowstring taut, ready to shoot the arrow. It was a terrifying sight and there wasn't a thing they could do about it. What would that fellow do next?

A big tear rolled down the cheek of the frightened rabbit. If only he hadn't made such unkind remarks, if he had not laughed so long and so hard, this awful thing would not be happening.

Hiawatha saw the big tear. What was a mighty hunter to do? He could not shoot a poor little rabbit like that. After all, it *was* funny for anybody to be afraid of a cricket, especially a brave hunter. He should have taken it as a joke and laughed with the rest of the animals. But no, he had to get cross!

"I—I'm sorry," whimpered the rabbit.

"Aw!" said Hiawatha. "Scoot! Scat! Be off with you. I can't shoot you, I haven't got the heart to do it."

The other animals were delighted to see that the little rabbit was safe and rushed out from their hiding places to thank the Indian boy. Hiawatha looked around in surprise. He saw their friendly faces and he saw they trusted him.

"I'll never hunt you again," declared Hiawatha firmly. "I like you, too." And to prove it, he broke his arrow and bow over his knees. There would be no more of hunting on this island.

Now they were friends, and romped and played together happily.

A thought came into Hiawatha's mind. He realized that since he wasn't going to hunt, he should do something else that was special—or what would he tell grandmother?

"Let me see," said Hiawatha. "Hmmm—" He was puzzled what to do.

"Look around the island," suggested the birds. "It is very pretty from above."

"I can't fly, so I will have to see it from the ground," said Hiawatha.

"The brooks are cool and blue; we like them," said the beavers.

"The trees are green, with leaves all summer long," said the raccoon.

"The bushes have lots of berries that are tasty to eat," said the chipmunks.

"In autumn there are lots of nuts. We gather them for winter," said the squirrels.

"Sounds good," said Hiawatha. "I will be an explorer! I will find out what and who lives here. Then I will have something interesting to tell grandmother."

The first thing for an explorer to do is to look for trails, of course. Oh, oh! Around the bend, in the middle of the path were paw marks so big that Hiawatha could hardly believe his eyes. He stepped into the first print with one foot, then with two feet—why, every paw print was so large they would hold both of his feet! There were long, sharp claw marks besides. This was indeed a time for caution.

Not a sound broke the stillness except that twig he accidentally stepped on, and those stones that rolled off the path, making a tinkling sound. Hiawatha crept along on his hands and knees. He approached a big round rock. The paw marks led around it. What was on the other side of the rock? He, Hiawatha, would find out!

But someone else, on the other side of the rock, heard that breaking twig and the sound of those

rolling stones. He, too, wanted to find out what was approaching so stealthily. Suddenly there they were, face to face, a frightened Hiawatha and a terrified bear cub. Hiawatha had often played with bear cubs, so he lost his fear immediately. This was a cute little fellow!

The bear cub had never seen a boy. He didn't know what a boy was. He only saw that this creature was something down on all fours, like an animal. But it also had a feather, so it was like a bird, too.

One quick look was enough for the bear cub. He squealed in fear and dashed away as fast as his fat little legs would carry him. He glanced back over his shoulder and saw that this strange thing was coming after him and now it was running on only two legs. What's more, it was yell-

ing at him. The cub didn't wait to listen. This was even more scary, if possible.

"Wait, wait," Hiawatha shouted to the cub. "Do not be afraid. I only want you to stay and play with us. Wait—wait," he puffed, "let me talk to you."

But the little cub headed for home and disappeared into the cave where he lived.

Hiawatha reached the bear cave. Something moved inside. Hiawatha jumped into the dark shadow, grabbing what he thought was the cub bear. "I caught you!" laughed Hiawatha and he held on tightly.

An angry, terrible roar almost burst his eardrums. A hot breath hit his face. He looked into a great mouth full of sharp teeth. This wasn't the cute bear cub he'd wanted to play with. This was the cub's very angry mother and he had grabbed her by the nose. Nothing could be worse!

The mama bear was furious at the stranger who had frightened her child. She did not know Hiawatha only wanted to play and that he meant no harm. Besides, her nose hurt when he grabbed it.

Hiawatha ran as he had never run before, but the huge mama bear, with her lengthy, pounding strides, gained ground at every step. She roared so loud that it could be heard all through the forest. Hiawatha was in deep, deep trouble—and all of his friends knew it.

Meanwhile, the fleeing Hiawatha saw a tree on the other side of a small stream. Maybe that would be safe. He crossed the stream quickly. The bear did not fear the water and splashed through it, too. The old tree had lost all its leaves and most of its limbs. The chipmunk and squirrel sat near the top, to observe the chase. The boy climbed almost to the top. The tree creaked with his weight, but he felt safe.

Not for long! Bears are good at tree-climbing, so up crawled the bear, as fast as she could. Two beavers came a-running and with their sharp teeth gnawed at the base of the tree.

The beavers sounded the first alarm by beating out the signal with their flat tails. The other animals heard it and ran to their secret meeting place. A chipmunk and squirrel were told to lead Hiawatha to the hidden clearing. The others knew what to do to help their friend and they would have everything ready—if the bear did not catch Hiawatha first.

As the bear reached out to grab Hiawatha, the old tree swayed with her extra weight. Then, weakened at the base by the two beavers who were gnawing frantically at the trunk, the old tree gave one deep shudder and toppled over—CRASH!

Down came the bear, the breath knocked out of her. Down came Hiawatha. But the squirrel helped the boy as he fell, so he landed on the ground gently.

"Follow us," said the squirrel.

"Hurry, hurry," said the chipmunk.

Hiawatha had to run away before the bear got back her breath and resumed the chase. The squirrel and the chipmunk were to guide him to the clearing.

From the moment the beavers had sounded the alarm, the other animals had been very busy. They dragged two fallen branches to be used as outer shafts for a simple cart. The raccoons and chipmunks found something that would serve as reins and a harness. They tied a crosspiece between the shafts for a footboard. The fawn, who could run almost as fast as the wind—and that is faster than a bear can run—stepped inside the harness. All was ready when the squirrel guided Hiawatha to the clearing.

"Here! Get on this! Take these reins." All the animals joined in showing him what to do. Hiawatha obeyed gladly.

"Giddap!" they shouted. "Now get going!" They could hear the big bear's roar getting closer and closer, closer and closer.

The fawn leaped ahead and in a flash Hiawatha was whizzing over the ground in the fastest ride he would ever have in his whole life. The forest closed in around the fleeing pair. The fawn and the small forest friends knew many shorter paths, and all the safe hidden trails, and these were the paths they used.

The other small animals had a hard time keeping up with the speedy deer. Some of them had to leap from tree to tree—and some had to hop, skip and jump. But they were all determined to be on hand to say good-by to their friend.

The roars and growls of the bear seemed more faint. At last they were only a whisper of sound and then they faded out completely. The bear was left far behind.

Hiawatha realized that now he was safe from the bear, but he still had to cross the lake to get home. The afternoon sun was sinking low in the sky as Hiawatha and his helpful friends arrived at the lake shore.

"Thanks, everybody," said Hiawatha. "I will never forget all you have done for me. I'll go home in my canoe and I will always remember you."

His canoe? Hiawatha looked where his canoe had been beached.

"My canoe! It's gone!" cried Hiawatha.

The animals pointed toward the middle of the lake. There was the canoe, drifting out of reach.

Hiawatha almost wept. "I didn't pull it up far enough, and I can't swim to get it. Without my canoe I can't go home."

"Don't worry, we will get your canoe," said the beavers. "We are good swimmers."

They dived gracefully in the water, swam out to the canoe and pushed it easily to shore. They held it steady as Hiawatha, using the turtle as a stepping-stone, got inside and settled down. And there he sat!

"Where is your paddle?" asked a beaver.

"Did you lose that, too?" asked another.

"Yes, I guess so," said Hiawatha, "but I didn't use it. The breeze brought me."

"Well, there's no breeze now," said the beavers, "and we may not have one for an hour, and maybe not until morning."

"Oh, my, how will I get home?" the boy asked anxiously.

The two beavers whispered slyly to each other and passed the word along. All the animals nodded their heads in agreement.

"We will be glad to help you, if you'll promise us something," said the beavers.

"Oh, I will," said Hiawatha. "But what should I promise?"

"That you will come again soon."

"I will," said Hiawatha gladly.

The beavers turned the bow of the canoe homeward, and using their flat tails as the paddles, they skimmed the canoe across the shining water, to Hiawatha's tepee. Then they bade him a fond good-by and swam back to their island.

Grandmother Nokomis was waiting at the tepee for him. She had his supper ready.

Hiawatha did not realize how hungry he really was until he saw all the good things grandmother had prepared. He felt tired, too.

"Today I was a mighty Hiawatha and so I hunted, but—" his voice drifted off.

"Ah, but now—" grandmother gathered a nodding child in her arms. "But now," she repeated with a loving smile, "now you are a mighty *little* Hiawatha, sound asleep."

And Hiawatha, mighty little Hiawatha, dreamed happily the whole night long.

Through the Picture Frame

THERE WAS no doubt about it. Hialmar had been good all day. He hadn't torn his shirt, or teased his little sister, or slammed the kitchen door. He hadn't spilled anything, or broken anything, or made an especially loud noise.

After supper, he went upstairs to his room. He finished his homework, and put all his toys away neatly in the cupboard. Then he stepped out on the balcony outside his window. It was a wonderful, a thrilling night. The trees were making strange, mysterious rustlings. The moon was out, and so were thousands of little dancing stars.

"Oh!" sighed Hialmar, "I do wish something

would happen! But I suppose I have to go to bed." He said good night to the moon and the stars, the birds and the crickets, and the hoarse old bullfrog down below in the pond. He waved good night to Gerda, the little girl across the way. Then he came back into his room and jumped into bed. He had scarcely closed his eyes when he was fast asleep.

Then something *did* happen. There was a sudden thump outside, then a scuffling and a shuffling. Footsteps on the balcony! Footsteps coming toward the window! Someone was cautiously pushing it open wide. The face of a little man with enormous spectacles peered into the room.

He looked searchingly all around, until he saw Hialmar asleep in his bed. Then he smiled and came tiptoeing in. He was a very strange and very little man. He had a tremendous big floppy hat with a blue feather, and white foamy whiskers that covered his whole chest like a bib. His heavy green coat came all the way down to the heels of his rough brown boots. Over his left arm he carried a large umbrella.

This very strange and very little man was very businesslike. He examined all of Hialmar's clothes, tidily laid out upon the chair. He went to the cupboard and counted every toy. Then he sat down at the table and studied every letter of Hialmar's homework in his school notebook. He even picked up Hialmar's report card.

"Always punctual, always present," he read aloud. "Mmmm . . ." he muttered, "that's satisfactory. Most satisfactory!"

"But who are you?" asked Hialmar, opening his eyes wide.

"I'm Ole Lukoie," said the little man. His voice was squeaky, but not unpleasant. "It's high time we got started."

"Started where?" Hialmar sat up straight.

"That depends," said Ole, "on how smart you are. How well do you spell your arithmetic?"

Hialmar laughed. "I don't *spell* arithmetic!"

"Too bad!" said Ole, strumming on the table, and looking very solemn. "I guess you'd better not go *there* on your trip. You'll have to spend the holiday somewhere else."

"Holiday!" cried Hialmar. "I didn't know it was a holiday."

"Tuesday's always a holiday," said Ole impatiently.

Hialmar felt very confused. "But today isn't Tuesday."

"Who said it was Tuesday? Dear me! You *are* confused. Do try to keep your mind on what you're doing. I hope you're all packed."

"Oh, I can get ready very quickly," said Hial-

Without another word, he seized his umbrella with both hands, and jumped up on the foot of Hialmar's bed. He snapped open the umbrella and hurled it toward Hialmar. "Grab on," he shouted. "You're on your way!"

Hialmar flung back the blankets. He reached up and caught the umbrella by the handle, just as it flew by over his head. In another instant, he went sailing through the air. Crash! He hit something. Hialmar had plunged right through the middle of a picture! It was an oil painting, the dull one with dark trees, that hung over the chest of drawers.

"Mmmm," said Hialmar, taking a deep breath. "It smells nice here inside this picture frame."

He picked himself up. There was grass all around him, tall and green. A gay little wind was blowing through the trees. It was making the leaves dance in strange, mysterious shadows. Some looked like long, thin people. Some looked like funny little waddling ducks. Some looked like elephants. The funniest shadow of them all was a small pug nose, all alone by itself, without any eyes or mouth. It was a lost nose. But Hialmar recognized it at once. It was the nose of his piano teacher, Miss Prill. Hialmar laughed aloud.

mar excitedly. "I expect I'd better take a lunch . . . some sandwiches and cake."

"*Cake*," cried Ole in a horrified voice. "Surely not cake! That would be most insulting to the King's pastry cooks."

"Oh . . ." stammered Hialmar. "I didn't intend to be rude."

"You must be very careful about that on your trip." Ole took off his spectacles and got down from the chair. He began pacing up and down, with the blue feather of his hat trailing behind him on the floor. "Dear me! How we've been wasting time! Do you know how to fly a horse?"

"Fly a horse! What kind of a horse?"

"An ordinary horse," said Ole. "You know . . . a talking horse . . . the kind that likes a dash of maple syrup on his oats."

"Well . . . er . . . I can *try* to fly him."

"Satisfactory," said Ole. He came up close to Hialmar and whispered in his ear. "Do you think you could manage a dragon . . . all alone?"

"Manage a *dragon!* What kind of a dragon?"

"Just an ordinary dragon," said Ole. "You know . . . the kind that snorts out fiery flames."

"Well . . . er . . . I've never met a dragon."

"Never met a dragon! Just imagine that!" Ole shook his head sadly. "Then let the trip begin at once!"

"Shhh . . . don't you know it's rude to laugh aloud when someone's singing?" said a voice just above him.

Hialmar looked up. Three silly little birds were frowning at him sternly. "I'm sorry," he said. "It *was* rude of me."

"Won't you run along and do your laughing somewhere else? This is the *only* place we have to rehearse." The birds looked really upset.

"You mean a bird can't sing any place he wants to in the forest?" asked Hialmar.

"Of course not! Please hurry along. In a few minutes the frogs will be tuning up . . . and then it will be time for the pheasants and the quail. Please go and let us rehearse!"

"Very well," said Hialmar, "if you'll just tell me what the rehearsal is for."

"For the spring concert, of course! For Easter! *Please* go! It won't seem at all like Easter if we don't sing." The birds were almost crying.

"No Easter! Then it *is* important for you to practice. But where shall I go where I won't be in the way?" asked Hialmar. "This picture is rather small, you know."

"Just anywhere back there in the sun! It's too noisy in the sun for us to rehearse."

"Too noisy in the sun!" thought Hialmar. "What nonsense is that?" Nevertheless, he thought he'd better not disturb the birds any more. He hurried off.

As Hialmar stepped back to a spot where the sun was shining brightly, his ears began to ring. The world inside the picture frame that he had always thought so stupid and dull was humming with a hundred kinds of noisy noises. The birds were right. It *was* noisy in the sun!

Below the earth, the roots of the trees were quarreling with the roots of the flowers, pushing them aside, and telling them to move somewhere else. Moles were objecting to the way ground

hogs came poking their noses into their tunnels. Great armies of ants made a low steady buzzing as they scurried along at their work.

Above the ground, the beetles were scolding the toads. "Why do you jump around so much? You get on everybody's nerves." And all the bees and all the butterflies seemed to be trying to sit on the very same leaves at the very same time.

Hialmar clapped his hands to his ears to shut out the noise. "Whew! This picture is too crowded!" He turned his back to it, and looked down into the room.

But strange things were going on there too.

The flowers in the room were jumping wildly up and down in their pots. Some were climbing the walls. Some were swinging merrily from the ceiling like circus trapezes. Suddenly, from out of the green vase in the corner, came the sound of stretching and yawns. Hialmar couldn't believe his ears. It was the vase in which he always hid the cores of the apples he took from Aunt Gussie's tree next door. The stretching and yawning grew louder! The base began to shake. It groaned. A tree trunk burst up through the top! It shot out in branches all hanging with fruit . . . apples and pears and ripe, juicy figs!

Bang! A hard green apple struck the portrait

of Aunt Gussie. It struck her right in the head, in the middle of her stiff black pompadour.

She blinked. "What's going on here?" She leaned out from her picture frame and looked crossly at Ole, who was standing there below.

"Oh . . . just a little fun," said Ole.

"Fun!" cried Aunt Gussie. "Why, it's the middle of the night!"

"So it is," said Ole. "It's high time Hialmar got started on his trip."

"*Trip!*" Aunt Gussie gasped. "With whom?"

"All by himself," said Ole. "He's plenty grown up."

"Grown up! Why, he's only a little child!"

"Madame," said Ole, "I regret to tell you that you are mistaken. Hialmar is *not* a little child. Ask the furniture what *they* think about it."

"Furniture!" snapped Aunt Gussie. "You mean that frightful new modern chair?"

"I am not frightful," answered the new blue chair. "You just think so because you have bad taste. And I say it's high time Hialmar went on a trip."

"Time?" interrupted the clock. "I'm the boss of when it's time. And I say it's not the time. He's got to stay and look after me. I need a winding. I feel I'm running down."

"That's very selfish," said the blue jug, opening and shutting its mouth faster than it could think of words to speak.

The furniture was now making such a noise that no one could hear anything. The footstools were stamping about. The chest kept opening and shutting its drawers. And the rug rolled and unrolled itself over and over again.

Suddenly a hush fell upon the room. Hialmar's great-great-grandfather leaned out from his portrait and spoke. His voice was so kind and great-great-grandfatherly, that even Aunt Gussie had to calm down. She straightened her hair and sat back in her picture frame. "Hialmar has the right to take a trip," he said. "All children have to go away sometimes. It says so in the

Hialmar hurried on. On the river's edge, a little red boat was tied to a tree. Its crisp white sails were all rigged up and ready to go. Hialmar climbed in and sailed off. He sped over the water like a fresh March wind, darting in and out among the islands. None of the river creatures had ever seen such a fast-sailing ship before. They came up from their watery nests to watch Hialmar rush by.

Suddenly the river turned a very sharp bend, and broadened out as wide as the open sea.

"I'm out of sight of land," said Hialmar aloud as he walked around his ship. "There's nobody here but the water and me."

"Nobody?" It was a voice from the air. "It seems to me there's quite a crowd."

As Hialmar looked up, the clouds all burst apart. Then he could see that the sky was filled with hundreds of gorgeous birds. It was a red one that had been speaking, the one with the long, hooked bill. "Who are you?" said Hialmar. "Where did you come from? Where are you going?"

"I'm a flamingo, of course," said the bird. "Can't you tell? I'm from Brazil. My friends and I are off for the holiday."

"Holiday?" said Hialmar, still confused about what day it was. "Maybe *you* can tell me . . . why is it a holiday?"

"I don't know," answered the flamingo. "For flamingos it is always a holiday. We like it that way. Toodle-oo!" The birds all flapped their wings at Hialmar and zoomed away.

Hialmar went on pacing round the ship. Then he heard a loud chuckle behind him. It was an enormous orange fish, with a smiling green face.

"What are you doing up here in the air?" said Hialmar. "You belong underneath, in the water."

"Why?" The fish looked very disappointed. "A little fresh air isn't against the rules on a holiday."

"Is it always a holiday for fish too?"

"Certainly," answered the fish. "Otherwise there'd be no time for blowing bubbles. So long!" He flipped his fins in a fancy twirl and dove down deep below.

Hialmar looked down at the splash, and dis-

rules." He waved good-by to Hialmar and pulled himself back into his portrait again.

Hialmar turned about and walked on farther into the picture. Beyond the wood, where the birds were still rehearsing for their concert, a river ran. It twisted around mysterious curves. In some places it was wide, and in some places very narrow. Way off in the distance, Hialmar could see little colored islands popping up like jack-in-the-boxes.

covered that he could see right through the waves. At the keel of the ship, a mermaid was swishing along. She had a cute turned-up nose, and golden hair like any pretty little girl. But instead of legs, she had a graceful fish's tail.

"I must say something clever," thought Hialmar. He cleared his throat, but he couldn't think of a single word to say. He paced around the ship and came back again. "I know. . . . I'll ask her up on board for a sail." He leaned down over the rail to speak. Now the water was *full* of mermaids!

Hialmar couldn't think what to do. He was just about to pace around the ship once more, when squash! Something wet was flung around his neck. It was pulling him down. He slipped and fell on the deck. He struggled. . . .

"Silly!" laughed someone. "It's no use to struggle. I've caught you and you're mine."

Hialmar stopped struggling and looked up. It was a necklace of sea-flowers that had him by the throat. A mermaid was pulling it tight. But Hialmar did not care to be caught. He felt like pushing her away. Then he remembered that Ole had cautioned him not to be rude. He smiled. "You've caught me all right, but you'll have to let me go."

"Why? Don't you like me?" The mermaid pouted.

"Oh yes . . . but you see, I'm on a trip. I'm in a hurry. There are places I have to go."

The mermaid pulled herself half out of the water and rested her chin on the deck of the ship. She sighed. "I suppose *you're* going to the tower, too. All the boys leave me to go to the tower."

"What tower?"

"The tower where the princess is locked up."

"Who said anything about a princess in a tower?" Hialmar whispered. He was breathless with excitement.

"The princess's pigeon. He tells me everything."

"What does he say . . . quick . . . tell me."

"He says the princess is so delicate she can't eat anything but hummingbirds' eggs. And she can't drink anything but the crystal tears of a weeping willow. That's what the pigeon says. But she'll never be rescued. There's nobody in the whole world that's strong or smart enough to do it. That's what the pigeon says."

"I'm strong and smart enough!" cried Hialmar. "I'll rescue the princess!" He tore off the necklace and threw it back into the water.

"So you're leaving me too!" The mermaid was crying now, and mopping her eyes with her long golden hair.

"Don't cry," said Hialmar. "I *have* to rescue the princess."

"All right . . . then good-by!" She threw Hialmar a kiss and glided off. "I'll hear about it, you know, if you're only just bragging. The pigeon tells me everything." The mermaid disappeared over the crest of a wave.

Hialmar stood up. He rushed forward to the prow of the ship and looked about. The river was narrow again. He sailed along under a high arched bridge. When he came out at the other side, he was right at the foot of an old stone tower.

"The princess's tower!" he gasped. 'Way up at the top, he could see her tiny window, locked with heavy iron bars. He could hear her dainty little footsteps pacing on the hard, stone floor.

"I must be brave and strong as a prince," said Hialmar to himself. Just at that minute, a sharp

wind came whizzing past. Round and round he
spun in a whirlwind. Then suddenly it was calm
again. Now Hialmar was dressed in the suit of a
prince. His own clothes had vanished! Hanging
at his waist was a heavy gold-hilted sword.

Hialmar tied up his ship and ran ashore. "If
only I had a horse!" he sighed.

"Always punctual, always present! Please remember that when you make out your report."
It was a horse! He came charging out from the
thicket. He bowed.

"I surely will remember it," said Hialmar.

"All right then . . . climb up in the saddle and
we'll talk things over."

"I'm certainly glad you can talk," said Hialmar.

"I not only talk, I talk back, too. Let me tell
you it's very dull being a horse, if you don't
know how to talk back."

"I expect so. Now hadn't we better get started?"

"All right . . . fine! Giddyap!" said the horse.

"You're not the one that says giddyap," said
Hialmar. "That's what I say."

"Oh, of course . . . pardon me. I keep forgetting.
You know . . . when I play horse with my little

son . . . he's just a little colt . . . he likes to be
the horse and I'm always the driver. So, naturally,
I'm always the one that says giddyap."

"I understand perfectly," nodded Hialmar.
"Now let's go. Giddyap!"

What a horse! He didn't run. He bounded.
Hialmar could hardly keep to his saddle. He
crouched down and clung like a jockey. "I'll go
around to the other side of the tower and see
if perhaps there's an entrance there," he thought.
He pulled on the rein to the left.

The horse stopped still. He turned his neck
all the way around and looked at Hialmar with
a very puzzled expression. "Is something wrong?"

"No, nothing's wrong," said Hialmar a little
impatiently. "I want to go left. Can't you feel
me pulling left on your rein?"

"*Pulling!*" The horse stamped a front foot. "Of
all the rude things I ever heard of! What a way
that is to talk to a horse! I'll have you know
right now I'm not the sort of horse you can pull
around by the nose."

"I'm terribly sorry," said Hialmar. "I guess I
don't know very much about talking horses."
Hialmar was beginning to feel very sad. He
could now see the pale white face of the princess

behind the bars of her window. She looked just like Gerda, his friend across the street. She was all alone. "I must get to her quickly," he thought. "This horse is delaying me so."

"Well," said the horse, "have you made up your mind where you want to go?"

"Yes . . . yes," answered Hialmar. "I want to get in the tower. I must rescue the princess!"

"Rescue the princess? . . . Why didn't you say so before? Quick . . . giddyap!"

"No . . . no . . . no . . . *you* don't say giddyap!"

"Oh! Just imagine my forgetting again! I do beg your pardon. Now if you'll just say giddyap, we'll have that princess down here in a twinkling."

"*Giddyap!*"

Like an arrow the horse sped through the air. Straight for the tower wall he plunged. Hialmar shut his eyes tightly. He braced himself. Crash! They hit. Enormous stones came thunder-

ing down. Clear through the shattered wall burst horse and rider together.

It was dark inside the tower. It smelled musty and damp.

"Well," sighed the horse, kicking himself free of the dirt, "I hope you don't expect me to do *that* every day." He brushed off Hialmar with his tail. "You'd better hurry on upstairs and get the princess."

"Aren't you coming with me?"

"No. Tower stairs, the winding kind, are very confusing to my hind legs. I'll be waiting for you at the entrance to the underground passage."

"Underground passage! To where?"

"It's the shortest way out to the town—unless, of course, you're afraid of the fiery dragon and the bats."

But Hialmar didn't even wait for the horse to finish what he was saying. He rushed up the stairs four at a time. Heavy oaken doors blocked his entrance to the tower chamber. Hialmar seized his sword and slashed his way through.

"It's Hialmar!" he shouted, as he plunged into the room. "You're rescued, Princess! It's Hialmar!"

The pale delicate princess flung herself into his arms. "Take me to my father, the King!" she sobbed. "Take me away from this lonely tower!"

Quickly Hialmar led the princess down the stairs. The horse was restlessly pacing up and down below. "Always punctual, always present," he called out as he heard them coming. Hialmar led the princess up to him and helped her to mount. Then he jumped up behind her in the saddle. "Giddyap!"

The horse did not stir. He turned his head toward Hialmar. He frowned. "Well . . . are you going to be rude again? I'm not accustomed to carrying people on my back when I haven't even been introduced."

"Oh!" said Hialmar. "I'm so sorry. I'd like to have you meet the princess."

"Pleased to meet you, Princess," said the horse, bowing. "It's been a pleasure to assist at your rescue. Now, we'd better be off." He sniffed. "Smell that heat coming up from below! The dragon must have been eating more hot coals. He'll be in *terrible* shape! Well . . . here we go!"

They went bounding down a long passage, past huge, mysterious doors.

Suddenly Hialmar heard a loud wheezing and snorting. "It must be the dragon," he whispered to the princess. "Don't be afraid. I'll slay him with just one thrust of my sword."

"I'll charge straight into him," said the horse. "That is, with your permission."

"Permission granted," said Hialmar.

Nearer and nearer they rushed toward the snorting. The air was filled with fiery sparks.

"Oh!" cried the princess, "I have cinders in my eyes!"

Hialmar leaned over and whispered to the horse. "This is no place for the delicate princess. Step back a little and await me. I must do away with this dragon alone!"

Hialmar dismounted. He gripped his sword and strode forward into the smoke. He could feel the animal's blistering breath.

"Not so close! . . . not so close!" rasped a voice just in front of him. "You'll singe yourself. Really you will! Don't you know I'm a dangerous dragon? Why don't you go away?"

"Why, you're a friendly dragon!" cried Hialmar. He beat back the smoke and looked right up into the dragon's face. Red-hot flames came spurting from his nostrils. "My!" gasped Hialmar. "You *are* in terrible shape. Doesn't it hurt your throat?"

"Yes, it does, but a dragon has to breathe, doesn't he?" The dragon began coughing so hard that Hialmar was afraid he'd choke.

"Can't I do something?" cried Hialmar. "Quick . . . let me climb up and slap you on the back."

"No . . . no . . . I'm really all right," gasped the dragon. "Would you care for a snack?"

"Well, I'll be jiggered!" cried Hialmar. As the smoke lifted a little, he saw that fresh roasted popcorn was popping on the dragon's breath. His long green backbone was hung with lollypops and all sorts of cake.

But Hialmar had no time for idling with pleasant, fiery dragons. From out of the darkness behind, where the horse was waiting, came terrified shoutings. "Help! Help! The bats! They're stealing the princess!" The long hallway echoed with the horsy shriekings.

Hialmar raced ahead into the blackness. Something brushed past him . . . an enormous something. It flapped. "A bat!" gasped Hialmar. For a moment, he didn't know what to do. "Horse, where are you?"

"Here! Right beside you! Always punctual, always present . . . jump on! Keep flashing your bright sword! It will dazzle the bats!"

And so it did. In the blinding light of the shining steel, the giant creatures flopped back. They plumped against each other, blinking and helpless. Hialmar clung to the saddle and held the delicate little princess safe. Off they galloped along the underground passage.

At length, they came up into the open air outdoors. It was dark. It was foggy, too.

Hialmar suddenly realized that he had no idea how far it was to the King's palace, or even how to get there.

"You *are* going to take me home, aren't you?" asked the princess timidly.

"Of course," said Hialmar. "But I do wish some one of us knew the way."

"Knew the way!" cried the horse. "There you go being rude again! *I* know the way! Whoever heard of a horse that didn't know the way home?"

"I'm sorry," said Hialmar. "I really didn't know that horses knew so much." He sighed happily. "Then all we have to do is sit back and ride to the palace."

"Sit back! I should say not! Rescuing a princess is not so easy as that. We have still to escape the invisible black horseman."

"Invisible black horseman? Who's he?" Hialmar felt of his sword to make sure it was safely there in his belt.

The horse looked cautiously up at the air. "The black horseman," he whispered, "is the guardian of the air that surrounds the forest that surrounds the town that surrounds the tower where the princess is supposed to be locked up."

"But if he's invisible," whispered Hialmar, "how'll we know when we see him?"

"Can you smell?" asked the horse.

"Certainly I can smell," answered Hialmar.

"Then you'll know when you see him," answered the horse. "You'll smell him. He has a smell like the inside of a drum . . . you know

. . . that old cracked drum in your Aunt Gussie's cellar."

"But I've never smelled the inside of that old cracked drum," said Hialmar.

"Too bad!" said the horse sadly.

"Never mind," said Hialmar. "If I can't see him, and I can't smell him, at least I'll hear him."

The horse shook his head. "No, you won't. The only noise the black horseman makes is the noise that tall grass makes in the middle of a field, just as it turns into hay. Nobody can hear that noise except a horse. . . . Shhh . . . I think I hear something!"

The horse drew in a great tremendous breath that seemed to come up from the very tip of his tail. Away he shot like a rocket! Over the roof tops, the tree tops, and the tops of twenty snow-capped peaks, went princess, Hialmar, and horse.

Then suddenly something seemed to go wrong.

"Look out!" panted the horse. "Prepare to crash!" He scraped past a church spire. Down he plunged through a roof. He sprawled out flat on a dusty attic floor.

"Sorry to do that, Princess," said the horse. He picked himself up quickly, and brushed off her little golden crown. "It was the only way I could get rid of that awful black horseman."

"Gracious!" gasped the princess. "Was he very close?"

"Close! I had to fight him tooth and hoof. You should see him now! Look, I still have bits of his mane in my mouth." He opened his mouth wide for the princess to look in.

"I don't see any mane."

"Well, you would," said the horse, "if it weren't invisible. Take my word for it."

Hialmar had climbed up to the attic window and was looking out. "I can see the King's palace! It's a beautiful, golden palace, with dozens of turrets and towers."

The princess jumped up beside him. "It's my father's house," she cried. "It's home!"

"Well," said the horse, "what are we waiting for?"

In another instant, they were off again. Everyone was happy now. Every now and then the

horse turned a somersault, just to show that he was having a very fine time. He pranced right up the main driveway to the palace.

A soldier stepped out and ordered him to halt.

"Halt?" cried the horse. "What a way *that* is to speak! Sir, you have offended a fine, loyal steed—the steed of the hero who has rescued your fair princess!" He whirled around.

"The princess!" gasped the soldier, as he caught sight of her in the saddle. "Sound the trumpets! Let the hero beg his loyal steed to come back!"

The horse turned around, and this time he pranced up the driveway in triumph. While the soldiers all stood at attention, he stepped right up to the palace doorway, and stood still while Hialmar helped the princess to dismount.

The King rushed out in his long ermine cloak and clasped the princess in his arms. He shook Hialmar's hand and smiled a broad kingly smile.

"Now, young man, what can I do to reward you?"

"I don't know," said Hialmar. "Let's go inside to the throne room and talk things over."

"And leave me standing here all alone on my four legs?" said the horse. "Rude, mighty rude!"

"Oh, I'm sorry," said Hialmar. "I thought you'd come along too."

"No," said the horse emphatically. "If His Majesty will pardon the suggestion, I'd like to be invited to enjoy the fresh air in the barn."

"Just make yourself at home," said the King. "I'll see that the royal coachman makes you comfortable. Possibly you'd like a dash of maple syrup with your oats."

"Perfect," said the horse. "Call me any time you need me. Always punctual, always present." He galloped away toward the stable.

"Now," said the King, taking Hialmar's arm,

and leading him and the princess into the palace, "You *must* tell me what I can do to reward you."

Hialmar tried to think quickly of all the things he'd like to be. He couldn't be king, because there was the King himself. "I'd like to be the Lord High Chancellor," he said.

"I'd like very much to have you for Lord High Chancellor," said the King. "But you see, it's impossible. You have no whiskers."

Hialmar stroked his chin. "So I haven't, Your Majesty." He thought for a minute. "I'd like to be the Keeper of the Royal Gold."

"I'd like very much to have you for Keeper of the Royal Gold," said the King. "But you see, that's impossible too, unless, of course, you know how to count in Chinese."

"But why must I count in Chinese?" asked Hialmar.

"I don't know," said the King. "It's just something it says in the rules."

Hialmar thought again. "I'd like to be the Chief-in-Charge-of-Cooks."

"Chief-in-Charge-of-Cooks! A splendid idea!" The King clapped his hands to summon a page boy. "Order the cooks to assemble at once! Their new chief is here to give them their orders."

A moment later, carved silver doors swung open. A hundred cooks in tall white hats clicked their spoons and stood at attention.

"Command them," said the King. "They are here to do your bidding."

Hialmar cleared his throat. "Bake me," he said, "a cake for the princess. Let it be the largest cake that has ever been baked in the palace. Let it have all the frostings that you have ever frosted, and a hundred new kinds of frosting that you have never frosted before . . . and, if

you please, I should like another cake, a smaller cake, made entirely of maple syrup. Send that one down to the barn."

"With such a cake," said the King, "we must have a party!" He clapped his hands for a page boy again. "Order the jesters and, jugglers to assemble at once! Put up the tents for the circus! Blow up ten thousand colored balloons!"

Then from the tents outside they heard the drums of the circus band. Hialmar and the princess rushed to their seats in the center of the royal box.

Bugles blew. On came the parade! Clowns! Tightrope walkers! Elephants, dancing elephants in little lace skirts! Giraffes and cowboys, midgets, and dozens of slippery black seals! Next came a horse and chariot. It came racing round the circus ring toward the royal box.

"Why, it's my horse!" cried Hialmar, "and Ole Lukoie is the charioteer!"

Ole's blue feather was standing out straight in the wind. Faster and faster thundered the chariot. Suddenly Ole opened his umbrella. He hurled it toward Hialmar in the royal box. "Grab on!" he shouted. "It's time you got started. Your ship is at the dock."

"Good-bye, Princess!" cried Hialmar. He caught the umbrella. "I'm on my way!" It carried him down to the racing chariot, to the shoulders of the white-whiskered charioteer.

The circus band stopped still. The jugglers stopped juggling. The clowns stopped clowning. The elephants stared as the chariot plunged

out through the tentside, with a boy and an umbrella riding on the shoulders of a little man.

They galloped down the steep river bank to the dock.

The wind was high. The ship was tugging at its rope. Hialmar leaped from the chariot. He threw the umbrella back to Ole. He cast off the anchor and jumped on board.

"So long!" called the horse. "Don't forget what I told you when you make out my report. Always punctual, always present." Then Hialmar faintly heard him speak to Ole. "Come now, giddyap!"

"Not satisfactory," said Ole. "I'm the one to say giddyap."

Their voices drifted away in the wind.

Hialmar sailed away.

A great gale was sweeping toward him from behind. It came in loud blasts like giant snorings. It *was* snorings! The houses alongside the river were sound asleep.

The ship rocked. It quivered. Hialmar shut his eyes. Crash! He hit something. He sat down with a thud. The wind had gone down.

Hialmar looked around. He was back again inside the picture frame, sitting with his legs dangling down into the room. The silly little birds were still perched on the same branch, still rehearsing for the Easter concert!

Hialmar began to feel very tired. He dropped down from the picture frame, walked across the rug, and got back into bed. The room was very quiet.

"Well," whispered his great-great-grandfather from his portrait beside the bed. "Did you have a good time?"

"Satisfactory," said Hialmar, "most satisfactory. I only hope I wasn't too rude to that wonderful horse."

"Did you tell him you were sorry?"

"Yes, I always did."

"Then it's all right. Nobody's ever rude if he says he's sorry. You'd better go to sleep now so you'll wake up in time for school."

"Always punctual, always present," mumbled Hialmar. He closed his eyes and slept.

The Story of Timothy's House

THIS is the story of the house of Timothy Mouse, just as he told it to Dumbo. Dumbo was the little circus elephant with the very big ears, and Timothy was his best friend.

Timothy told Dumbo all about it one rainy afternoon when the circus show was over and little Dumbo, with his clown clothes on, was waiting for the second performance.

Timothy had traveled from town to town with the circus as long as he could remember. And as long as he could remember, Timothy had wanted a little private place in the circus that he could call his own.

It was all very well digging his way into a nice warm spot inside one of the bales of hay they always carried around for the elephants, but it was rather tiresome having to pick out a different bale each night. He even had a couple of narrow escapes when an elephant unexpectedly made up his mind to lie down on the hay.

Added to that, Timothy sometimes got hay fever. And a little mouse just doesn't dare sneeze at the wrong time. So Timothy wanted a regular home, a safe home, a home of his own.

"I stumbled on the idea of building a house," Timothy told Dumbo, "when I fell over an empty cheese carton outside the clowns' tent, in the dark."

The clowns had been eating cheese and crackers before they went to bed, and Timothy went to see what was left of the feast. The cheese was gone, but the container was there. It had a peaked roof and it *looked* like a house. Timothy put it on the framework under the floor of the ringmaster's car, right by a knothole so he could pop in and out easily.

That was a fine beginning, but of course Timothy needed a great many things to make it homelike.

First, he fixed up the outside. Naturally, he needed a chimney. So he hunted and he hunted and he hunted—and finally he found an old corncob pipe.

Then he found a thimble. He didn't know exactly how he could use it, but he knew it would come in very handy. So he took it with him.

And on his way home he saw a broken necklace of orange beads, so he brought that, too.

And still he needed a thing or two. He hunted and he hunted and he hunted—and finally he found a walnut shell and two gold-headed hatpins . . . some feathers from an old feather boa . . . and a cork . . . and a big clothespin. And he took them all.

On his way home he saw a broken necklace of blue beads, so he brought that too.

They didn't look like much, all lying in a heap, but Timothy went to work because, more than anything else, he wanted his own home.

And after a while he had everything in place —and he stood off and looked at it and he beamed with delight and threw out his arms and cried, "It's a mansion!"

BUT IT WAS EMPTY INSIDE!

So Timothy started out again. And he hunted and he hunted and he hunted and he found just what he wanted! A half-opened sardine can. So he took that.

And on his way home he saw a fat hairpin . . . and another cork.

The cork and the hairpin were easy to carry home, but the sardine can was heavy for just a little mouse. Then a boy came along, saw the can, and kicked it as he walked. His last kick sent it into a clump of grass not five feet from Timothy's home, and Timothy pulled it the rest of the way.

But his house wasn't half furnished yet, and off Timothy went again. And he hunted. And this time he found an overturned wastebasket. It had lots of very important things in it. There were safety pins . . . and a bottle top . . . and a piece of broken comb . . . and a collar button . . . and a beautiful postage stamp. And Timothy took them all.

He hurried back to the wastebasket and found what was left of a sock with broad red stripes.

He found more hairpins—they were *very* use-

Timothy pasted the beautiful postage stamp which, with the golden button to balance it on the other side, made as fine a decoration as you can imagine. The old sock became a beautiful rug.

"There," said Timothy, "is a very fine living room for a mouse."

Next morning, Timothy made a rare find—a big stickpin! With an almost-real diamond in it!

"What could be better," cried Timothy, "as a mirror for my bathroom!" But then he remembered that he didn't have a bathroom. "Dear me," he said to himself, "I *must* have a bathroom, or however can I take a bath?"

So he hunted and he hunted and he hunted and finally he saw an old paper cup with a drinking straw beside it. And on his way home he found a playing card. Then he saw a half-empty packet of paper matches. He propped open the lid—and there he had a fine washstand. He stuck his almost-real diamond stickpin above it for a mirror. Then he put the playing card on the floor for a mat.

And so he added to his home. Another pipe, with a lid, gave him a nice stove, and a key served as a poker.

Timothy loved music, too, so he made himself some lovely musical instruments. Some assorted pins, stuck through the side of a boxlid and supported by a spool, gave him a zither to play.

He had a harp, too, made from more pins in a cork with a safety pin as a frame. (This was mostly for looks, because Timothy could never

ful—and a bright gold button, which he polished until it shone.

And on his way home he found an old, cracked safety-razor blade. So he picked that up very carefully and took it home too.

Now he really had a great deal to work with. So Timothy began to make things for the inside of his house. First he made a rocking chair. He used two safety pins, a cork, and the big hairpin.

Then he made a table out of two smaller hairpins and the bottle top. But best of all, so far, was his fireplace. There, right in the center of the side wall, was the sardine can with its lid rolled back to frame a hearth, and the piece of comb just fitting the front as a perfect fender.

Beside the fireplace was a bit of shingle with the razor blade handy to chop it up for firewood. The walnut shell was a wood basket. On the wall

get much music out of it—it just added a good deal of elegance to the corner of his living room.)

But Timothy's prize possession was his chest for cheeses. This was a small candy box which still had its lacy paper frills around the edges. Partitions ran across it, and when Timothy stood it on end and filled it with bits of his favorite cheeses, carefully arranged to give the most delightful combinations of fragrant odors, it was, Timothy felt, the most wonderful thing of all.

Timothy's house was nearly complete. He made clothestrees by notching matches and standing them up straight. He picked some dandelions and put them in the thimble. It made a lovely vase.

But when night came and Timothy was very tired from all his work, he couldn't get a good rest. He didn't have a good bed. It was a nice springy scrubbing brush, with four old pencils for posts. But it had no mattress and no covers.

The rest of his bedroom was fine, Timothy thought. A matchbox was a bureau, and he had found a broken mirror for it. He had a chair, a rug—made of someone's lost handkerchief—and a beautiful cigar band for a wall decoration.

After a rather uncomfortable night, he decided that he *must* find some way to improve his bed. He hunted and he hunted and he hunted, but he could find nothing that was just right. He *did* find two more matchboxes, some buttons, and a bright penny. He made a table, with a drawer, from one matchbox. The other became a cabinet on one side of the living room. It contained his fine collection of buttons, the prize one of which Timothy had daringly gnawed off the best uniform of the ringmaster himself.

But he did not forget his bed. In the afternoon he did not go to the circus performance because he was so busy hunting. Finally he found it! A big, soft pocketbook with a plush lining!

Home he brought it, tugging it through the front door past its two pin pillars, past the sardine-box fireplace and his safety-pin rocking chair, through the bathroom with its paper-cup shower and the beautiful, almost-real diamond mirror, into his bedroom and up on top of the springy scrubbing brush.

"There," said Timothy, "is a royal bed for a mouse!"

And he climbed right in.

But somehow he couldn't get comfortable. First he tried to sleep on his right side. Then he tried to sleep on his left side. Then he tried to sleep on his back. And that was worst of all.

And then suddenly he had an idea. He sprang out of bed. He ran into the living room. He seized—very carefully—his razor-blade hatchet. And he rushed back to his pocketbook bed.

One—two! And there was a little hole right through the top side of the pocketbook.

Three—four! And there was his hat hanging on the post at the head of his bed.

Five—six! And there was Timothy himself back inside his bed.

Seven—eight! And there—look!—*there was his tail,* at last comfortable, sticking out through the hole in the pocketbook!

Nine—ten! And there was—ho-hum—oh, dear me, excuse me—there was—hmm—eh? What was that? Oh! Yes—Timothy—hum—There was Timothy Mouse sound asleep in his own bed in his own house. Ho—hum!

GOOD NIGHT!

The Case of the Light-fingered Fiddler

"It's a disgrace!" exploded Pongo, the Dalmation dog.

"What's a disgrace, Papa?" asked Lucky Puppy.

Pongo glared at the newspaper which was spread out on the floor of his dog house. "The royal jewels are missing!" he said. "It's all here in the paper. Yesterday the jewels were sent out to be cleaned. There were emerald rings, a sapphire necklace, ruby bracelets, a diamond tiara and enough pearls for the world's biggest marble game. On the way to the jeweler's, they were stolen. There's no sign of them! Scotland Yard is baffled! It's a disgrace, that's what it is! It's an affront to every decent Englishman."

"And every English dog," put in Lucky, helpfully.

"Right!" agreed Pongo. His tail thumped impatiently on the floor. "We should do something about it," he said firmly. "We dogs, I mean. We have ways of knowing things that our humans . . . ." He left the sentence unfinished. Then he said, "The Twilight Bark! That's it! We'll rally all the dogs in England!"

So, that evening, the dogs in London were alerted. A Kerry in Kensington heard Pongo's message and passed it along. A St. Bernard in Bayswater, a spaniel in Soho and a collie from Chelsea helped spread the word.

News of the missing jewels was passed from the dogs in the city to dogs in the outlying villages until, at last, the Twilight Bark came to the shaggy ear of an old sheep dog known as the Colonel. With the Colonel was his trusted friend, a lean and lively cat named Sergeant Tibs.

"What's that?" exclaimed the Colonel. He cocked his good ear. "Loyal fools?"

"Royal jewels, I think, sir," said Tibs respectfully. "Yes, three short barks and one long. Royal jewels. Pongo's sent word from London that we're to keep alert for signs of the scoundrels who took the royal jewels."

"Good show!" huffed the Colonel. "Obviously I'll be in charge of this area. Tibs, we must set up a headquarters, organize a staff, establish an officer's club . . ."

Sergeant Tibs interrupted. "Hadn't we better concentrate on looking for the jewels, sir?"

"Yes, yes! All in good time. But first things first. I think Hell Hall would be a logical command post."

Sergeant Tibs shuddered. "That scarey old place?"

"Why not? It's been empty since that awful Cruella de Vil woman moved out. Let's get over and inspect it."

Tibs wasn't too pleased at the idea, but he followed the Colonel out of their warm, cozy stable and across the fields toward the run-down mansion called Hell Hall.

As they approached the old manor house, however, they went more carefully, for there were lights in some of the windows.

"Odd!" muttered the Colonel. "The place is supposed to be vacant!"

An eerie sound floated from the house—a sound like wind moaning in the trees, and yet not like that at all.

Moving like shadows, the dog and the cat crept up to a lighted window. Sergeant Tibs leaped to the Colonel's back. The Colonel raised his head and looked in through the dusty panes of glass.

"'Pon my word!" gasped the Colonel.

For inside the house were their old enemies, the villainous Badun brothers, Horace and Jasper.

There was a third man with the Baduns—a tall, thin, scarecrow of a man with a pointed, bald head and the nose of a vulture. He was sitting on a high stool playing a bass violin. A melancholy voom-voom-voom filled the air as he drew a heavy bow across the strings. On the floor near his feet was a big case for the violin.

Tibs and the Colonel retreated to the end of the garden.

"Something's up, Tibs!" announced the Colonel. "Mark my words, where those Baduns are, there's trouble!"

Tibs was about to agree when, suddenly, the sound of the bass violin was stilled. Moments later the tall, bald man and the Baduns left the house, got into a car and drove away.

"Now's our chance!" cried Sergeant Tibs, scampering toward the back door.

The door was ajar. The Colonel nosed it open, and Tibs flashed through and began sniffing around. The violin case seemed interesting. It looked too big even for the huge bass fiddle.

"Colonel, sir," said Tibs. "I think this has a false bottom."

"Yes, yes!" scoffed the Colonel. "It's to carry music in."

"Music—or stolen jewels?" suggested Tibs.

The Colonel nodded. "I was just about to think of that."

Tibs prodded the case with his paw. "If there *were* jewels here, they aren't here now," he announced. "I suggest we search the premises thoroughly."

"Good show. Carry on!" ordered the Colonel.

They went all through the house. When they got to the cellar they found footprints leading across the dirt floor to a door which was bolted, chained and padlocked.

"I think we should see what's behind that door, sir," said Tibs.

"Carry on," said the Colonel.

"But how, sir?" asked Tibs.

"Good heavens, Tibs!" huffed the Colonel. "Do I have to think of every little detail?"

"If I might suggest, sir," said Tibs soothingly, "we can send word back to London by the Twi-

light Bark and get Pongo here. He'll know what to do."

"Just what I was about to say, Sergeant!" replied the Colonel. And they slipped out of the house and ran to send for Pongo.

It was late the next day when Pongo arrived. He had Lucky Puppy in tow. The Colonel glared at the Dalmation pup. "What's this raw recruit doing here?" he demanded.

Pongo replied airily, "It will be good training for him."

So the four of them—the Colonel, Tibs, Pongo and Lucky—went warily across the fields to Hell Hall. Outside the library window they stopped and listened. Horace and Jasper Badun were inside, talking.

"I can't stand that bloomin' scratchin' on the fiddle!" Horace was saying.

"Aw, but all great geniuses have their little quirks," Jasper countered. "Besides, Sherlock Holmes fiddled. Einstein fiddled. Why can't the Fiddler fiddle?"

The droning of the bass violin went on and on. Pongo beckoned the others away from the window and led them toward the back of the house, and the open kitchen door. Hardly breathing, they made their way into the house and down to the cellar.

"We're safe for a while," said Pongo. "The Baduns are busy arguing. And as long as we can hear the bass violin playing upstairs, we know the Fiddler won't bother us. Let's get busy."

The locked door which had so dismayed the Colonel was no problem at all to Pongo. The Dalmation started tunneling under it, digging away the soft earth of the cellar floor.

Before long, Lucky Puppy piped up. "That tunnel's big enough for me now, Papa," he said. "I can get through there."

Pongo backed away from the door. "Okay, son. Crawl inside and see what you can see."

The Colonel, Tibs and Pongo waited, listening to the voom-voom of the bass violin. Lucky Puppy wriggled under the door.

A moment later Lucky called, "There are some big funny marbles in here!"

"Marbles?" echoed the Colonel.

Lucky appeared again in the tunnel. There was an emerald the size of an egg gripped in his jaws, and a platinum bracelet was wrapped around his neck.

"The royal jewels!" exclaimed Pongo.

"Good show! We've found them!" said the Colonel. "Don't forget to put that on the morning report, Sergeant."

Pongo immediately took charge. "I'll go to the village for the police," he said. "I know how to get them out here right away. Lucky, you put the jewels back behind the door so the police will find them all together. Then all of you leave! Don't stay here in the house."

Lucky disappeared behind the door, and Pongo ran up the stairs toward the kitchen. The Colonel and Tibs remained on guard. Upstairs, the voom-voom of the violin continued.

"I say, Lucky," growled the Colonel. "Do hurry up."

Just then, complete quiet enveloped Hell Hall.

"Come on, Lucky," whispered Sergeant Tibs nervously. "Let's get out of here!"

The cellar door was swung wide and the two Baduns loomed large at the top of the steps. "Wha . . . ?" cried Horace. "A dog!"

"And a cat!" yelled Jasper.

Tibs and the Colonel scrambled up onto a packing crate and then out through an open window. They streaked away toward the bushes that edged the field.

Only there, in the safety of the sheltering branches, did they stop. For once, words failed the Colonel. They had succeeded in finding the royal jewels, but they had failed, too. Lucky was trapped in the locked room in that horrible old house. Poor little Lucky. He was at the mercy of the Baduns and that criminal genius, the Fiddler!

"We must rescue young Lucky from the Baduns and the Fiddler!" the Colonel announced. The old sheep dog was pacing his command post at the edge of the field.

Sergeant Tibs agreed. "Let's go!" he urged.

"Not so fast, Sergeant! This is a military operation! We've got to plan our campaign!"

Tibs saluted.

"We must have a meeting of the general staff," the Colonel pointed out. "We've got to plan strategy, send out patrols, have the ladies' auxiliary stand by with coffee and donuts, prepare . . ."

Tibs knew only too well that the Colonel's planning session might last longer than Lucky Puppy's luck, so he innocently reminded the Colonel of his famous campaign at the Battle of Waterpup.

"A great victory!" the Colonel exclaimed. "Er . . . what did I do?"

"You attacked from all sides and so confused the enemy that they were helpless when the reinforcements arrived!"

"Of course!" The Colonel thought for a moment. Then, "Tibs, I have a plan," he announced. "I will remain here at my command post. You will attack from all sides and so confuse the enemy that . . ."

Before he had finished, Tibs was racing toward the fearful house known as Hell Hall.

Meanwhile, Pongo had reached the village and set up a howl that brought every dog in town hurrying to meet him. He quickly explained that they must help lead the police to Hell Hall, where the jewel thieves were hiding.

A dachshund spoke up. "What if the police don't understand what we want them to do?"

"Do whatever you must," Pongo instructed, "but get the police to Hell Hall."

113

Immediately the dogs fanned out through the village streets. The dachshund found a man in blue, then began nipping at his heels. A cocker spaniel pushed over a coal scuttle practically under the nose of another officer. A French poodle sought out the Chief Constable himself. She fluttered her long, silky eyelashes at him, then bit him lightly on the ankle to make sure he got the message. He chased her down the street to the village square, where he found himself face to face with the rest of his force. The police were all surrounded by happily barking dogs.

Suddenly the other dogs were silent. Only Pongo barked and jumped and growled and snapped. Then he stood absolutely still and de-

liberately raised one paw to point down the road toward Hell Hall.

The Chief Constable shook his head with wonder. "Men," he said, "I do believe these dogs are trying to tell us something."

At that, the dogs broke into delighted barks of agreement and raced down the road. After a moment of hesitation, the mystified policemen followed them.

While Pongo had been busy getting the police, Sergeant Tibs hadn't been idle. The intrepid cat had crept back into the frightening old house. Sure enough, the Baduns were there trying to

work the rusty padlock on the door of the basement room where Lucky was trapped. Tibs surveyed the situation for a second, then dashed in to claw Horace's ankle and bite Jasper on the knee.

The two evil-doers howled with pain and rage. Jasper reached for Tibs, but the cat streaked away across the room and leaped onto a workbench. From there he scrambled up onto a stack of fruit baskets. From the top of the baskets he launched himself onto Horace's back, claws exposed.

"Get this crazy cat off me!" cried Horace.

Jasper swung at Tibs with a large stick just as the cat jumped to the floor. Unfortunately for Horace, Jasper's aim was very good. The stick landed squarely between Horace's sixth vertebra and his fourth cat-scratch!

"Not me, you fool!" Horace raged. "Hit the *cat!*"

But Tibs was already launching a new offensive. This time he overwhelmed Jasper with a barrage of spitting and snarling. Each time one of the thieves tried to get away, the Sergeant attacked again, chasing the Baduns in circles, squares, ovals, oblongs and patterns of helpless confusion.

"Help!" Jasper yelled at last. "Someone—HELP!"

The words were hardly out of Jasper's mouth before the front door of the house burst open and a small army of policemen, accompanied by Pongo, the Colonel and all the village dogs, came charging down the cellar stairs. Sergeant Tibs smiled and retreated from the field of combat to lick his whiskers in triumph.

"What's going on here?" the Chief Constable demanded.

"Oh, nothing," the Baduns replied, trying to hide their surprise and fear. "Uh—just a little game."

But Pongo was already posed with one paw pointing to the locked door. "Help me!" he called to the other dogs. "We have to make the policemen understand where the stolen jewels are hidden!"

The other dogs quickly followed Pongo's example. Even the Colonel did his bit, though he wasn't very athletic and he fell over twice before the Chief Constable got the idea.

When the police forced the lock and the door swung open, there was Lucky cheerfully playing with the world's largest pigeonblood ruby.

"Lucky!" cried Pongo, trying to be stern. "You should have more respect for the royal jewels!"

"I thought it was a glass Easter egg," Lucky answered with an innocent smile. "Who are your friends, Papa?"

Before Pongo could explain that his friends were the police, the Chief Constable had seen the gems heaped under Lucky's paws and was snapping heavy-duty handcuffs on Horace and Jasper Badun.

The dogs were congratulating themselves on the capture of the thieves when Sergeant Tibs suddenly stopped and frowned. "There was a third thief," he whispered to Pongo. "The man who played the bass violin!"

Pongo was puzzled. "I don't know how we can tell the policemen about him," he told Tibs. "And I'll bet the Fiddler is the brains of the gang!"

"I say!" The Chief Constable, who had been sorting through the jewels, looked up with a very unhappy expression on his face. "The Star of Liverpool necklace is missing! It's the most valuable item of them all!"

It was then that Tibs remembered the Fiddler's big fiddle case! No doubt the Fiddler had hidden the necklace there, hoping to fool the Baduns and keep the necklace for himself.

Tibs dashed up the steps from the basement and crossed the hall to the room where he had first seen the fiddle case. Sure enough, there it was, lying open and empty on the floor. The cat nosed around the case, sniffing and snuffing. Then he stepped carefully into the case. There was something very strange here—something that . . .

What the brave cat did not know was that the evil man known as the Fiddler had hidden behind the kitchen cupboard when he heard the policemen thunder down to the basement. He had guessed that the stolen jewels had been discovered. Now he was stealing silently into the room where he had left his fiddle case. And . . .

WHOMP!

The cover of the case snapped shut, trapping Tibs inside! And a secret compartment snapped open, spilling a necklace of emeralds and moonstones about the cat's neck. A second later, Tibs

fell against the side of the case as it was lifted from the floor.

"YEEE-OWWW!!"

Tibs rocked from side to side. He yeowled and yelled and screeched and spit. Cats hate to be cooped up in small places, and Sergeant Tibs was no exception. His voice was shrill with terror.

The Fiddler was taking a desperate chance. He had to be silent to steal through the house, collect his violin case and escape without being seen by dog or man. When the pent-up cat began to snarl, the master criminal panicked. With the violin case bumping clumsily on the floor, the Fiddler ran for the hallway.

There in the doorway was Pongo, staring at him. Behind Pongo were several large policemen, and they were staring at him, too. And to one side of the policemen were Horace and Jasper.

Before the Fiddler could say a word, the Chief Constable seized the violin case and opened it. Still complaining at the top of his voice, Tibs streaked out. Spitting and hissing, he glared at the Fiddler. The Star of Liverpool necklace was draped loosely over his ears.

Lucky Puppy padded forward and nuzzled Tibs in a friendly way. "The newspaper photographers are coming," warned Lucky. "Don't you want to take off the necklace before they take your picture? Who ever heard of a tom cat wearing emeralds?"

At this, Tibs *did* take off the necklace. Rather, he let the Chief Constable take it off. The police took the Fiddler and the Baduns to jail, and Tibs and the dogs had their pictures taken for the newspapers. Then the Colonel congratulated all the dogs for having done their duty. Lucky Puppy got a very special commendation from the Colonel. Not only had he been the first to discover the jewels, but he had kept Sergeant Tibs from being a very embarrassed hero!

At last Pongo said it was time to start for home. Lucky Puppy was very pleased. "I'm glad we were proper, patriotic dogs and captured those thieves," he said to his father, "but it will be awfully nice to be back home with my own favorite dog-blanket!"

The Emperor's New Clothes

Many years ago there lived an Emperor who liked beautiful new clothes more than anything else in the world, and he spent all his money on adorning himself. He had no interest in his army, or in the theater, or in going for a ride in the country, unless of course it gave him a chance to show off his new clothes. He had a different costume for every hour of the day, and just as it can usually be said of a king that he is in the council-chamber, it could always be said of this Emperor that he was in his dressing room.

Life was gay in the great city in which he lived; every day there were visitors from everywhere in the world, and one day two swindlers arrived. They pretended to be weavers and told everyone that they could weave the most beauti-

ful cloth imaginable. Not only were the colors and the patterns extraordinarily beautiful, but the clothes made from it had a most remarkable property. They would be invisible to any person unfit for his position or more stupid than he had any right to be.

"How wonderful," thought the Emperor, "to have clothes like that. Simply by wearing them I could find out which men in my realm are unfit for their positions; I could tell the clever from the stupid. Yes, I must have some of that cloth woven for me immediately." And he gave the two swindlers a large sum of money in advance so that they could start work at once.

And so the swindlers set up two looms and pretended to be hard at work, but actually there was nothing on the loom at all. They demanded the purest silk and the finest gold thread, which they hid in their bags, and went on working into all hours of the night on their empty looms.

"I wonder how they're coming along with the cloth," thought the Emperor, but he felt a little queasy when he remembered that it would be invisible to anyone unfit for his position or simply stupid. Not that he himself had anything to fear, of course, but it might be better to send someone else to find out how the work was progressing. Everyone in town knew of the miraculous power of the cloth, and everyone was eager to find out how stupid or unfit his neighbor was.

"I'll have my good old honest Prime Minister look in on the two weavers," thought the Emperor. "He'll be the best one to judge how they're coming along with the cloth, because he's very sensible and no one knows his job better than he does."

So off went the good old honest Prime Minister to the weavers, who were busily working at the empty looms.

"Bless my soul," thought the Prime Minister, his eyes widening, "I can't see a thing." But he did not say a word.

The two swindlers begged him to step a little closer and asked if he didn't think the pattern and colors were beautiful. They pointed to the empty loom, and the poor old Prime Minister stared and stared, but he still couldn't see anything, because there was nothing to see.

"Merciful heaven," thought the old man, "could I be stupid? I never thought I was, and no one must find out about it now. Maybe I'm not even fit for my job! No, it won't do for me to admit I can't see the cloth."

"Well," said one of the weavers, "you're not saying anything."

"Oh, it's beautiful—quite lovely," said the Prime Minister, peering through his glasses. "This pattern, those colors! Yes, I'm going to tell the Emperor how pleased I am with it."

"We're glad to hear that," said the weavers, and they named the colors and explained the unusual design. The old minister listened carefully, so he would be able to repeat it all when he returned to the Emperor, and that he did.

Now the swindlers demanded more money, and more silk and more gold thread they needed for weaving. They put everything in their own pockets, and not a single thread on the loom, but they went on as before, weaving on the empty loom.

Soon the Emperor sent another trusted old
official to see how the weaving was coming along,
and if the cloth would soon be ready. The same
thing happened to him as had happened to the
Prime Minister. He looked and looked, but since
there was nothing there to see except the empty
loom, he couldn't see anything.

"Isn't that a lovely piece of cloth?" said the
two swindlers, and they pointed out and explained the pattern which wasn't there at all.

"I know I'm not stupid," thought the man, "so
it must be that I am no good at my job. It's ridicu-
lous, of course, but it's not the kind of thing you'd
want known."

And so he praised the cloth he didn't see, and
assured them he was most happy about the pretty
colors and the lovely pattern.

"It's perfectly enchanting," he later told the
Emperor.

The whole town was talking about the magnificent cloth, and now the Emperor wanted to
see it for himself while it was still on the loom.
Accompanied by a flock of trusted officials,
among whom were two men he had sent before,
he went to see the sly weavers, who were weaving away for all they were worth without a single
thread or shred of fabric.

122

"Isn't it magnificent?" said the two good old officials who had been there before. "Observe, Your Majesty—the colors, the design." And they pointed to the empty loom, because they thought that the others could surely see the cloth.

"What!" thought the Emperor. "I can't see a thing! But this is terrible! Am I stupid? Am I not fit to be Emperor? This is the most terrible thing that could happen to me!"

"Oh, it's very handsome," said the Emperor. "It has my most gracious approval," and he nodded with satisfaction as he contemplated the empty loom; he didn't want to say he couldn't see anything.

All the others stood there and looked and looked, and although they got no more out of it than anyone else, they said, just like the Emperor, "Oh, it's very beautiful," and advised him to have clothes made of this superb material immediately, and to wear the new garments at the next Royal Procession.

One after another, they repeated, "*Magnifique! Perfectly lovely! Simply enchanting!*" And they were very pleased with it all.

The Emperor presented the two swindlers with the highest decoration of the land and gave them each the title of "Sir Weaver."

The swindlers worked all through the night before the procession by the light of more than sixteen candles, and everyone could see how busy they were getting the Emperor's new clothes ready. They pretended to take the cloth off the loom, they cut the air with huge scissors, they sewed with unthreaded needles, and finally they said, "Look! Now the clothes are ready."

The Emperor, together with the highest nobles of the court, went to the weavers, who held out their arms in the air as if they were carrying something, saying, "Look, here are the breeches, Your Majesty. Here is the robe. And here is the cloak. They are as light as cobwebs. They're so light you would almost think you were not wearing anything at all, but that's the beauty of it."

"Yes," agreed the nobles, but they couldn't see a thing because there was nothing at all to see.

"If His Imperial Majesty will now be gracious enough to remove his clothes, we'll fit him out with the new ones, in front of the mirror over here," the swindlers said.

The Emperor took off his clothes and the swindlers pretended to be fitting him, piece by piece, with the clothes they supposedly had made. They reached around his middle as if they were tieing something tightly on—that was the train. And the Emperor kept turning and admiring himself in the mirror.

"My, how superbly they fit you!" cried everyone. "Such a beautiful pattern, and those colors! What a sumptuous costume!"

"The canopy that is to be carried over you is in readiness outside, Your Majesty," said the Master-of-Ceremonies.

"I'm ready, too," said the Emperor. "Don't you

think it fits beautifully?" And he turned once more before the mirror, to give the impression that he was really admiring his finery. The nobles who were to carry the train fumbled along the floor with their hands, as if they were picking it up. Walking along, they clutched the air, not daring to show that they couldn't see anything.

And so the Emperor walked in the procession under the magnificent canopy, and all the people who lined the streets and leaned out of their windows said, "My, how marvelous the Emperor's new clothes are! What a lovely train! How well it fits."

No one would admit that he couldn't see anything, because that would be to admit that he was stupid or unfit for his position. None of the Emperor's clothes had ever been such a success.

"But he doesn't have anything on," said a little child.

"Merciful heaven, listen to the voice of the innocent!" said the child's father, and a whisper ran through the crowd: "A little child says he doesn't have anything on."

"Yes, he doesn't have anything on!" all the people cried out at last.

The Emperor's heart skipped a beat, for he thought they were right. But he also thought, "All the same, as long as I'm in the procession, I must carry on." And he held himself prouder than ever, while the nobles walked behind him carrying the train that wasn't there at all.

The Steadfast Tin Soldier

Once upon a time there were twenty-five tin soldiers. They were all brothers, so to speak, because they all had been made from one and the same old tin spoon. Shoulder arms! eyes front!—that's how they stood in their handsome red and blue uniforms.

The very first thing they ever heard, when a happy little boy took the lid off the box in which they were packed, was "Tin soldiers!" The boy jumped for joy and clapped his hands. He had been given the soldiers for his birthday, and now he took them out one by one and put them on the table. Each looked exactly like the others, except for one, who had only a single leg. That was because he was the last to be made and there just wasn't enough tin left to make two legs. But he stood just as straight on his one leg as his brothers did on two, and it is this one-legged tin soldier that our story is all about.

There were many other toys on the table, but the finest of them all was a beautiful castle made of cardboard. It had windows through which could be seen all of the elegant rooms. In front of the castle, little green trees surrounded a lake made from a mirror, on which swam wax swans, gazing at their own reflection. It was all very lovely, but loveliest of all was the figure of a young girl standing in the castle door. She was cut out of paper, but she wore a skirt made of the sheerest muslin. Around her shoulders she had a narrow blue ribbon, fastened with a glittering spangle as large as her face. She held her arms outstretched, for she was a ballet dancer. And she kicked one leg so high in the air that at first the tin soldier did not see it and thought that she, too, had only a single leg.

"There is the wife for me," he thought. "But she is a lady—she lives in a castle. I live in a box that I share with twenty-four others, and that's no place for her. But I must try to get to know her."

129

Then he lay down on the table and hid behind a snuff box. From here he had a fine view of the little ballet dancer, who was still standing on one leg without losing her balance. Later in the evening, all the other tin soldiers were put back in the box. The little boy and his family went to bed, and the house was still. Now the toys began to play games with each other. The tin soldiers rattled in their box, trying to get out and join in the fun, but they couldn't get the lid off. A funny-looking nutcracker turned somersaults, and the sticks of chalk danced on the blackboard. There was such a racket that the canary woke up and began chirping poetry. Only the tin soldier and the little ballet dancer remained in their places, not moving an inch. She stood straight and tall on tip-toe with arms out-stretched, and he stood just as straight and tall on his one leg, his eyes never leaving her for a moment.

Now the clock struck twelve and *crack!* off flew the lid of the snuff box, but there was no snuff in it. Instead, a little black troll popped out.

"Tin soldier," said the troll, "keep your eyes to yourself."

The tin soldier pretended not to hear.

"All right, you just wait until tomorrow," said the troll.

And the next morning, when the children of the house got up, they put the tin soldier on the windowsill, and whether it was a gust of wind that did it or the troll, the window flew open and the tin soldier fell head first out of the window. It was a terrible fall, all the way from the third floor. His leg went straight up in the air and he landed right on his tall hat, the bayonet on his gun sticking between two paving stones in the sidewalk.

The little boy immediately came down to look for the tin soldier, but, although he almost stepped on him, he could not see him. If only the tin soldier had cried out, "Here I am," the little boy would have found him, but the soldier thought it was bad manners to raise his voice, since he was in uniform.

131

Suddenly the boat sailed under a wide board that had been placed over the gutter, making a long, dark tunnel. It was as dark there as it was at home in the box. "I wonder where the boat will take me?" thought the tin soldier. "I'm sure this is all because of that troll. If only the little ballet dancer was here in the boat with me, I wouldn't care if it was twice as dark."

Just then a big water-rat tried to stop him.

"Show me your pass!" said the rat.

The tin soldier didn't bother to answer. He just stood a little straighter and held his gun even more tightly. The boat was moving faster now,

It started to rain, the drops falling closer and closer, faster and faster, in a tremendous shower. When the shower was over, two boys came walking by. The taller of the two said, "Hey; look! There's a tin soldier! Let's give him a boat ride!"

So they made a boat out of a folded newspaper, put the tin soldier aboard, and sent him on his way. The boat floated down the gutter, going faster and faster, and the boys ran alongside clapping their hands with joy. How the paper boat bobbed up and down in the big waves! Sometimes the swift current rocked the boat and spun it completely around, which made the tin soldier dizzy. But he didn't bat an eye or move a muscle, and stood steadfast in the middle of the boat with eyes front, his rifle on his shoulder.

and the rat chased it, gnashing his teeth and yelling and screaming to the sticks and straws, "Stop him, stop him! He didn't pay the toll! He doesn't have a pass!" But the current became swifter and swifter, and the tin soldier could begin to see daylight at the end of the tunnel. He could also hear a roaring noise that was enough to frighten even the bravest man. Just imagine, at the point where the tunnel ended, the water plunged into a large canal, as dangerous for him as a great waterfall would be for us. He was already so close that there was no way for him to stop.

The boat shot out of the tunnel into the canal, and the soldier stood as steadfast as ever. No one could say he even blinked an eye. The boat spun around two or three times and filled with water—in a moment it would go to the bottom. The tin soldier stood up to his neck in water as the boat sank deeper and deeper. The soggy paper began to come apart and the water closed over his head.

The tin soldier thought of the lovely little ballet dancer whom he would never see again, and an old song ran through his mind:

Soldier, soldier, danger ahead,
Soon, too soon, you will be dead.

Now the paper came completely apart, and the tin soldier dropped straight down—and was immediately swallowed by a huge fish. How dark it was in there! It was even darker than in the tunnel, and terribly narrow. But the tin soldier, lying at full length, was as steadfast as ever, his rifle on his shoulder and eyes front. The fish leaped and thrashed about, but finally became still. The tin soldier saw a flash of light—then it was broad daylight and someone was shouting, "The tin soldier!"

The fish had been caught, taken to the market and sold, and was now on a kitchen table where a cook was cutting it open with a big knife. With two fingers she picked up the tin soldier by the waist and carried him in to the living room, where everyone crowded around to see the extraordinary creature who had traveled in the stomach of a fish. The tin soldier, however, did not think this was anything to be proud of He was put on a table and—how strangely things sometimes turn out in this world!—he found himself in the very same room, in the very same house, with the very same family, where he had been before.

135

The same toys were still on the table. There before him were the cardboard castle and the lovely little ballet dancer. She was still standing on one leg with the other high in the air. She, too, was as steadfast as ever. The tin soldier was so touched by this that he almost shed tears of tin, but of course he didn't. He looked at her and she looked at him, and neither of them said a word.

Suddenly one of the children snatched up the tin soldier and threw him into the stove. He had no reason to do such a thing. Very likely the troll in the snuff box was behind it all.

The tin soldier stood in the glow of the blaze. He could hardly bear the heat, but whether it came from the fire of the stove or from the fire of his love, he did not know. His bright colors had disappeared, but whether it had happened because of his terrible adventure or from grief, no one could tell. He looked at the little dancer and she looked straight back at him, and he felt himself melting—but he still stood steadfast as ever—*eyes front! shoulder arms!*

A door flew open and, caught in the draft, the little ballet dancer flew straight into the stove, burst into flames, and was gone. Then the tin soldier melted down completely, and the next day, when the maid took out the ashes, she found he was only a little lump in the shape of a heart. There was nothing left of the little ballet dancer except the spangle from her dress, and that was scorched black as coal.

Further Adventures
of Peter Pan

It all began the day the crocodile got sick. As everyone knows, the crocodile who lives in Never Land once ate Captain Hook's hand. He liked it so much that from that time on he followed Hook everywhere, hoping to get the rest of him. Luckily for the pirate, the crocodile had also swallowed a clock. The clock continued to tick merrily away inside the croc, and the ticking warned Hook when the crocodile was near. Hook soon became expert at making quick departures whenever he heard the tell-tale ticking.

One day, when the crocodile was practicing his backstroke in the lagoon, he met the lost boys. They were having a picnic on the beach. The lost boys rather liked the crocodile. Any enemy of Captain Hook was a friend of theirs. So they offered the croc some bran muffins which they had baked themselves. Sad to say, they had misread the recipe and put in too much mustard. The poor crocodile immediately got indigestion.

The lost boys were very upset, so they led the groaning croc to their home and dosed him well with bicarbonate of soda.

That morning Captain Hook awoke in fine fettle. "It's a beautiful day," said he, when Mr.

Smee brought his breakfast. "I think I'll go out and stir up some trouble!"

"Watch out for the crocodile," warned Mr. Smee.

"Aye," said Hook. "That beast is always on my trail. If he hadn't swallowed that clock, he'd have gotten me long ago. That blasted tick-tocking has saved me many a time."

Then Hook firmly put all thoughts of the crocodile out of his mind. He hoisted anchor and set sail for Skull Rock. When he got there he listened carefully for the ticking of the clock. All was silent. The crocodile wasn't about. So Hook carved his initials on Skull Rock. It was something he'd always wanted to do.

On sailed the pirate ship to Mermaid Lagoon. Hook couldn't hear the crocodile ticking there, so he stole all of the mermaids' coral combs.

Hook then gave orders to sail to the Indian camp. When he arrived there he did not hear the tick-tock of the croc, so he stole two Indian totem poles and a teepee and made off in his ship, chuckling an evil chuckle.

"That awful crocodile must have left Never Land!" chortled Hook. "I don't have a care in the

TICK TOCK

world! Oh, what nasty thing shall I do to celebrate?"

"Why not kidnap the lost boys?" suggested Mr. Smee, who liked to be helpful.

"Just the thing!" cried Hook. "Mr. Smee, let us plot!"

While Hook was plotting, the Indian Chief came to the tree house where Peter Pan and the lost boys lived. "Wicked pirate steal totems," complained the Chief. "Where is crocodile who keeps wicked pirate in line?"

Peter had to admit that the crocodile was right there in the tree house. What's more, the croc was still too sick to thwart Hook's evil plans. Peter and the lost boys held a conference.

"Since the croc can't stop Hook, we'll have to find some other way," said Peter.

"What way?" wondered Foxy. "We don't have long sharp teeth like croc. Hook isn't afraid of us!"

"Wait." said Peter. "We don't really need the croc to scare Hook. All we need are a lot of loud clocks. If Hook hears anything tick, he'll run so fast he'll never look to see whether the crocodile is behind him or not."

"But we don't have any clocks," Cubby pointed out.

"There are lots of clocks in London," said Peter Pan. "We can borrow some from Wendy."

So Peter Pan flew off to London and talked to Wendy Darling. She was very helpful. She borrowed an alarm clock from her mother. She gave Peter the clock that stood on the shelf in the nursery. When the cook wasn't looking, she took the kitchen clock. She even borrowed a clock from Nana, the nursemaid dog. Soon Peter had his arms full of clocks, all ticking loudly. Well satisfied, Peter flew back to Never Land.

He was just in time, for night was falling and Captain Hook had sailed his ship right up Crocodile Creek. He planned to land and march his pirate crew straight to the lost boys' tree home. Peter quickly put a clock in the tall grass on the bank of the creek. When Hook stepped ashore

141

he heard the ominous "Tick-tock!" He turned and rushed back to the safety of his ship.

"Hah!" said Hook to himself. "Now I know that the crocodile is in Crocodile Creek, I'll land at the Indian camp."

But as Hook came within sight of the Indian village he heard a "Tick-tock!" from the clock which Peter Pan had hidden under the bluffs. Hook turned five shades of green and ordered a quick retreat.

The pirate ship sailed toward Skull Rock. But Peter had hidden Mrs. Darling's alarm clock in one of the hollows of the rock. When Hook approached, the clock not only ticked—the alarm went off with a clanging jangle!

Hook's hair stood on end. He clutched at Mr. Smee in terror. "Save me, Smee!" he pleaded. "That crocodile is everywhere!"

Smee ordered the ship back to Pirate Cove, and there Captain Hook took to his bed with a bad case of nerves. By the time Hook was able to sail abroad again, the crocodile was feeling well and healthy and was looking for Hook with renewed relish.

As for the clocks, Peter Pan flew to London with them, arriving just before dawn. Wendy put every clock back where it belonged, and Mrs. Darling's alarm clock rang in time to awaken the Darling family for breakfast. So no one was the wiser. Except Wendy, of course.

Rumpelstiltskin

THERE was once a miller who had a mill at the edge of the forest. He was a good enough miller, but he was poor, and he had nothing to be proud of—except his beautiful daughter. One day the king went hunting in the forest, and on his way back to the palace, the hunting party came riding by the mill.

"Who is this?" asked the king when he saw the miller's daughter.

"She is my daughter, Your Majesty," said the miller.

"Indeed?" said the king. "She is very beautiful."

"None more so," the miller said, "and she is just as clever as she is beautiful."

"Indeed?" said the king.

"Indeed," said the miller. "Among other things, she can spin straw into gold."

Just why the miller said this he did not know, but say it he did, no doubt out of pride in his daughter.

"Then she can be of service to me," said the king, for, although he was young and handsome, he was as poor for a king as the miller was for a miller. "Bring her to my palace, and I will put her skill to the test." And, without another word, he rode off.

"Oh, father," said the miller's daughter, and the poor girl trembled with fear, "I can no more spin straw into gold than I can fly like a bird. Whatever shall I do?"

145

"If I knew, I would gladly tell you," said the miller. "But I can tell you this. You had better think of something, or it will be very unpleasant for us. . . . Yes," he added, rubbing his neck as if he could already feel the hangman's noose, "most unpleasant."

And so he brought her to the palace, where the king led her to a room filled with straw. In a corner of the room was a spinning wheel.

"This is the finest straw," the king said, "and it must be spun into the purest gold by morning. If not—well, we shall see."

The king went out, locking the door behind him, leaving the girl alone. She looked at the straw, and she looked at the spinning wheel, and she thought, "Perhaps, if I try hard, I can really do it."

Picking up a handful of straw, she spun as hard as she could, but of course it did no good. Not one little straw turned into gold. She stopped spinning and burst into tears.

Suddenly she heard a voice, saying:

"Why are you weeping, miller's daughter?"

Before her stood a little man with a long beard.

He was quite an ugly little man, but his voice was kind.

"Oh," she said, "I must spin this straw into gold, and I don't know the first thing about it."

"What may be difficult for one," said the little man, "may not be difficult for another. What will you give me if I spin it for you?"

"My necklace," said the girl. "It was left to me by my grandmother."

The little man examined the necklace carefully.

"Not of the best quality," he said. "But a bargain is a bargain."

Seating himself at the spinning wheel, he began spinning—*whir, whir, whir!* And *whir, whir, whir* went the spinning wheel all night, and by morning he had spun all the straw into the purest gold. He quickly vanished, and soon the king came into the room.

"Amazing!" said the king, his eyes glittering as brightly as the gold. But still he was not satisfied. He led the girl to an even larger room filled with

straw, and told her it must be spun into gold overnight.

"If not—well, I'd rather not talk about it," he said.

Once again he left the girl alone, once again she wept—and once again the little man appeared.

"What will you give me this time?" he asked.

"The ring from my finger," the girl answered. "It, too, was left to me by my grandmother."

"Hmm," the little man said. "Again, not of the best quality. In fact, it's not even as good as the necklace. But a bargain is a bargain."

And *whir, whir, whir* went the spinning wheel,

and by morning the room was filled with gold. The king was delighted, but he led the girl to a room larger than the other two together and, like the others, filled with straw.

"Spin this in one night, my dear," he said, "and you shall be my wife. You are indeed as clever as you are beautiful, and I shall be the richest man in the world."

The girl smiled happily, for the king was young and handsome, and she would be queen. But the moment the king had left the room, she wept and wailed louder than ever.

"Weeping again?" said the little man as he appeared for the third time.

"Yes," the girl sobbed, "for I have nothing left to give you."

150

"Will you promise to give me your first child after you are married to the king?" the little man asked.

The girl agreed, for there was nothing else she could do. And *whir, whir, whir* went the spinning wheel all night, and by morning the room was filled with gold.

"Splendid," said the king, and they were married that very day.

And so the miller's daughter became queen, and a year later she had a little daughter of her own. She had all but forgotten the little man, when one day he suddenly appeared.

"I have come for the child you promised me," he said.

The queen wept bitterly, and pleaded with him. She now had many things she could give him, if only he would leave her the child. She offered him gold. She offered him precious jewels. She offered him a high position at the court.

"No," he said, "you can give me no greater treasure than a child."

But the queen wept so piteously that at last he said, "A bargain is a bargain. But I am not a cruel man. I will give you three days in which to guess my name, and if you can do it you will keep the child. If not, the child is mine."

The queen spent the night making a list of all the names she could think of, and the next day the little man was back again. She read through the whole list of names, but after each one the little man shook his head and said:

"That is not my name."

The next day the queen ran about, asking everyone in the palace to tell her the most unusual names they had ever heard. When the little man appeared, she repeated them all, one after another.

"Spindleshanks?" she said. "Roast-ribs? Kiliklankey? Fiddleydiddle? Bodger? Todger? Willowaleywallee? Snip-snap Zyx? Gaboo?"

"That is not my name," he said.

As soon as he had vanished, she sent messengers throughout the land to see if they could find any new names. They were back the next morning, and one of them said:

"I found no new names, Your Majesty. But as I went through the woods, I saw a high hill. On the hill, was a little house. Near the house burned a fire, and around it danced a little man. He was an ugly little man, and as he danced, he sang,

'Today I brew, today I bake,
'And tomorrow the queen's child I take,
'For she'll never guess—oh, what a shame!—
'That Rumpelstiltskin is my name!'"

"Thank you," said the queen, and sat down with her little daughter on her knee to wait for the little man. He soon appeared.

"What a beautiful child!" he said. "And she'll soon be mine, for this is the third day, you know, and a bargain is a bargain."

"Could your name be Harry or Parry or Peter-billybones?" she asked.

"No, that is not my name," the little man said, smiling.

"Jack?"

"That is not my name."

"John?"

"That is not my name."

"Then . . . could it be . . . let me see . . . Could it be . . . Rumpelstiltskin?"

The little man let out a terrible shriek.

"Who told you that? He stamped his feet so hard that he stamped himself right through the floor, and never was he seen again.

Lambert the Sheepish Lion

Afterward, the sheep all said that the whole thing would not have happened except for Mr. Stork. The stork wouldn't admit that. Not for a second. It was the dispatcher's fault, said Mr. Stork. The dispatcher had wrapped the bundle. The dispatcher had addressed the label to the flock of sheep that lived in Tully's meadow.

The address couldn't be plainer. And underneath, to make sure there would be no mistake, the dispatcher had written, "Baby lambs. Handle with care."

Of course Mr. Stork *did* handle them with care.

He hadn't been delivering babies for years and years without learning a thing or two or three. Even when he was caught in a strong down-draft on the way to the meadow, he never jostled his precious bundle.

Mr. Stork had started out at sunset. He liked to make his deliveries during the night. The full moon had risen by the time he circled above the meadow where the sheep were at pasture. He tilted his great wings this way and that way and floated down through the trees.

Mr. Stork put his bundle down on the ground and began to unwrap it. "Kind of a bumpy trip," said he, to anyone who might care to listen.

No one answered. In the meadow all around Mr. Stork, the mother sheep waited eagerly. Not one of them stirred as the stork finished unwrapping the bundle.

"Well, here we are now," said he.

The mother sheep smiled. One, two, three, four, five little lambs lifted their heads, opened their sleepy eyes and looked around them.

155

"Up you get!" ordered Mr. Stork. "Now don't crowd. Just pick out the ewe that you like best, and she'll be your mother."

One, two, three, four, five little lambs got to their feet. They wobbled as they began to walk. But after a few steps they were more steady. In a moment or two five little lambs were snuggling up to five happy mother sheep.

But, "Oh, dear me!" said Mr. Stork. "Oh me, oh my!"

For the stork saw a sixth sheep. And he saw that she had no little lamb. She stood to one side and watched the ewes caress their new babies, and she looked as lonely as lonely can be.

"What could have happened?" wondered the stork. "I was sure I had enough to go around."

He picked up the bundle and shook it, hoping as hard as a stork can hope that there would be a baby lamb left in the bottom.

Sure enough, out tumbled a soft little ball of fluff!

"Why, you lazy little lamb!" exclaimed Mr. Stork. "Come on! It's time you were awake!"

The cuddly little thing unrolled itself. A pair of

pale green eyes looked up at Mr. Stork. A rough pink tongue licked at a shiny black nose. A mouth opened wide in a yawn and Mr. Stork saw little needle-sharp teeth.

"Goodness!" exclaimed Mr. Stork. "That's not a lamb. That's not a lamb at all!"

Mr. Stork looked at the label on the bundle. Sure enough, it was addressed to the flock of sheep. So that was no help.

Next Mr. Stork took off his spectacles and polished them. Then he took out his order book. "There has to be some mistake," said he, and he turned the pages, reading orders for baby leopards and young lizards, tiny lynxes and infant llamas and little lambs.

"Aha!" said he at last. "That's it! You must be

Lambert! And you're a lion. You don't belong here at all!"

Mr. Stork looked up from his order book. "Lambert?" said he.

But Lambert the baby lion wasn't there. He had made his way to the lonely mother sheep and had nestled up to her, just as the little lambs had nestled up to the ewes they had chosen to be their mothers. The lonely mother sheep was nuzzling Lambert, and she didn't look at all lonely any more. In fact, she looked like a very happy mother sheep.

Mr. Stork took out a pencil and made a notation in his order book. "Lambert," said he to himself. "Lion. South Africa. My stars! I have to do some flying!"

158

He put away the pencil and tucked the order book back into his vest pocket.

"Come, Lambert," he called.

Lambert paid not the slightest attention. He pressed closer to the mother sheep and purred.

Mr. Stork strode up to the sheep. "I'm very sorry that we've had a slight mix-up, Mrs. Sheep," he said, tipping his cap. "No need for you to worry about this vicious little brute. I'll just take him away and drop him in the jungle, where he belongs."

With that, the stork tried to pick Lambert up.

The next thing Mr. Stork knew, the mother sheep had butted him right straight up into the air. She had found a baby, and she did not intend to let him go again. And if he didn't look like every other little lamb in the pasture, she thought he was all the dearer for that!

Mr. Stork rubbed his damaged tailfeathers. "Heavens to Betsy!" said he.

Mrs. Sheep lowered her head as if she might butt Mr. Stork again. As for Lambert, he opened his little mouth and showed his sharp little teeth.

"Well, all right!" exclaimed Mr. Stork. "You can have him. You can have anything you want. After all, I'm only a delivery service!"

And he flew back to headquarters, no doubt intending to have a word or two with the dispatcher who had made up his bundle.

As for Lambert, he snuggled down to sleep

next to Mrs. Sheep. And when morning came and all the little lambs were being tidied up by their mothers, Lambert stood patiently while Mrs. Sheep smoothed down his little dark mane and fluffed out his tail. When Lambert was as neat and handsome as she could make him, Mrs. Sheep nudged him toward the little lambs.

And weren't those little lambs having a good time! Lambert scampered up to them with his rough little pink tongue hanging out. He was all ready to jump and gambol the way they did.

"Baaa!" The little lambs bleated a welcome to Lambert. "Baa. Baa."

Lambert tried to say "Baa." He knew it was

the thing to say. But when he opened his mouth, all that came out was a small "Meow!"

The little lambs had never heard such a thing. They tried bleating again, and again Lambert meowed.

The little lambs began to laugh. They laughed and laughed. And they leaped into the air, for little lambs love to leap. And they butted each other with their hard little heads, for little lambs love to butt.

At last, the little lambs began to sing a rather nasty song—the way small folk the world over sing when they want to make fun of someone who is different.

"*Lambert!*" sang the little lambs.
"*Lambert! Lambert!*
"*You can't even baa and you can't even bleat.*
"*Your ears are too big, and so are your feet.*
"*Your tail is too short, and so is your wool.*
"*There isn't enough for one bag full!*"

Lambert felt simply dreadful. At first he crept back to his mother to be comforted. It was true. It was too true. Lambert's feet *were* too big. And his wool *was* too short. Strictly speaking, he didn't have wool at all. He was a very strange lamb indeed.

Lambert's mother fluffed up his fur and smoothed down his mane, and Lambert began to feel better. That's when he decided that he might be a strange-looking little thing, for a lamb, but that he would do the very best he could to act properly, the way a lamb should act.

So Lambert practiced gamboling and leaping —even though he fell over his own big feet.

Lambert practiced butting heads with the little lambs—even though he kept getting knocked silly when he collided with the hard, hard heads of the little lambs.

And Lambert practiced bleating. After a while he would manage to get half a bleat out before it could change into a "Meow!"

And while all this was going on, Lambert grew and grew and grew and GREW.

Lambert's mother was very proud of him. No one in the flock had ever had such a big lamb.

But Lambert wasn't proud. Deep down in his heart he knew that he was good for nothing.

He couldn't leap and he couldn't bleat.

He couldn't gambol and he couldn't butt.

He couldn't do a single earthly thing, except hide behind his mother when the lambs teased him too badly.

And after he got very large, he couldn't even hide very well.

In short, Lambert was a strange, yellow, cowardly, sheepish lion, and not a wild and woolly sheep.

Time passed. Spring became summer and summer became autumn. The little lambs were grown now. They really weren't little lambs any more.

They were practically sheep. But they were still young and they still liked to gambol and butt, and they still made fun of Lambert and played jokes on him and sang about him.

Lambert kept right on being a good sport about it, but he *was* getting tired of it. He was

tired of being butted into the pond every time he bent over to take a drink. He was tired of grinning his sheepish grin whenever his playmates sang their nasty little song. Most of all, he was tired of being different.

Then, one night when all the sheep were fast asleep in the meadow, Lambert awoke in a terrible fright. He had heard an awful sound. He had heard a wolf howling in the forest just beyond the meadow.

Lambert raised his head and pricked up his ears and listened as hard as he could listen.

There it was again! And now Lambert could see the wolf. The lean, hungry animal came slink-

ing out of the shadows. Its cruel yellow eyes glinted in the moonlight. It drew back its lips and Lambert could see horrid fangs.

A killer had found the flock!

Lambert was petrified. He hadn't the faintest idea what to do. He trembled and pressed himself close to his mother. He hoped the wolf wouldn't notice him.

Nearer and nearer came the wolf. Lambert saw that the terrible beast was passing by some of the sleeping sheep. It was headed straight for him!

Lambert cowered behind his mother. The wolf had come for him; there was no doubt of it. He closed his eyes in terror.

Suddenly there was a scramble and a struggle next to Lambert.

"Lambert!" The cry echoed in the night.

Lambert opened his eyes and looked around. The wolf had seized his mother by the leg and was pulling her away from the flock toward the darkness of the forest.

"Lambert!" she bleated.

Now every ram and ewe in the flock was awake. The lively ones who were so quick to butt at Lambert were quite different now that a hungry wolf was on the scene. With a clatter of their sharp feet and a flit of their white tails, they jumped to hide behind rocks and trees.

"Lambert!" called Lambert's mother. The wolf had her almost to the edge of the forest now. In a moment she would be gone forever.

With a desperate kick, Lambert's mother managed to free herself from the wolf. Still the hungry beast stood between her and the safety of the flock. He advanced on her slowly, step by step. Without pity, he drove her back. Now she was not retreating toward the forest. She was going toward the edge of the cliff. Behind her was a

straight drop of hundreds and hundreds of feet.

"Lambert!" she cried. At the very edge of the cliff, she stopped.

It was too much. At the sight of his mother crouching in terror before the wolf, something snapped inside of Lambert. He forgot that he was a poor, miserable, cowardly, sheepish creature. In a twinkling, he became a raging lion.

Every hair in Lambert's huge, dark mane bristled and stood upright.

Lambert took a great breath. His enormous chest swelled.

Then he opened his mouth and he roared a mighty roar. It was a roar that would have made the most ferocious lion in Africa proud.

171

Having announced his intentions in this way, Lambert unsheathed his huge claws and sprang at the wolf.

The wolf had never before heard anything like Lambert.

The wolf had never before seen anything like Lambert.

Moreover, the wolf never wanted to hear or see anything like Lambert again. With a whimper, the wolf leaped over Lambert's mother and tried to hide.

Lambert was no sheepish coward now. He was a jungle monarch. He stepped past his mother and quietly butted the wolf off the cliff.

The rams and the ewes came out from their hiding places one by one. After a moment or two, Lambert's mother stopped trembling. She was so proud of Lambert that she didn't quite know what to do.

What a celebration the sheep had then! How glad they were that Lambert was one of them. They made up a brand new song that very moment, and they hoisted Lambert onto their shoulders and carried him around the meadow singing:

> "*Lambert, the sheepish lion,*
> "*Lambert, there's no denying*
> "*Now he's a wild and woolly sheep*
> "*Instead of a sheepish,*
> "*Wailing and weepish,*
> "*Little Bo-Peepish lion!*"

So Lambert became the hero of the flock, and he and his mother lived happily ever after.

As for the wolf—well, he was lucky too, after a fashion. He didn't fall straight to the bottom of the cliff. He managed to catch hold of a bush that grew out of a narrow crevice half-way down. For all we know, he's there still. He may be quite hungry by now. But then, he won't starve. The bush has berries every spring!

The Little Match Girl

It was bitterly cold; it was snowing; it was already beginning to get dark. It was the last evening of the year, New Year's Eve. In this cold and this darkness there walked along the street a poor little girl with bare head and bare feet. True, she had been wearing slippers when she left home, but what good did that do her now? They had been her mother's cast-offs, and much too big for her. They fell off her feet when she had crossed the street and a carriage drove by so fast that she had to jump to avoid being hit. One slipper she couldn't find at all, and the other was snatched up by a boy who ran away with it. He called back to her that he would take it home to use as a cradle when he had children.

So now the little girl walked along on her small, bare feet, which were red and blue with cold. She carried a lot of matches in her old apron and held a bunch of them in her hand. She had been trying to sell them all day, but nobody had bought any, or even given her a penny. Hungry and cold she walked along; she looked miserable, poor child. The snowflakes fell on her long golden hair, which curled so prettily around her shoulders, but that kind of thing was far from her mind now. Lights shone from all the windows, and the street was filled with the wonderful smell of roast goose. It was New Year's Eve, you see, and yes, that's what she was thinking about.

175

In a corner between two houses—the wall of
one came further into the street than the other—
she crouched and tucked her legs under her. But
she only grew colder and colder, and she didn't
dare go home, for she hadn't sold a single match,
nor earned a single penny. Her father would beat
her, and besides it was almost as cold at home.
They lived in the attic, and the wind whistled
through the holes in the roof right over their
heads, although they had tried to stuff rags and
straw in the largest cracks.

Her small hands were almost dead with cold.
Ah, even one little match would do her so much

good. If only she dared to pull one out of the
bunch and strike it on the wall, and warm her
fingers! She pulled one out—scratch! how it sputtered and burned. It was a warm clear flame, like
a tiny candle when she cupped her hands around
it. It burned with a strange light; it seemed as if
she sat in front of a big iron stove with shiny
brass knobs and a polished grill. The fire burned
so blissfully, it warmed her so well; wait, what
was that?—she had already stretched her feet
out to warm them, too, when the flame went out.
The stove vanished—and there she sat, with just
a little burnt-out matchstick in her hand.

She struck a second match, it flared up, and where the light fell on the house, the wall became transparent, like a veil, and she could see right into the room. The table was covered with a glistening white tablecloth and set with fine china, and there, steaming deliciously, was the roast goose stuffed with apples and prunes. And what was even more fantastic, the goose jumped off the table and waddled along the floor, with the serving fork and carving knife still sticking up from its back. Then the match went out and all there was to see was the thick cold wall.

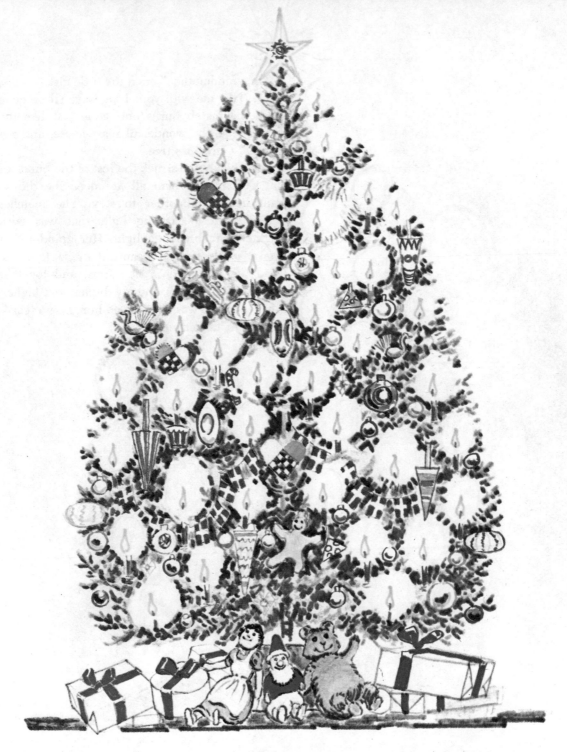

She lit another match, and now she was sitting under the most lovely Christmas tree. It was even larger and more beautifully decorated than the one she had seen through the glass door at the rich merchant's house at Christmas. A thousand candles blazed on the green branches, and many colored pictures like the ones that hang in shop windows were gazing down at her. She held out both her hands—then the match went out; the Christmas candles rose higher and higher until they became bright stars shining in the sky. One of them fell, leaving a long fiery trail.

"That means someone is dying," said the little girl.

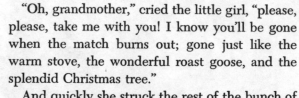

"Oh, grandmother," cried the little girl, "please, please, take me with you! I know you'll be gone when the match burns out; gone just like the warm stove, the wonderful roast goose, and the splendid Christmas tree."

And quickly she struck the rest of the bunch of matches and lit them all at once. She did so want her grandmother to stay. The matches burned with a dazzling light that was even brighter than broad daylight. Her grandmother had never looked so beautiful or so tall. She lifted the little girl in her arms, and together they flew in splendor and joy, higher and higher, to where there was no cold, no hunger, no fear— they were in heaven.

Her old grandmother, who had been good to her, but now was dead, had always said that when you see a falling star it means that a soul is going to heaven. She struck another match, and in the beautiful light she could clearly see her old grandmother standing there, so gentle, so kind, so blessed.

But in the cold of early morning, huddled in the corner between the two houses, still sat the little girl, with red cheeks and a smile on her face—dead, frozen to death on the last night of the old year. The new year dawned on the little body that sat there with all the matches in an apron, the burnt ones in its hand.

She probably wanted to get warm, people said; nobody knew the lovely things she had seen, and with what glory she had gone with her grandmother into the happiness of the New Year.

The Sheperdess and the Chimney Sweep

Hᴀᴠᴇ you ever seen a real old-fashioned cabinet made of wood, almost black with age, and covered with all kinds of fancy carvings? One just like that stood in the living room; it had been handed down from great grandmother, and was carved from top to bottom with roses and tulips. There were the strangest curlicues between which could be seen the heads of deer and stags with big antlers; in the center of the cabinet had been carved the figure of a man. He was funny to look at, laughable in fact, and laugh he did—or rather, grinned. He had horns on his head and a long beard, and the legs of a billy goat. The children in the house always called him Commander-in-Chief-Private-First-Class-Sergeant-Billy-Goat-Legs, because that was a difficult name to pronounce and there are very few persons in the world who are given a title

like that; and to be carved in wood besides was also something to be reckoned with.

Yes, there he was, always staring at the table under the mirror, for on it stood a lovely little porcelain figure of a shepherdess. Her shoes were of gold, her dress was prettily gathered and caught up with a red rose. She wore a gold hat and carried a shepherd's crook. She was enchanting. Right next to her stood a little chimney sweep. His clothes were black as coal, but he, too, was made of porcelain, and was just as neat and clean as anyone else; he wasn't a real chimney sweep after all, he was just a porcelain figure. The porcelain maker might just as easily have turned him into a prince.

There he stood so nicely with his ladder, his face as pink and white as a girl's, and that was really a mistake, for his face should have been

at least a little smudged with soot. He stood quite close to the shepherdess; they both stood where they had been placed, and since they had been placed so closely to each other they had become engaged. Besides, they suited each other; they were both young, they were both made of the same kind of porcelain, and they were equally as fragile.

Near them stood still another figure. It was three times as big as they were. It was an old Chinaman who could nod his head. He,

too, was made of porcelain, and he claimed to be the little shepherdess's grandfather, although he couldn't prove it. He insisted he had authority over her, and that is why he nodded his head when Commander-in-Chief-Private-First-Class-Sergeant-Billy-Goat-Legs asked permission to marry the little shepherdess.

"Now there's a man for you," said the old Chinaman, "a man I'm almost sure is made of real mahogany. You will be Mrs. Commander-in-Chief - Private - First - Class - Sergeant - Billy -

Goat-Legs. He owns a whole cabinet full of silverware, not to mention what he has hidden away in a secret compartment."

"I don't want to live in a dark cabinet," said the little shepherdess. "I've heard that he already has eleven porcelain wives."

"Then you can be number twelve," said the Chinaman. "Tonight, as soon as you hear the old cabinet creaking, you will have your wedding, just as sure as I am an old Chinaman." Then he nodded his head and fell asleep.

But the little shepherdess cried and cried and looked at her sweetheart, the porcelain chimney sweep.

"I think I have to ask you," she said, "to please run away with me. Let us go out into the wide world, because we cannot remain here any longer."

"Whatever you want, I want," said the little chimney sweep. "Let us go now. I'm sure I can support you with my profession."

"I wish we were already safely off this table," she sighed. "I won't be happy until we are out in the wide world."

The chimney sweep comforted her, then showed her where to put her little feet on the carvings and the gilded foliage which ran down the legs of the table. His ladder was also a help, and soon they reached the floor.

But when they looked towards the old cabinet, there was a fearful commotion. All the carved stags were stretching out their necks and shaking their antlers, and Commander-in-Chief - Private - First - Class - Sergeant - Billy-

Goat-Legs jumped high in the air and shouted to the old Chinaman, "They're running away, they're running away!"

The little shepherdess and the chimney sweep were so frightened that they jumped up to the big drawer of the window-seat. In the drawer were scattered a number of playing cards. There was also a rickety little toy theater, on the stage of which a play was going on. The Queens of Hearts, Diamonds, Spades, and Clubs sat in the front row, fanning themselves with their roses; in back of them stood all the Jacks with their two heads, one up and one down, as is customary with playing cards. The play was about two young people who were not allowed to marry each other, and the shepherdess wept, for it was like her own story.

"I can't bear this," she said, "I must get out!"

But when they were on the floor again and looked up at the table, they saw that the old Chinaman was awake and that his whole body was shaking with rage.

"Here comes the old Chinaman," screamed the little shepherdess, and fell on her porcelain knees, so miserable was she.

"I have an idea," said the chimney sweep. "Let's hide in the big pot-pourri jar over there in the corner. Then we can lie down among the rose petals and lavender, and throw the salt in his eyes when he comes after us."

"That won't do," she said. "Besides, I know that the old Chinaman and the pot-pourri jar were once engaged, and after a relationship like that, there is bound to be some good feeling between them. No, there is only one thing for us to do, and that's to go out into the wide world."

"Do you really have the courage to go with me out into the wide world?" asked the chimney sweep. "Have you thought about how big the world is, and that we may never be able to come back here?"

"I have," said the little shepherdess.

The chimney sweep looked steadily at her and said, "my road leads through the chimney. Do you really have the courage to creep with me through the stove, up the flue, and into the chimney? Once we're there, I'll know what to do. We'll climb so high that they cannot reach us, and way up there we'll come to a hole which opens onto the whole wide world."

And he led her to the stove and opened the door.

"How dark it is in there!" she said, but still she went with him, into the stove and through the flue, where it was as dark as night.

"Now we are in the chimney," he said, "and look, look! Way up above you can see a lovely star."

And there really was a lovely star shining down on them through the chimney, as if to show them the way. They crawled and climbed—it was terribly hard, but up and up they went—and he helped her all he could, and showed her the best places to put her tiny porcelain feet. Finally they reached the top of the chimney and sat down on the rim, for they were very tired, which is not really surprising.

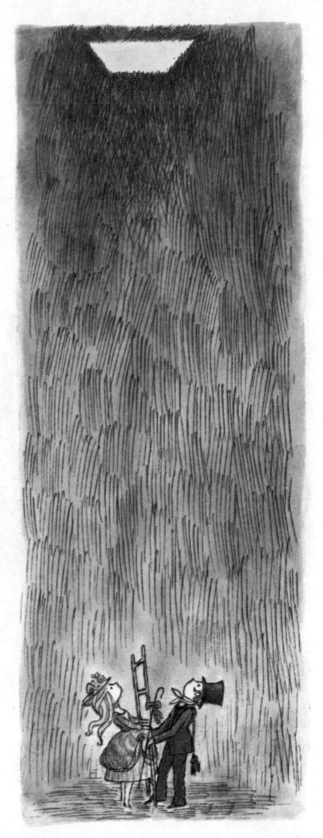

189

Above them was the sky with all its stars, and below them lay the roofs of the town. All around them stretched the wide, wide world. The poor little shepherdess had never imagined it this way. She put her little head on the chimney sweep's shoulder and cried so hard that the gold paint on her belt flaked off.

"This is too much for me," she said. "I can't bear it, the world is much too big, I wish I were still standing on the little table under the mirror!

190

I'll never be happy until I'm back there again! Now that I've followed you out into the wide world, the least you can do is follow me back home again—that is, if you like me even a little bit."

The chimney sweep tried to talk sensibly to her. He reminded her of the old Chinaman, and Commander - in - Chief - Private - First - Class - Sergeant - Billy - Goat - Legs. But she sobbed dreadfully, and kissed her little chimney sweep

191

so that he could not help giving in to her, foolish as it was.

And down again they went, with great difficulty, down the chimney, through the flue—it wasn't at all nice—and then they were in the darkness of the stove. They stood behind the door of the stove, hesitating. They peered out—oh, my! there in the middle of the floor was the old Chinaman. He had fallen off the table when he tried to follow them, and was lying there broken in three pieces. His head had broken off his body and had rolled into a corner. Commander - in - Chief - Private - First - Class - Sergeant - Billy - Goat - Legs stood where he had always stood, deep in thought.

"This is terrible," said the little shepherdess. "Poor old grandpa is broken into pieces, and it's all our fault. I'll never forgive myself." And she wrung her tiny little hands.

"He can still be mended," said the chimney sweep. "He can very easily be mended. Just keep calm. When they glue him back together again and put a strong rivet on his neck, he'll be as good as new, and will still be able to say many disagreeable things to us."

"Do you really think so?" she asked, and then

they climbed back up on the table where they had stood before.

"Well," said the chimney sweep, "this is as far as we've got. We could have saved ourselves all that trouble."

"If only old grandfather were all put together again," said the shepherdess. "Do you think it will be very expensive?"

And put together again he was; his back was glued and his neck was given a fine rivet, and he was as good as new, except that he could no longer nod his head.

"You've become awfully standoffish since you were broken into pieces," said Commander-in-Chief - Private - First - Class - Sergeant - Billy-Goat - Legs. "I certainly don't see that that was anything to be proud of. Are you going to let me marry her or not?"

The chimney sweep and the little shepherdess looked beseechingly at the old Chinaman, afraid that he would nod, but of course he was not able to do that, and he was, as a matter of fact, embarrassed to admit that he had a permanent rivet in his neck. And so the two little porcelain people remained together, and they blessed the old grandfather's rivet, and they loved each other until they broke into pieces.

The Musicians of Bremen

T<small>HERE</small> was once a donkey who had worked on a farm all his life. He had worked faithfully and well, but now he was old, and one day he overheard the farmer saying:

"Our old donkey no longer has the strength to work. We'll have to do away with him and get another."

"It's true," thought the donkey. "I am too old for farm work. But if I stay here, it's the end of me, and I wouldn't care for that at all."

So he ran off—or, rather, hobbled off, for his legs were as stiff as boards. After he had gone a little way on the road, he stopped.

"This is all very well," he said, "but what will

194

I do to earn a living?" He thought for a moment, then said, "I know! Although I have lost the strength to work, my voice is as strong as ever. I will go to Bremen Town and be a musician."

He let out a long bray, and said, "Beautiful, if I do say so myself. I'll make a fortune."

And he hobbled on, feeling quite cheerful. He had not gone very far before a dog came running up to the road. Puffing and panting, the dog lay down to rest and catch his breath.

"My friend," said the donkey, "you seem well past the age for running so fast. Why are you running, may I ask?"

"Because," the dog said between puffs and pants, "I am running for my life. My master wants to do away with me, because I am too old to go

hunting with him. But whatever will become of me now? How will I make a living?"

"How is your voice?" the donkey asked.

"As loud as ever."

"Fine," said the donkey. "I am running away, too. I am going to Bremen Town to be a musician, and two can make better music than one. Why not join me?"

The dog quickly agreed, and they walked along together. Soon they came to a cat sitting dismally in the center of the road.

"Madam Cat," said the donkey, "you seem to be in trouble. May we be of assistance?"

"Thank you, but I'm afraid not," the cat answered. "You see, I am getting too old to catch mice, and my mistress said she was going to do away with me. I ran off, but whatever will become of me now?"

"How is your voice?" asked the donkey.

"As sweet as ever."

"Then come with us," the donkey said. "We are going to Bremen Town to be musicians, and three can make better music than two."

"I would be most pleased," said the cat.

The three walked along, chatting of this and that, until they came upon a rooster hurrying up the road, running and hopping and flapping his wings.

"Friend rooster," the donkey said, "you seem to be in a great hurry."

"I am," said the rooster. "If I am not far from here by tomorrow morning, I will be made into soup, for I am getting too old to be good for any-

thing else. But what will become of me now I don't know."

"How is your voice?" asked the donkey.

"As magnificent as ever."

"Splendid!" said the donkey. "Why not come with us? We are off to Bremen Town to be musicians, and four can make better music than three. Our music will be the talk of the town, and we will be rich and famous."

"Nothing would suit me better," said the rooster. "I have always thought I should be a musician."

And the four of them went on together, talking about the wonderful music they would make. But when darkness came they had not yet reached Bremen Town, and they prepared to spend the night in the woods. The donkey and the dog lay down at the foot of a tall tree, while

the cat stretched herself out on a limb above their head and the rooster flew up to the topmost branch. He called down to the others:

"I see a light in the woods. There must be a house nearby."

"Let us go there," the donkey said, "for this place is none too comfortable."

"And if there is a house, we may be able to get something to eat," added the dog.

They went off in the direction of the light, and came to the house. The donkey, who was the tallest of them all, peered in through the window.

"What do you see?" asked the rooster.

"A table loaded down with all kinds of things to eat and drink," said the donkey.

"Good! Good!" the dog said.

"I also see four men sitting at the table," the donkey said. "And they must be robbers, for on the floor are chests of gold and bags of coins, not to mention pistols and swords and clubs such as robbers use."

"Not so good," said the cat. "How will we get the food? Oh, dear! And I'm so hungry!"

"We must drive the robbers away," the donkey said, and soon they hit upon a plan. The donkey stood at the window, his two front feet on the sill. The dog stood on his shoulders. The cat

climbed up on the dog's back, and the rooster perched on the back of the cat.

"Ready?" whispered the donkey. "One, and two, and—"

Then the donkey brayed, "Hee haw! Hee haw!"
The dog barked, "Woof, woof!"
The cat meowed, "Meow, meow!"
The rooster crowed, "Cock-a-doodle-do!"
"Help!" shouted the frightened robbers, rushing out of the house and into the woods.

The donkey and his three friends went into the house, sat down at the table, and had a feast. When they had eaten and drunk as much as they

could hold, they put out the light and went to sleep.

After a while, one of the robbers came creeping up to the house. He had been sent by his companions to see if it was safe for them to return.

"Everything seems quiet," he said. "We were fools to run away and leave all that gold behind."

Quietly he pushed open the door and went in-

side. But in the darkness he stumbled over a stool, which fell to the floor with a clatter. Hissing and spitting, her eyes gleaming, the cat leaped up at the robber and scratched his face. The dog bit him on the leg. The donkey kicked him, and the rooster flapped his wings and crowed, "Cock-a-doodle-do! Cock-a-doodle-do!"

The robber burst out of the house and limped back to his companions as fast as he could, trembling with fear.

"We can never go back to the house!" he said. "A witch with terrible eyes scratched my face! A dwarf stabbed me in the leg, a monster with long ears beat me with a club, and someone clapped his hands and shouted in a voice loud enough to be heard for miles, 'Catch the scoundrel, do! Catch the scoundrel, do!' We must get away from here before they come after us!"

And so the robbers fled, never to return. The donkey, the dog, the cat, and the rooster decided not to go to Bremen Town. They remained in the house, and there they are to this day. And if you ever pass by in the cool of the evening, you will hear them making music together—*Hee haw! Woof, woof! Meow, meow! Cock-a-doodle-do!*

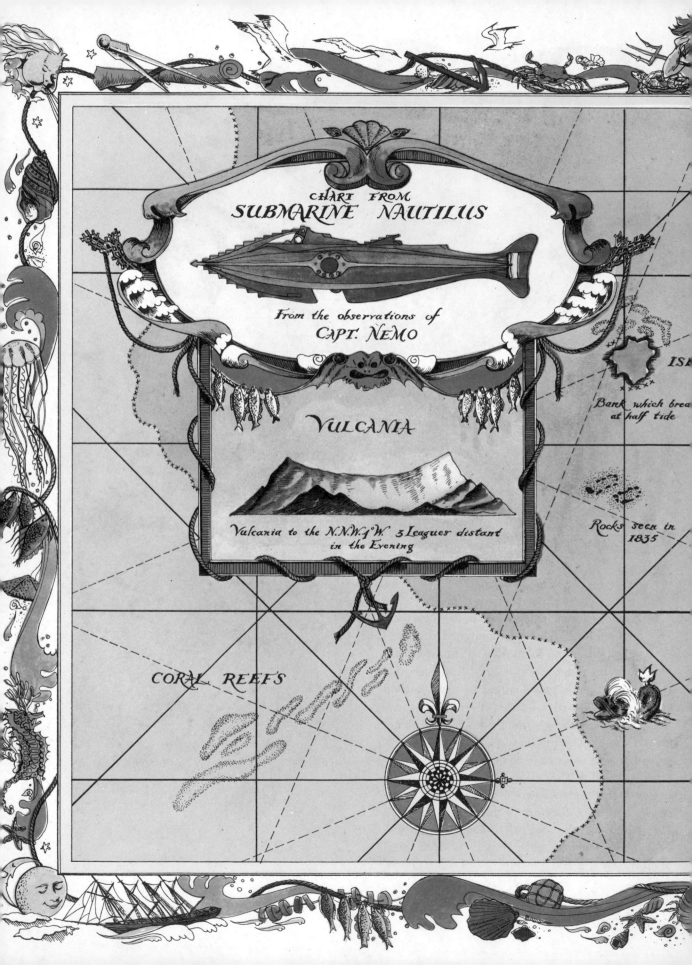

CHART FROM
SUBMARINE NAUTILUS

From the observations of
CAPT. NEMO

VULCANIA

Vulcania to the N.N.W. ¼ W. 3 Leagues distant
in the Evening

ISL

Bank which brea
at half tide

Rocks seen in
1835

CORAL REEFS

20,000 Leagues Under the Sea

It was a night in the year 1868. The steamship "Golden Arrow" was churning through the rolling waters of the South Seas. There was no moon. Only a few lonely-looking stars hung in the midnight sky.

On the deck of the "Golden Arrow" a group of sailors were singing to the music of a concertina. Now and then the music faded. When it did, the sailors' singing faded, too. And fear came into the eyes of all the men as they looked out at the restless ocean.

Once when the music and singing faded, the concertinist turned to the man beside him. "They say The Monster appears on nights like this," he whispered.

The second sailor shuddered. "'Tis bad luck to speak of It," he said, making a sign with his fingers. It was a sign used by sailormen to keep bad luck away.

The other sailors saw the sign and knew why their shipmate had made it. So each of them made it, too, and each scowled at the concertinist because he had mentioned The Monster.

None of them knew exactly what The Monster was. They only knew it roamed these South Seas and had sunk many ships. Most of the ships had gone down with all on board.

However, there had been a few survivors. From these men, the world had learned The Monster was a creature that breathed fire and

ripped apart strong ships as easily as a child might rip a piece of paper.

It was no wonder, therefore, that the men aboard the "Golden Arrow" stared at the sea with frightened eyes.

Could they have seen below the ocean's surface they would have been even more frightened. For they would have seen a great, ghostly shape slipping silently through the depths. Seaweed dripped from its hideous head and jagged beak and huge, frog-like eyes.

Suddenly a sighing sound rose from the ghostly shape. And it shot upwards, breaking the ocean's surface with its jagged beak.

Now the frog-eyes lighted up, sending long beams of blinding whiteness across the waters.

On board the "Golden Arrow" the sailors froze in terror.

"The Monster!" screamed the concertinist.

The other sailors took up the cry.

"The Monster! The Monster!" they screamed.

A tremendous roar rose above their screams. Then the ocean frothed as the horrible creature streaked toward the steamship. Behind it a strange yellow glow spread over the water.

A moment later the creature struck the "Golden Arrow" squarely amidships. Then it raced on, apparently unharmed by the collision.

The "Golden Arrow" tipped crazily. The foremast crashed to the deck, pulling sails and rigging and spars down with it. With thunderous noises, the ship's timbers came apart. And her engines hissed as the sea waters rushed over them.

Some of the crew ran for the lifeboats. Others jumped overboard. Some men screamed, and others prayed.

Suddenly the "Golden Arrow's" bow dipped into the water. Lower and lower it dipped until the ship looked as if she were standing on her bow. For a long moment she teetered there. Then she plunged downward.

And on the broad, black ocean nothing moved except a bobbing lifeboat.

In the bottom of the boat lay two men. Their names were Billy Johnson and Mike Magee. They were the only survivors of the "Golden Arrow."

Two days went by. By the morning of the third day, Billy and Mike were weak from hunger and thirst. They were too weak to row or to care where the lifeboat drifted.

Suddenly Billy saw smoke on the horizon. It looked like a broad black ribbon against the cloudless sky. "Look, Mike!" he cried. "A boat!"

Mike squinted in the direction Billy was pointing. "She's coming this way!" he exclaimed.

Billy took off his jacket and tied it, by the

sleeve, to one of the oars. Then he raised the oar to an upright position. The jacket caught the wind and bellied out like a sail.

By this time the ship was closer. Finally she was close enough for Mike and Billy to read her name—"Nancy Lee."

"Suppose the lookout doesn't spy us?" fretted Mike.

Billy swallowed hard. "Then we're done for, matey," he said.

However, the lookout of the "Nancy Lee" had sharp eyes—and a fine telescope. He had already spotted the bellying jacketsail and had reported it to the captain. And, at that very moment, some of the "Nancy Lee's" sailors were preparing to lower a longboat.

In a short while, friendly hands were helping Billy and Mike up the ship's ladder to the deck of the "Nancy Lee."

Three weeks later, Billy and Mike—and the "Nancy Lee"—were back in San Francisco.

An Invitation

Several weeks went by. More stories of ships sunk by the dreaded Monster reached San Francisco, and sailors refused to ship out even at double wages.

Every day an agent of the Great Western Company went out into the streets to talk to the sailors. He tried to persuade them to ship out on one of the Great Western's boats. But the sailors would not listen to him. Instead, they did their best to outshout him.

One day a giant of a man named Casey Moore not only shouted but waved a stout stick. This scared the agent and he ran away down the street.

Casey climbed to the back of a nearby wagon. "Listen to me, mates!" he yelled, waving the stout stick wildly. "If you ship out, you'll never get back to 'Frisco alive!"

"Who says so?" came a voice from the crowd. A broad-shouldered man pushed through to the

front row, crossed to the wagon and stood there, looking up at Casey.

"I say so!" Casey bellowed. "Who are you?"

"My name's Ned Land," replied the other man. "I'm a master harpooner. I don't believe in The Monster."

"Men have seen it," scowled Casey.

"Men see many strange things when they've been at sea a long time," said Ned Land.

Billy Johnson, who was in the crowd, stepped forward. "That's true," he said. "But this monster is as real as the hair on your head. 'Tis a cable length long from beak to tail, and has eyes like lighthouses. Its teeth are as big as a mainsail and—"

"And that's the tallest tale I ever heard," interrupted Ned. He faced the sailors. "You're fools for believing such a yarn!"

Cra-ack! Casey brought the stout stick down on Ned's head. The blow knocked Ned, face first, into the gutter.

At that moment, the agent came back up the street. Several policemen were with him.

"There he is!" yelled the agent, pointing at Casey.

The policemen started to run toward him.

"The cops!" yelled Billy, racing for a nearby alley.

Casey jumped from the wagon to follow Billy. But by now Ned had scrambled to his feet. He

grabbed Casey, whirled him around and smashed a hard fist against Casey's jaw. The blow knocked Casey back across the sidewalk into a large window.

The window broke into a hundred pieces. And Casey fell in through it! Immediately, two policemen grabbed him.

Two more policemen grabbed Ned Land, who was running across the street.

But nobody grabbed Billy Johnson. He was safely hidden behind a barrel in the alley.

A large crowd had been attracted by the excitement. It was so large it blocked the street and forced the driver of an open carriage to stop.

In the carriage, behind the driver, sat two men. The elder of the two was Professor Pierre Aronnax of the French National Museum. His companion was Conseil, his servant, who also assisted the Professor in his scientific work.

Professor Aronnax was paying no attention to the crowd. He was calmly reading a book.

However, Conseil stood up in the carriage and watched the policemen taking Casey and Ned Land away. "What a town!" he exclaimed. "I shall not be sorry to leave it."

Professor Aronnax looked up from his book. "Neither shall I, but for a different reason," he smiled. "The sooner we sail from here, the sooner we reach Saigon."

"Humph!" snorted Conseil. "Unless this carriage gets under way soon, we shall miss our boat."

"We can move now," said the driver. He cracked his whip and the carriage rattled on toward the dock.

A few minutes later, the driver pulled up in front of the shipping office. Professor Aronnax and Conseil hurried inside. Here they learned their ship would not sail because the crew had deserted.

"But we must get to Saigon," Conseil said to the shipping agent. "Isn't there another ship?"

"No," the agent replied. "There won't be any ship sailing out of this port until The Monster is destroyed."

When Professor Aronnax and Conseil turned away from the desk, three men stepped up to them. These men were newspaper reporters. They wanted to know what the Professor thought about The Monster.

"I have not thought much about it at all," the Professor told them.

"Do you believe such a creature exists?" asked one of the reporters.

Professor Aronnax smiled. "Many strange creatures exist in the depths of the sea."

Another reporter spoke up: "Could any of them drag a ship under the water?"

"If it were big enough," replied the Professor.

"Do not print *that* in the newspaper," said Conseil.

The reporters smiled at Conseil and said nothing. Conseil wondered why they smiled. Late that afternoon he found out.

Professor Aronnax had gone for a short walk. When he returned to the hotel room he was so indignant he neglected to close the door behind him. He slapped a newspaper down on the table and pointed to a drawing on the front page.

"Look at that!" he exclaimed.

Conseil peered at the drawing. It showed a hideous creature flying over the waves, carrying a large ship in its huge jaws. The words under the picture read:

"MONSTER EXISTS!" SAYS FRENCH SCIENTIST IN WARNING TO WORLD

Professor Aronnax paced the floor. "I did not say that!" he declared. "I—"

A voice from the doorway interrupted him. "Excuse me. I am looking for Professor Aronnax." The speaker was a tall, dignified-looking man.

Conseil bustled toward him. "I am the Professor's assistant," he said sharply. "He is too busy to see any more reporters."

The man came on into the room. "I'm not a reporter," he smiled. "My name is John Howard. I represent the United States Government."

Professor Aronnax indicated a chair. "Please sit down," he said.

Howard did so, and Aronnax sat down close by.

"When must you be in Saigon, Professor?" asked Howard.

"By the first of the year," Aronnax replied. "But the way things look now, I doubt that I will *ever* get there."

"The United States Government will get you there—on one condition," said Howard.

The Professor frowned. "What is that?"

"The Government is sending an armed frigate —the 'Abraham Lincoln'—to search for The Monster," explained Howard. "We hope to prove whether it exists. You are the world's greatest authority on the sea and its mysteries. If you will sail on this search, we will land you and your assistant at Saigon by the first of the year."

Aronnax thought a moment. Then he said, "Thank you. We will be happy to accept."

"Good!" said Howard. He stood up as he added, "Captain Farragut will command the 'Lincoln.' He is downstairs now. I would like you to meet him."

"I would like it, too," said the Professor.

When Aronnax and Howard had gone, Conseil looked again at the drawing of the winged monster.

"Humph!" he snorted. "I, for one, do not believe any such creature exists!"

A Wild Goose Chase

A FEW DAYS later the "Abraham Lincoln" steamed out of San Francisco harbor and headed south.

Professor Aronnax enjoyed talking to Captain Farragut and spent much time on the bridge.

Captain Farragut did not believe in The Monster. He thought the ship disasters had been caused by storms or hidden reefs. He thought

The Monster was nothing more than a narwhale, sometimes called a "sea unicorn" because of its long, ivory tusk. He told Professor Aronnax so.

"But I have never heard of a narwhale sinking a ship," said Aronnax.

Captain Farragut frowned. "Neither have I," he said. "However, whatever the creature is, he will not catch us napping. The 'Lincoln' is fully manned and well-armed. We also have a master harpooner named Ned Land aboard. We bailed him out of jail to sign him on."

When Conseil saw Ned Land, he recognized the harpooner as one of the street brawlers in San Francisco.

"Such riffraff!" snorted Conseil to himself. "I'll have nothing to do with *him!*"

When the "Abraham Lincoln" reached the South Seas, excitement gripped all on board. Day and night, the rigging was crowded with sailors. Each man hoped he would be the first to sight The Monster.

Professor Aronnax kept constant watch, too.

But Conseil was more interested in the warship's guns than in The Monster. He did not believe in the creature. The "Lincoln's" guns were big ones. They were able to hurl their cone-shaped balls almost ten miles. Conseil thought they could sink any monster of the deep.

A month went by. The warship steamed in circles, crossing and recrossing her course. Still there was no sign of The Monster.

A second month passed. And a third. The Monster did not appear.

One night Captain Farragut called Professor Aronnax, Ned Land and Conseil to the wardroom.

"I am calling off the search," said the Captain bluntly. "It has proved to be only a wild-goose chase." He looked at the Professor. "We will set you and Conseil ashore in Saigon very soon." With that, he strode from the wardroom.

"What do you think about the Captain's decision?" Aronnax asked Ned Land.

"It's all right by me," grinned Ned. "I'll be glad to go back to whaling. Not that I'll get rich at it but it's better than sitting around, letting my harpoon get rusty." He turned to leave the wardroom.

As he did, Conseil said, "Perhaps we are lucky, Professor. If we had met The Monster, it might have sunk us."

Ned turned back. "I doubt that, matey," he laughed. "I've been around some, and I've never seen a whale, or dolphin, or sea unicorn strong enough to sink a warship." He hitched up his trousers and took the companionway stairs two at a time.

Conseil sighed. "It is too bad, Professor. I know you have dreamed of seeing that monster mounted and stuffed—and in the French National Museum."

"It would probably have been too big for that," said Aronnax.

When Aronnax and Conseil reached the deck, Ned was playing his guitar and singing to a group of sailors.

At the sight of Aronnax and Conseil, Ned began to sing:

"There's no sea monster big enough
"To ever frighten me . . ."

Aronnax hooked his arm in Conseil's. "Come," he said. "Let us go below. Nobody on board seems to take The Monster too seriously. So perhaps I shouldn't, either."

The words were hardly spoken before a brilliant flash lighted the entire ship. But only for an instant. Deep darkness followed it. Then came an even brighter flash.

Ned dropped his guitar. The sailors jumped to their feet. Aronnax and Conseil ran for the rail to stare off into the night.

Captain Farragut, who was on the bridge, snatched up his telescope.

Boom! The sound—like that of a giant explosion—echoed across the ocean. On the horizon a pillar of flame shot up into the sky.

"A ship blew up!" yelled Conseil.

A second blast boomed across the waters. More flames shot up into the night.

On the bridge Captain Farragut lowered his telescope. "Hard over," he said to the helmsman. "Bear for that ship."

The helmsman obeyed and spun the wheel.

The Captain turned to First Mate Hardy. "Mr. Hardy, pipe all hands to quarters."

"Aye, sir," said Hardy, leaving the bridge on the run.

Now Captain Farragut stepped to the engine telegraph and jammed it over to "Full Ahead." Bells jangled loudly. Above their noise, the Captain shouted into the speaking tube leading down to the engine room. "Full speed ahead!" he bellowed.

The frigate shuddered from stem to stern as the engineer obeyed the Captain's orders.

The shrill piping of the bo's'n's whistle rose from the deck. Mingled with the piping was shouting and the thump-thump of feet as the sailors scurried to their stations.

The frigate swung in a wide halfcircle. Then she straightened out and steamed toward the flaming horizon.

Attack in the Night

WHEN THE "Abraham Lincoln" reached the scene, nothing was left of the flaming ship except floating debris. The frigate's engines slowed and the crew lined the rails to look for survivors.

No one spoke. No one moved. The silence and the darkness were as frightening as the explosions and the flames.

Aronnax stood at the rail with Conseil and Chief Gunner Carson.

After several moments, Chief Gunner Carson said, "I'm thinking she went down with all hands. But I can't figure out what made her blow up."

"Perhaps something struck her," suggested the Professor.

"It must have been The Monster!" shouted one of the sailors.

Captain Farragut heard the sailor's shout and yelled from the bridge. "There is no such creature!"

But at that moment . . .

"Ahoy the deck!" shouted the lookout from high above. "Floating object to starboard!"

"Which side is starboard?" Conseil asked the Professor.

"To the right as you look toward the bow," said Aronnax. He hurried to the starboard rail.

Conseil followed and saw a huge, dark shape rising out of the water. It looked like a great sea mammal.

Instantly wild cries rang out. Some were cries of fear; others were cries of excitement.

Conseil made no outcry. For the first time, he found himself compelled to believe in The Monster.

Ned Land darted into the nearest hatch, quickly returning with his harpoon.

The deck was cleared for action. The sailors rushed to their gun stations. Captain Farragut again sent orders to the engine room for "Full Speed Ahead!"

Meanwhile The Monster had pulled ahead of the warship. It was racing off into the night, leaving a strange yellow glow behind it.

"Into the longboat, Mr. Land!" shouted Captain Farragut when he saw Ned running along the deck, waving his harpoon.

"Aye, sir!" cried Ned. He climbed the rail and leaped into the longboat, now swinging free from the ship's side. And there he stood, holding his harpoon in striking position.

The frigate's guns thundered. But their shells fell short of The Monster, which was zooming away at terrific speed.

"It behaves very strangely for a monster," Professor Aronnax said to Conseil.

Conseil looked surprised. "You mean it may not *be* one?"

"Well, it is not a narwhale," replied Aronnax.

"I am sure of that. Why, it must be going more than fifty miles an hour!"

The guns thundered again. Black smoke poured over the deck. The frigate picked up speed. Chief Gunner Carson leaped up into the rigging and peered into the night.

"What's the matter, Carson?" yelled Captain Farragut.

Carson cupped his hands and yelled back, "She's showing us her heels, sir."

"Then hit her in the heels!" the Captain ordered.

Carson dropped to the deck to help the gun crews load and prime the cannons.

The guns roared and bucked. Orange fire

lighted the blackness as cannon balls whizzed off to straddle The Monster. When the cannon balls hit the water, they sent towers of white froth shooting high into the air.

Again the guns roared. And The Monster suddenly stopped.

"A hit!" yelled Carson. "She's turning!"

With Conseil's help, Professor Aronnax climbed up into the lower shrouds so that he could get a good look at the terrifying creature.

A terrible moaning sound rose above the roar of the guns. Long beams of blinding whiteness swept over the frigate. The Monster gathered speed and came charging toward the warship.

"Get your helm up!" shouted Captain Farragut.

Conseil did not have to ask what that meant. He knew. It meant that the helmsman should turn the ship.

The helmsman spun the wheel. The warship started a turn. But The Monster was moving too fast. It struck the frigate on the starboard side. There was a grinding crash, and the ship tilted crazily. Timbers flew in all directions.

The force of the crash broke the ropes holding the longboat. It tumbled bow-first into the sea,

throwing Ned Land into the water where an enormous wave carried him away.

A tall ventilator toppled over, smacked into the starboard rail and swept Professor Aronnax overboard with guns and gear and ammunition.

Although half-blinded by the salt water, Aronnax managed to grab hold of a floating spar.

On deck, Conseil was peeling off his coat. "Hang on, Professor!" he screamed.

He climbed up on the starboard rail, took a deep breath and jumped. He was under water only a few seconds. When he came to the surface, he struck out for Aronnax, who was still clinging to the spar.

Conseil grabbed the spar, too. Then both men looked toward the frigate.

The "Lincoln" lay partly on its side. Its engines were stilled, and it was drifting away.

Conseil waved one arm. "Help!" he shouted. "Don't leave us!"

Professor Aronnax sighed. "They cannot help us, Conseil."

Conseil knew the Professor was right, so he did not yell again. He just clung to the spar and, with Aronnax, drifted slowly away into the darkness and silence of the endless sea.

Amazing Discoveries

Aʟʟ ɴɪɢʜᴛ long Aronnax and Conseil clung to the floating spar. When daylight came they found themselves surrounded by fog. They were both numb from cold.

"If we could only see something!" gasped Aronnax.

Conseil squinted through the fog. Were his eyes playing tricks on him? Or did he actually see a dark mass ahead? He kicked his feet vigorously to force the spar forward. Suddenly he cried, "Look, Professor!"

Aronnax raised his head. The dark mass could be plainly seen now. It looked something like a giant fish with a tall back fin. But it was not a fish; it was a vessel made of iron plates riveted to a hull. It was nearly two hundred feet long, with jagged prongs at the bow. Behind these prongs was a turret in which was a large, glassed-in porthole.

"It's The Monster!" gasped Conseil.

"I do not care what it is," said Aronnax weakly. "Let us get aboard."

Conseil pulled himself onto the strange vessel. Then, using both hands, he hauled Aronnax aboard. For a moment both men lay still, too exhausted to move. Then Conseil got unsteadily to his feet, and Aronnax sat up and looked around.

Conseil walked to the porthole in the turret. Peering through it, he exclaimed, "What a strange-looking wheelhouse!"

Aronnax stumbled to Conseil's side, and stared at the levers and dials and steering gear that almost filled the inside of the turret. "Conseil," he said hoarsely, "this vessel is a submarine."

"A what?" gulped Conseil.

"A boat that sails under water," Aronnax explained. "Men have dreamed of such a boat for many years. I wonder who made this one. He—"

"It can't be a boat!" interrupted Conseil. "It's breathing. Listen."

The Professor did so and heard a slow, sighing sound. It seemed to come from the other side of the turret. "Let us see what it is," he said.

When they rounded the turret they saw that several of the iron plates were tilted up from the deck. The slow, sighing sound came from openings below these plates.

"What are those?" asked Conseil.

"You might call them breathing-flaps," replied Aronnax. "The submarine is taking in a fresh air supply." He walked to an open hatch behind the first tilted plate and looked down. He could see a flight of stairs at the end of which was a patch of bright light. "Ahoy!" he called. "Is anybody aboard?"

No answer came from below. Aronnax called again. There was still no answer.

"It seems quite deserted," said Aronnax, starting down the stairs. Conseil followed.

The stairs ended at a narrow balcony from which more stairs led to a room below. This room was lighted by glowing balls in wall brackets. Other lights winked on a large control panel set into a bulkhead. At the far end of the room, a circular stairway wound up toward the wheelhouse. Through a side door a corridor could be seen.

"Why, it's as bright as day in here!" exclaimed Conseil. "And there isn't any gas or oil in those strange lamps, either."

"True," Aronnax said. "There is a great mind behind all this."

"And great evil," said Conseil with a shudder.

Aronnax did not answer. He was hurrying down the second flight of stairs.

Again Conseil followed—but more slowly. By the time he reached the lower room, the Professor was studying the many dials and winking lights on the control panel. Conseil went straight to the side door and yelled into the corridor.

"Hello!" he called hoarsely. "Ahoy!"

"Ahoy!" came a very faint voice from above.

Hurrying back to the balcony stairs, Conseil listened closely. The very faint voice came again. "Ahoy! Anybody aboard?"

"Professor!" cried Conseil. "Somebody's up on deck! Come on!" He darted up the stairs.

Aronnax did not follow Conseil. He went out into the corridor.

When Conseil reached the deck, he could scarcely believe his eyes. An over-turned longboat was bobbing alongside the submarine. Straddling it, and paddling with one oar, was Ned Land!

"The harpooner from the 'Lincoln'!" gasped Conseil. He was so glad to see another familiar

face that he forgot about thinking of Ned as riffraff.

"The Professor's handy man!" exclaimed Ned. "Was he saved?"

"Yes," Conseil replied. "I do not know about the others."

Ned paddled the longboat closer and leaped aboard the submarine. "Well," he grinned, "so this is the Professor's monster! I suppose he's below looking it over."

Conseil nodded.

"Anybody else aboard?" asked Ned.

"Not that we know of," said Conseil.

Ned pointed to the longboat. "Let's turn that right-side up," he said. "We may need it for a getaway."

Conseil hurried to help. Just as the longboat was righted and tied to the submarine's hull a rumbling noise sounded behind the two men.

The hatch was rolling shut!

Ned and Conseil rushed toward it but they were too late. It was tightly closed.

Ned tried to pull it open. "It won't budge," he said. "Let's see if there's another one aft."

"Aft?" frowned Conseil.

"At the back," said Ned.

They started down the deck, hanging onto the railing alongside the tall back fin. Suddenly Ned stopped. Caught in the railing was his harpoon. Eagerly he seized it. Then he hurried to join Conseil who had discovered another hatch behind the fin. They raised the hatch cover, propped it open with Ned's harpoon and hurried down winding stairs.

At the bottom of the stairs, Ned and Conseil found themselves in a hollow steel room with a heavy door at the opposite end. This door led them into a narrow corridor.

"We must find the Professor and get away before the crew returns," said Conseil. "I have a feeling they are evil men."

"So have I," said Ned, following Conseil down the corridor.

This corridor had steel doors on both sides. One of the doors was open. Conseil peered through it. "It's the kitchen," he said.

"You mean the galley," chuckled Ned. He went into the room. "We'll be needing water and food. I'll get them."

"And I will find the Professor," said Conseil, moving on down the corridor.

At the end of the corridor hung red velvet curtains, richly embroidered.

Conseil parted them and gasped in amazement. He was looking into a magnificent cabin. Rich Oriental rugs covered the floor. Beautiful tapestries and paintings hung on the walls. On both sides of the cabin were couches, upholstered in red velvet. Handsomely bound books lined wall shelves beside these couches. A large glass case, supported by iron legs, stood in the center of the cabin.

However, these rich furnishings were not entirely responsible for Conseil's amazement. Centering each side of the cabin were great, round, glass windows. Professor Aronnax was standing in front of one of these windows. He was staring, open-mouthed, out into the ocean depths.

"Professor!" cried Conseil.

"Quiet!" said Aronnax. "I am watching a funeral."

Conseil gulped and joined the Professor. Then his mouth fell open, too, as he saw what was taking place outside the submarine. He could see clearly because the sun's rays were piercing the water like huge, bright columns.

Dark figures, wearing strange-looking diving suits and helmets, were moving through the arches of a coral forest. The tallest of the figures

walked alone; apparently he was the leader. The others were carrying an oblong object wrapped in white cloth. And they were walking toward a tall cross of coral held upright by large stones. The leader stopped at this cross and folded his arms as the white object was lowered into a shallow grave.

Conseil could keep quiet no longer. "Professor," he whispered, "are those men the crew of this submarine?"

"They must be," replied Aronnax. "Look! They are filling in the grave with pieces of coral."

Conseil shuddered. Then he said, "Ned Land is here with a boat. We must get away before those men return."

"Of course," said Aronnax, watching the dark figures as they knelt around the grave.

Conseil tugged at the Professor. "We must go now!" he declared.

"Very well," sighed Aronnax.

When Conseil turned, he had another surprise.

Alongside the curtained doorway, through which he had entered, stood a magnificent gold organ. Its golden pipes fanned upward to the ceiling, which was a mass of iron and steel. A second curtained doorway was on the other side.

"Unbelievable, is it not?" said Aronnax as he and Conseil hurried toward the corridor.

"Indeed it is," said Conseil nervously.

As the curtains fell behind Aronnax and Conseil, the men kneeling by the grave rose to their feet. They bowed their heads while the leader raised his arm. It was his last farewell to their dead companion. Then they all began their slow trudging back toward the submarine.

Suddenly the leader signaled for a halt. He pointed upward and the men lifted their helmeted heads to look that way.

Above them was the clearly outlined bottom of the longboat.

The leader waved his arm. And the group moved on, swiftly now, toward the submarine.

Sentence of Death

As Aronnax and Conseil hurried up the corridor, Ned Land came out of the galley. He was carrying a jug of water and a large sack of food.

The three men hurried up to the deck, and Conseil and the Professor went directly to the longboat. Seizing his harpoon, Ned followed them.

"Shove off, lads!" shouted Ned, leaping into the boat. He snatched up the oar and began to paddle vigorously.

At that moment six of the helmeted divers popped up out of the water and seized the sides of the longboat.

Wham! Ned smacked the oar down on the head of the nearest diver. The blow did not even dent the man's helmet. So Ned dropped the oar and picked up his harpoon. With the harpoon, he jabbed at the diver. The man fell back, wounded. One of the other divers grabbed

the wounded man and pulled him to safety. A third driver yanked the harpoon out of Ned's hands.

In the meantime, Conseil had snatched up the oar and struck out at a diver with it. The diver ducked the blow. Then he grabbed the oar and jerked it away from Conseil.

The other two divers were forcing the longboat back toward the submarine. Professor Aronnax could not stop them because he had no oar or harpoon, only his bare hands.

Now more crewmen popped out of the hatch and swarmed across the deck to the longboat. And in a very few moments the Professor and Conseil and Ned were prisoners. They were marched along the deck to the hatch behind the turret. Then they were marched down the stairs to the room below the balcony.

Here a tall man in a sea-captain's uniform was waiting. His bearded face was stern and his eyes were burning. "Are you men from the warship that attacked me?" he asked Professor Aronnax.

"Yes," replied Aronnax. "We thought this was

a sea monster. We did not know it was a submarine."

"And what are your names?" asked the Captain.

Aronnax told him.

"I have heard of you, Professor," said the Captain. "I have read your books, too. I am Captain
Nemo and this submarine is the 'Nautilus.'" He
looked at the crewmen who were guarding the
prisoners. "Take Land and Conseil on deck," he
ordered.

The crewmen seized the two men and started
to drag them toward the stairs.

"What are you going to do with us?" cried
Ned.

Captain Nemo's eyes flashed. "Destroy you,"
he said, "because you came here to destroy me."
He motioned to the crewmen. "Take them away,"
he ordered.

The crewmen forced Ned and Conseil back
up the stairs.

Aronnax watched them go. Then he turned to
Captain Nemo. "You cannot kill them," he said.
"They have not done any harm."

Captain Nemo shrugged. "The sea brought
them," he said. "The sea shall have them back.
Come! Let us go to the salon." He walked toward
the door at the side of the room, and Aronnax
followed.

The salon turned out to be the magnificent
cabin.

When Nemo and Aronnax reached it, the Professor said, "If Ned and Conseil are guilty of
wrong-doing, so am I."

Nemo did not answer. He took a book from
one of the shelves. It was a book written by Professor Aronnax.

"You have a great deal to learn about the
depths of the ocean, Professor," said Nemo as he
flipped the book's pages. "I know everything
about them—all their secrets. I will share my
knowledge with you."

"But what about Conseil and Ned?" frowned
Aronnax.

"They will die," replied Nemo calmly.

Professor Aronnax squared his shoulders and
looked Nemo fearlessly in the eyes. "Then I
choose to die with them," he said.

Again Nemo shrugged. He flipped a wall
switch and, in the distance, a bell jangled.

"I am sorry you feel that way, Professor," said
Nemo. He turned to a crewman coming through
one of the curtained doorways. "Take him away,
Mate."

"Aye, sir," said the Mate.

"Then prepare to dive," Nemo added, as the
Mate led Aronnax toward the doorway.

The Mate saluted. "Aye, sir."

Nemo put the Professor's book back on the
shelf. Then he went into the chartroom to check
the dials on the large control panel. After this,
he climbed the stairs to the wheelhouse.

The helmsman was at the wheel. Two other
crewmen stood silently at the control levels.

Captain Nemo walked to the large porthole
through which he could see the after part of the
"Nautilus." The hatches and breathing flaps were
tightly closed now. Clinging to the tall back fin
were Professor Aronnax, Conseil and Ned Land.

Ned saw Captain Nemo at the porthole and

shook his fist angrily. Professor Aronnax saw Nemo, too, and lifted his head high as if he were not afraid to die.

Over his shoulder, Nemo spoke to the helmsman. "Ahead—slow," he said.

Bells jangled. The control levels clanked as the crewmen pushed them forward. And the "Nautilus" began to move through the water.

Captain Nemo gave the order to dive—but *very* slowly. The deck of the submarine slanted downward a little. Waves poured over the wheelhouse and over the three men clinging to the back fin.

The deck slanted a little more. The water swirled higher and higher . . . until it reached the waists of the men on the deck. Still Professor

Aronnax gave no sign that he had changed his mind about dying with his companions.

Suddenly Captain Nemo turned away from the porthole. "Stop all engines," he said. "Then surface."

The levers clanked again. Slowly the "Nautilus" started to rise to the surface.

The Mate came up from the chartroom into the wheelhouse. "Take the prisoners below," Captain Nemo said to him. "Lock them in a cabin."

"Aye, sir," said the Mate.

Out on deck, Ned Land stared at the Professor. "He isn't going to drown us!" Ned exclaimed. "He's changed his mind."

Aronnax nodded and said, "Before this is all over, we may wish he had *not* changed it."

Conseil shuddered. He almost wished he had not been saved. For he knew Captain Nemo was an evil man. And evil men did evil things.

A Strange Meal

It was an hour later.

The "Nautilus" was moving through the ocean depths. It moved so slowly it scarcely disturbed the hundreds of brightly colored fish swimming there.

Aboard the submarine Captain Nemo was in the salon eating dinner. There were three empty chairs at his table; apparently he was expecting company.

The salon was ablaze with light. The great round side windows no longer looked out upon the ocean. They were shuttered with metal panels. A steward was waiting on the Captain. He served the food from dishes on a nearby sideboard.

All at once, a large seal flopped into the salon. He was Snoopy, Captain Nemo's pet. He clapped his flippers together and flopped over to the table.

"Hello, Snoopy," smiled Captain Nemo. "Are you hungry?"

Snoopy clapped his flippers again and sat up on his tail. It was his way of saying "yes."

Nemo chuckled and popped a piece of fish into Snoopy's mouth.

At that moment, a sailor came through one of the curtained doorways. Behind him came Professor Aronnax, Conseil and Ned. They had changed from their wet clothes and were now wearing uniforms like those worn by the crewmen of the "Nautilus."

"Be seated, please." Captain Nemo nodded at the three empty chairs.

"Thank you," said Aronnax.

While the steward was bringing food to the newcomers, Captain Nemo said, "Your own clothes are being dried. They will soon be returned to you."

"Thank you," said Aronnax again. Then he added, "We are grateful to you for sparing our lives."

Nemo scowled. "Never mind that!" he snapped. "Just do not try to escape."

None of the other three answered him. They began to eat. The Professor and Conseil ate quietly—as well-mannered people always eat. But Ned Land ate noisily and smacked his lips over every mouthful. He also shoveled his food into his mouth with his knife.

"Mr. Land!" barked Captain Nemo. "You have been given a fork. Why don't you use it?"

"I get more food faster this way," chuckled Ned.

Professor Aronnax looked a little worried. He did not want Captain Nemo to grow angry with them, so he said quickly, "This is a delicious dinner, Captain."

"I'm glad you like it," said Nemo. "All our food comes from the ocean."

"Even this veal?" asked Ned.

Nemo smiled. "That is not veal. It is fillet of sea snake."

"Wh-what is this?" stammered Conseil, pointing to his plate.

Captain Nemo leaned over to look. "That is blowfish," he said, "with sea squirt dressing. Those preserves are made of sea cucumbers. And the cream is milk from the giant sperm whale."

Ned Land frowned at a dish of pudding the

steward was placing in front of him. "I guess I don't want any of that," he said.

"But it is very good," said Nemo. "It is octopus."

"Ugh!" cried Ned. He jumped to his feet, backed away from the table—and tripped over Snoopy!

When Ned crashed to the floor, Snoopy clapped his flippers delightedly.

By the time Ned scrambled to his feet, Captain Nemo was walking to one of the metal-shuttered windows. He pressed a wall button and the shutter opened. But not as a shutter usually does. It opened like the shutter in front of a camera lens.

"That window is a great invention," said Professor Aronnax.

Nemo nodded, pleased. "I call it a viewport," he said. He turned to Ned. "We are nearing the island of Crespo, Mr. Land. If you wish, you may join my men on a short hunting trip."

"I do wish," grinned Ned.

Conseil stepped forward. "I would like to go, too," he said.

"Very well," said Nemo. He pressed another wall button and almost immediately two crewmen appeared. Nemo pointed to Ned and Conseil. "Prepare those two men for the trip to Crespo," he ordered.

Snoopy flopped after the four men when they left the salon. The seal seemed to like Ned Land, because he kept close to the master-harpooner's heels.

Captain Nemo and Professor Aronnax lighted seaweed cigars and sat down on the couch in front of the opened viewport.

"I am curious, Captain," said Aronnax. "Why did you save our lives?"

"I may have use for you."

"Use?" repeated the Professor. "I do not understand."

Nemo puffed on his cigar in silence for a moment. "I am not ready to explain now," he finally said. "I do not know when I shall be ready to do so, either. In the meantime, you should find life on the 'Nautilus' pleasant and interesting."

"The submarine itself interests me most," said Aronnax. "I can scarcely believe I am sailing under the water—"

"—where all is peaceful," said Nemo. "The sea is a beautiful place, Professor."

"True," nodded Aronnax. "But aren't you ever homesick for land?"

"No!" Nemo's eyes flashed. "There is hunger up on earth. And fear, and fighting and slavery. Here, in the ocean, my men and I are free!"

Again the salon was filled with silence. Nemo broke it by saying, "I dread to think what men of the earth would do with an underwater boat like this one."

"You mean in a war?" asked Aronnax.

Nemo nodded. "I hope they never learn to make such boats," he said. "I hope they keep on thinking the 'Nautilus' is a sea monster."

"They will," declared Aronnax, "as long as you use those blinding lights and terrifying sounds."

Nemo's eyes twinkled briefly. "They are fine protection," he agreed.

At that moment, the "Nautilus" came to rest on the sandy ocean floor. In the viewport, Aronnax saw the wreck of an ancient ship. It lay some distance from the submarine.

Aronnax glanced, puzzled, at Captain Nemo.

"Why are we stopping?" he asked.

"We have reached the island of Crespo," replied Nemo.

Surprise swept over the Professor's face. "It is an underwater island?"

"Yes." Nemo waved his hand at the viewport. "There go my men now."

Aronnax peered out at the ocean. A party of helmeted divers were crossing the sandy bottom. Some of them carried axes and hoes and sharply pointed poles. Others were towing floating baskets that looked like fish-net balloons.

Only two of the divers carried nothing. They seemed to be having trouble just walking in the water. As Aronnax watched, one of these two fell to his knees. His companion helped him back to his feet and together, they hurried to catch up with the rest of the party.

"The two at the rear are Conseil and Land," said Nemo. "They will soon learn how to walk under water."

"I would like to learn how, too," Aronnax smiled. "I would like to meet the wonders of the sea face-to-face."

"Then come with me," said Captain Nemo, leading the way toward the curtained doorway on the right.

A Battle for Life

In the outfitting room, crewmen helped Professor Aronnax and Captain Nemo into diving suits.

"Take this, too," Nemo said to Aronnax as he handed the Professor a strange-looking object. "It is an underwater gun."

The gun felt odd in the Professor's gloved hand. The metal helmet, which was slipped over his head by one of the crewmen, felt even more odd. The helmet was very heavy. Aronnax knew he would not be able to hear through it. But he would be able to see because the front of the helmet was glass.

After putting on his helmet, which had a light on it, Captain Nemo led the way to the diving chamber. This was a round room behind a watertight door. In the ceiling was a large iron ring and in the floor was a round escape tube from which a ladder led downward.

Nemo and Aronnax gripped the ceiling ring tightly while air was forced into the chamber. When the air stopped coming in, water foamed up in the escape tube. Nemo started down the ladder, and Professor Aronnax followed.

The ladder ended at a small, sloping platform under the submarine's keel. Aronnax trailed Nemo down this platform to the ocean's sandy bottom. They both walked on the broad stub toes of their boots; it was much easier than trying to walk flat-flooted.

Captain Nemo led the way toward a great forest of coral as beautiful as any forest of trees on land.

Aronnax saw much that interested him.

Schools of brilliantly colored fish were everywhere. A barracuda charged into one of these schools, scattering the smaller fish right and left.

A giant grouper fish swam up to the Professor and peeked through the glass front of his helmet. Then, unconcernedly, it swam away again.

A shadow passed overhead, and Aronnax looked up to see a huge manta ray soaring by.

At the top of a little rise, Captain Nemo halted and waited for Aronnax to join him. When the Professor did so, he saw some of the divers trudging out of a tangle of underwater growth. They carried the fish-net balloons, which were now filled with clusters of seaweed and great quantities of shellfish, such as shrimp and lobster.

Off to the left, other divers were using their sharply pointed poles to dig more shellfish out of the coral. Ned Land and Conseil were with this group.

Suddenly Ned threw down his pole and scrambled up on a nearby coral ledge. He peered beyond it, then motioned wildly for Conseil to join him.

Conseil gulped when he saw what lay beyond the coral ledge. It was the wreck of an ancient Spanish galleon. In the shimmering water and tall, waving, sea grasses, it looked like a ghost ship.

Ned stepped around to face Conseil. Behind the glass front of his helmet, his lips were moving. Conseil knew Ned was suggesting that they take a closer look at the ancient wreck.

Conseil shook his head. He was afraid to get too far from the others. But Ned grabbed his arm and practically forced him down the other side of the ledge and across the sand.

Captain Nemo saw the two men moving away in the direction of the wreck.

But Aronnax, a few steps behind Nemo, did not see them. He was watching a great hermit crab burrowing deeper into the ocean floor.

In a very few moments, Ned and Conseil reached the galleon. The ship lay deep in the sand. Hundreds of fish were swimming through her rotted timbers . . . around the stumps of her broken masts . . . over and under her great rusted anchor.

When Ned climbed over the rail onto the deck, Conseil followed. He was afraid to board the wreck but he was even more afraid to be left alone. The sight of a skeleton sprawled on the deck sent shivers up and down his spine. And when Ned calmly stepped over the skeleton to duck into the main cabin, Conseil was so frightened he could hardly follow the harpooner.

But he did. He followed Ned through the main cabin and down a rickety stairway to what had once been a grand dining salon. Here were more skeletons, piled in dark corners.

"I am a fool," Conseil told himself. "I should have stayed in the coral forest. There I would have been safe."

At that moment Ned picked up a heavy timber and, with all his might, swung it against a door that led forward—toward the ship's bow. The blow splintered the door. Beyond it Conseil saw a ladder leading down to a lower room.

Slowly Ned backed down this ladder. And much more slowly Conseil followed.

The lower room was a clutter of old weapons, boxes and furniture. Amid this clutter, at the far end of the room, stood a large, brass-bound chest. Near it lay an ancient cutlass. Ned snatched this cutlass up and smashed the lock on the chest. Then he and Conseil lifted the lid.

In amazement, the two men fell back a step. The chest was filled with gold and silver Spanish

coins. On top of the coins lay a beautiful crown set with pearls.

Ned slammed down the lid, lifted the chest in both arms and started back toward the ladder. He had taken only a few steps when the room was suddenly darkened by a huge shadow.

Ned glanced up. A monster tiger shark was swooping toward him.

Conseil saw the shark, too, and fell to his knees behind an upended table.

As the shark lunged, Ned ducked, dropping the chest which cracked and spilled some of the treasure. The shark circled and lunged again. This time, the harpooner threw himself on the floor—and saw the cutlass lying only inches from his fingers. Seizing it, he jumped to his feet and struck out at the ferocious monster rushing him for the third time. The blade of the cutlass tore a long gash in the under-belly of the man-eater.

Maddened by pain, the shark zoomed away into the shadows at the back of the room.

At a signal from Ned, Conseil helped him push a rickety table under the ladder. Ned boosted the chest up onto this table. Then he climbed a few rungs of the ladder, Conseil climbing up behind him. Stooping, Ned tried to lift the chest but he did not get it off the table.

For the shark was back!

He hurled his thirteen hundred pounds of fury at the ladder, jarring Ned and Conseil off onto the table.

Under their weight, the table collapsed. And Ned, Conseil and brass-bound chest crashed through the rotting floor timbers to the ocean bottom. The chest broke wide open, spilling the rest of the treasure.

Although stunned, Conseil and Ned managed to struggle to their feet. They started to stumble

away . . . but again the shark found them. Jaws agape, he glided swiftly toward them. Helpless, Conseil and Ned fell back.

Closer and closer came the sharp-toothed killer.

Conseil closed his eyes, mumbled a little prayer and waited for the death blow. When it did not come, he opened his eyes. To his great relief and amazement, he saw the shark had gone limp and was rolling over on the sand.

Beyond the dying monster stood Captain Nemo and Professor Aronnax on a little rise of coral. Bubbles were rising from the muzzle of the underwater gun in Nemo's hands. He had shot the tiger shark, and just in time!

Now several divers marched up and over the little rise of coral. They seized Ned and Conseil and began to lead them away. Ned made wild motions at the spilled gold and silver coins. When the divers paid no attention to him, he tried to break away from them to go back for the treasure. At that, the divers seized him by the back of the neck and the seat of the pants, and frog-walked him back toward the "Nautilus."

Nemo and Aronnax followed. The Captain wore a grim expression that worried the Professor. There was no telling what this burning-eyed man of the sea was apt to do because Conseil and Ned had left their work to go treasure hunting.

Land, Ho

Nᴇᴅ Lᴀɴᴅ was angry. "Why didn't you let us bring back that treasure?" he barked at Captain Nemo.

"You were sent to get food," scowled Nemo. "You cannot eat gold and silver."

The men were in the submarine's outfitting room.

As soon as Nemo was out of his suit, he strode to a door at the forward end of the room and yanked it open. The compartment beyond was crammed with gold bars, baskets of jewels and chests filled with golden coins.

Nemo pointed to this treasure and said, scornfully, "We use such stuff for ballast aboard the 'Nautilus.'" He slammed the door shut. "After this, Mr. Land, when you are sent for food, *get* food! Or I shall certainly do what the tiger shark failed to do." He clattered up the stairs to the chartroom.

Professor Aronnax eyed Ned sternly. "I want to see you and Conseil in my cabin," he said as he headed for the stairs.

When Ned and Conseil joined the Professor, they found him worriedly pacing the cabin. Aronnax closed the corridor door and frowned at Ned.

"Nemo was not fooling," Aronnax declared. "He will surely kill you if you disobey his orders again."

"What about him?" Ned nodded at Conseil. "He disobeyed, too."

Conseil's face reddened. "But I—uh—didn't know you were going after treasure," he stammered.

"That's a lie!" shouted Ned. He clenched his fist as if he were going to strike Conseil.

Aronnax stepped between them. "We must not quarrel among ourselves," he said. "And we must do nothing to anger Nemo. It is our only chance to survive."

"Humph!" Ned snorted. "I know a better way. Let's take over the 'Nautilus' and that treasure."

Aronnax gasped and turned a little pale. "That

would be insane, Ned. You must promise me not to try it."

Ned shook his head. "No, Professor. I won't promise that. But I'll promise not to try it—yet!" He started for the door but turned back to add, "Nemo's crazy—like a mad dog. You can't be nice to a mad dog. You have to muzzle or shoot him."

Before Aronnax could reply, Ned was gone.

Aronnax sank into a chair and stared at Conseil for a long moment. "There is only one thing to do," he finally said. "You will have to move into Ned's cabin and keep a close watch on him."

"Oh, no!" exclaimed Conseil.

"Oh, yes," said the Professor firmly.

So, of course, Conseil moved into Ned's cabin. Neither he nor Ned liked being cabin mates. But Ned did not feel like arguing with the Professor, and Conseil did not dare to do so.

During the days that followed, Conseil kept a close watch on Ned. And Ned, who knew what Conseil was up to, chuckled every time he managed to give the smaller man the slip. Ned did this at least every other day. He was determined to learn the layout of the "Nautilus" and how the ship was operated. He also hoped to steal some of the treasure from the compartment in the outfitting room. He did not want Conseil to spy on him while he was doing these things.

Professor Aronnax was busy throughout these weeks. He was keeping a daily journal of this strange underwater voyage. Every night he wrote in this journal. He wrote about the underwater wonders he saw through the viewports, and of how amazingly the "Nautilus" rode out a heavy tropical storm. He wrote of Nemo's skill in steering the submarine safely through huge, jagged formations of coral.

But most of all he wrote about the ship itself; and of the secret power that ran it.

Once Captain Nemo took Aronnax down to the power room, a narrow place centered by a heavy-looking block. This block was topped by flashing lights and moving flaps. From behind heavy shields made of lead, they watched the lights and flaps for several moments. Then, without a word, Nemo led the way back up to the engine room.

That night, Aronnax wrote in his journal:

"Captain Nemo seems to have discov-

Elevation plan of the Nautilus

A: Forward Hatch
B. Arronax's Cabin
C: Nemo's Cabin
D: Wheel House
E: Forward Ballast
F: Chart Room
G: Outfitting Room
H: Diving Chamber
I: Main Hatch
J: Pump Room
K: Salon
L: Power Supply
M: Passageway
N: After Ballast
O: After Hatch
P: Arsenal
Q: Galley
R: Chain Locker

ered the secret power of the universe. This makes him not only master of the seas but of the world and all its peoples."

League after league, the "Nautilus" cruised . . . through vast submarine grottos . . . over black, yawning pits of the deepest oceans. Now and then, it surfaced to replenish the air supply. Once this occurred in the middle of a sea of towering icebergs. However, under Captain Nemo's skillful handling, the submarine sailed through them safely.

The next time the "Nautilus" surfaced, the morning air was warm, the sky was blue and sunny.

Captain Nemo and Professor Aronnax went up on deck. Ned Land saw them go and followed—but at a safe distance.

An island lay off starboard. From it, a long finger of land reached out into the sea.

Nemo pointed to this finger of land. "Will you go ashore with me, Professor?" he asked. Aronnax nodded.

Nemo strode down the deck, the Professor at his heels. From the open main hatch, Ned watched them. He was careful not to let them see him, though.

Near the rear hatch, several crewmen were opening a section of the deck. This action disclosed a small metal boat snuggled against the submarine's hull. The crewmen slid this boat down a groove into the water, then steadied it until Nemo and Aronnax—and two oarsmen—climbed aboard.

As the little boat moved away from the "Nautilus," Ned Land smiled to himself. Now he knew how he would escape.

Another for Davy Jones

THE OARSMEN beached the little metal boat on a small beach below a rocky headland. Professor Aronnax stepped ashore at once. But Captain Nemo delayed to take a telescope from under the stern sheets. Then he and Aronnax climbed up a narrow path to the summit of the headland.

Reaching the summit, Aronnax saw there was a large bay on the other side. Into this bay a wharf jutted. A large cargo ship was tied up to this wharf. A number of men, each one carrying a heavy sack, were moving up the vessel's gangplank. At the same time more men, with empty sacks hanging from their hands, were moving down the gangplank. These latter men headed for a train of loaded ore cars that stood on the beach. Guards, wearing white helmets and bearing rifles, were stationed at the gangplank, at the ore cars, and along the route where the men with the sacks were moving.

Off to the right were some unpainted wooden buildings and, off to the left, what looked like the entrance to a mine.

"That is the prison camp of Rorapandi," said Nemo. "It is called 'the white man's grave'."

"I have heard of it," Aronnax said slowly. "I thought it no longer existed."

"It will exist as long as it can make money for the hated nation that owns it," said Nemo. He handed the telescope to the Professor. "Look through this. You will see what a horror it is."

Through the telescope, Aronnax could see that the men with the sacks were chained together. When he saw a guard strike one of them with a whip, he shuddered and returned the telescope to Nemo. "What is in those sacks?" he asked.

"Nitrates and phosphates to make ammunition," Nemo replied. "Those pitiful wretches are loading a cargo of death."

At the strangeness of Nemo's voice, Arronax turned to look at him. The Captain's face was a mask of hate, terrible to behold.

motionless in the water. When this happened, the Professor began to pace the cabin floor. He knew what was coming and was filled with despair.

Suddenly, from the salon, came organ music. It was so loud and angry-sounding that it made the Professor's blood run cold. No one but Nemo could be playing the organ. And Aronnax realized that, through the music, Nemo was giving voice to his terrible, bitter hate.

In Ned's cabin, the harpooner and Conseil also heard the crashing music. Conseil shuddered and even Ned looked grim.

"Another one for Davy Jones' locker," said Ned.

The music ended abruptly on a thunderous chord.

"Now the horror will begin," thought the Professor.

He was right. A moment later, bells clanged deep within the "Nautilus." The submarine began to move—slowly at first. Then faster and faster it sped toward the nitrate ship, dark and ugly against the sunset-reddened sky.

A low whine echoed through the air. The blinding lights streamed across the water. And the whine swelled to a tremendous roar.

The nitrate ship began to turn as those on board awoke to their danger. But the ship was too big to move rapidly.

Nearer and nearer zoomed the "Nautilus," the sea curling past her hull like a giant, watery serpent.

Then she dove, striking the nitrate ship at bilge-level. The vessel tilted way over, rolled back and exploded with a deafening blast. Pieces of deck, hull, paddle wheels and masts filled the air. A great ball of fire rose into the sky. A second explosion set the shattered hulk afire from stem to stern.

Aronnax, Conseil and Ned rushed from their cabins in wild alarm, and hurried to the salon.

The viewports were closed. As Ned snapped the switch to open them, the "Nautilus" submerged.

At the same moment, the nitrate ship pointed her stern straight up in the air and plunged under the water.

"Professor," Nemo went on. "Once I was one of those pitiful wretches. When I escaped, I did not leave alone. Those who left with me are still with me—as my crew. We seized one of the cargo ships and fled to a place called Vulcania."

Aronnax frowned. "I have never heard of it."

"It is not on any map," said Nemo. "We built the 'Nautilus' and developed its secret power there. You will see it for yourself one of these days. When our work is done, we are going back."

Turning abruptly, Nemo started back down the path. He did not speak again during the return trip to the "Nautilus."

The Mate met them as they reached the deck. He saluted Captain Nemo and pointed toward the island where a black column of smoke was rising into the sky beyond the headland. "They are getting up steam," he said.

Nemo looked at the Professor. "That nitrate ship will sail with the tide, but the evil it carries will never reach its destination," he said.

"You—you are going to sink it?" gasped Aronnax.

Anger flamed in Nemo's cheeks. His eyes flashed. "That is my business!" he barked. "Go below to your cabin and stay there!"

As ordered by Nemo, Professor Aronnax stayed in his cabin the rest of the day.

At sunset the "Nautilus" surfaced, but lay

Through the viewport, Aronnax and his two companions watched the wreck float downward. Like a leaf tumbling from a tree, it rolled over and over while the "Nautilus" cruised closer as if to gloat over the death of its enemy.

When the battered ship was halfway to the ocean floor, another explosion came. The wreck flew apart. The blue of the water turned to flaming red. The "Nautilus" whirled upward.

Aronnax, Conseil and Ned were thrown to the floor of the salon. Furniture and lamps crashed about them.

Very slowly, the submarine leveled. The three men staggered to their feet. They were too dazed to speak—even when Captain Nemo entered.

Nemo eyed them and the disordered room. Then he snapped the switch to close the viewports and said, wearily, "Go to your quarters."

Ned and Conseil quickly left the salon but Aronnax was still too dazed to move. He leaned against an overturned table and stared at Nemo.

The Mate came briskly into the room. "The diving planes are damaged, sir," he said.

"We will make temporary repairs here," said Nemo. As the Mate left, Nemo turned to Aronnax.

"Did I not ask you to leave me?" His voice sounded as if he were very tired.

"Yes," said Aronnax. Taking a deep breath, he continued: "And you took me ashore today to show me a horror. I just saw a worse one, you—you murderer!"

"That was not murder you saw!" shouted Nemo angrily. "That was justice! Those men were dealers in death!" He clenched his fists and took a step toward Aronnax.

The Professor did not flinch. He, too, was angry. And his anger made him unafraid.

"The men of that hated nation took everything from me!" Nemo stormed. "They put me in prison! They killed my wife and young son!"

To Aronnax's amazement, Nemo suddenly sank onto one of the couches and covered his face with his hands. After a few seconds, he looked up at the Professor. "You do not understand the power of hate," he said in a quieter tone. "It can fill the heart as fully as love can." Again he buried his face in his hands.

For a long moment, Aronnax stared at the Captain. Then he said softly, "I am sorry for you." Turning on his heel, he walked out of the salon.

Destination Vulcania

WHEN NEMO ordered Ned Land and Conseil to their quarters, the latter went straight to the Professor's cabin. He found it most untidy, just as he had thought it would be. A chair was overturned. The bunk pillow was on the floor, which was additionally littered with papers and books.

"That explosion certainly upset things," Conseil murmured.

He began to tidy up but stopped when he came across Aronnax's journal. He knew he should not read it, but he was very curious.

Suddenly the Professor entered. He frowned when he saw his journal open in Conseil's hands. Snatching the book angrily from his assistant, he threw it on the desk.

"I—uh—was straightening up," stammered Conseil.

Aronnax did not answer. He sat down at the desk and stared into space.

"What a terrible man Nemo is," said Conseil after a moment. "He seems to enjoy killing."

Aronnax swung around in his chair. "It is not your place to judge him!" he snapped. "He will not harm you if you do as you are told. However, if you wander away with Ned Land again—"

"There is no danger of that," Conseil interrupted.

"Good," said Aronnax. "And stop worrying about Nemo. The world can use him and his genius. I must make him realize that—and I will!" He slapped the desk emphatically. "Do you understand, Conseil?" When Conseil nodded, Aronnax turned away, saying wearily, "Now please leave me alone."

Conseil shrugged, and hurried to the cabin he shared with Ned Land.

Ned was lying face-down on his bunk.

"Uh—Ned," said Conseil hesitantly. "I have been reading the profesor's journal."

Ned rolled over and growled, "So what is that to me?"

"I know where we are going," said Conseil.

238

At that, Ned sat bolt upright. "Where?" he rasped.

"To a place called Vulcania," said Conseil. "It is Nemo's home base. Nemo told the Professor about it. He has told the Professor many things. They are all in the journal. What is worse, the Professor seems to believe them. He has grown blind to our danger and—"

"Stop babbling!" interrupted Ned, getting to his feet. "Tell me more about this Vulcania place."

"I do not know any more," said Conseil.

Ned started for the door. "Come on," he said. "Let's try for a look at Nemo's charts."

Conseil did not wish to go, but he did not wish to anger Ned, either. So he went.

While Ned and Conseil were stealing toward the chartroom, Nemo and all the crew—except the Mate—were putting on their diving suits. They were preparing to leave the "Nautilus" to repair the damaged rudder.

"You stay aboard and keep watch," Nemo told the Mate.

From the corridor outside the chartroom, Conseil and Ned heard Captain Nemo's words and crouched back in the shadows.

When the Mate left the room, Ned hurried in. He went to a rack, pulled out several charts and spread them open on the table. "Keep your eyes peeled for the Mate," he told Conseil.

Conseil took up his watch at the entrance to the corridor leading aft to the salon. He was there only a minute or so when he saw the Mate part the curtains at the salon doorway and start down the corridor toward the chartroom.

Conseil whirled toward Ned. "He's coming!" he gasped.

Ned slammed the charts back into the rack, looked around wildly and saw a half-open door nearby. Shoving Conseil toward this door, he rasped, "Get in there! Hurry!"

They ducked through the door, closing it behind them, and found themselves in Nemo's private cabin. It was as magnificently furnished as the salon. On the bulkhead was a large chart. Ned rushed to this.

Conseil joined him. "Have you found something interesting?" he asked.

"Maybe," said Ned. "See this big 'V'?" He pointed to a large letter on the chart. It was circled in black and was halfway between the Equator and the Antarctic Circle. "I've got an idea it marks Vulcania." He scribbled on a piece of paper. "Find me the calipers."

Conseil knew what calipers were; they were like a compass, and used for measuring. He found a pair on the center table. As he reached for them, Snoopy the seal reared up from a settee at the far end of the cabin. When he saw Ned, Snoopy barked and clapped his flippers together.

"Pipe down, you noisy beggar!" cried Ned. Picking up a round float—the kind used to hold fish nets afloat—he threw it at the seal.

"Oh, dear!" wailed Conseil. "He wants to play!"

Snoopy slithered off the settee and, barking happily, came flopping toward Ned. The harpooner picked up a chair.

"Wait!" cried Conseil. "Talk to him!"

Ned scowled. "Talking won't do any good. If we only had some fish!" He snatched up a humidor filled with seaweed cigars and thrust it at Conseil. "Feed him some of these!"

To Conseil's surprise, Snoopy eagerly gobbled the first cigar and barked for more. So Conseil gave him more—one at a time—while Ned figured and scribbled.

"Hurry up, Ned," Conseil urged as Snoopy finished his tenth cigar. "I'm running out of cigars."

Ned nodded and went on scribbing. At that moment voices were heard in the chartroom.

"The rudder is repaired, sir?" That was the Mate's voice.

"For now," came Nemo's voice in reply. "We will complete our repairs at the base."

Dumping the rest of the cigars on the floor, Conseil headed for the side door. Ned was right behind him. They gained the corridor just as Nemo entered from the chartroom. He was looking back at the Mate so he did not see them.

"Whew! That was close!" exclaimed Ned when he and Conseil were back in their own cabin.

Conseil sat down on his bunk and mopped his face with his handkerchief. "Too close for me," he panted. "I'm through with prowling—"

"Wrong, matey," Ned interrupted. "You're going prowling again—right now."

"I am not." Conseil declared.

Grabbing Conseil's shoulders, Ned stood him on his feet. "I say you are! You're going to the salon and getting me some specimens from Nemo's big glass case."

"Wh-what kind of specimens?" gulped Conseil.

"The kind in bottles!" Ned pushed Conseil from the cabin and slammed the door. Then he went to the desk and again began to scribble.

When Conseil returned, six pieces of paper were lined-up on the desk in front of Ned. Each had a message scribbled on it. Each message read:

"Aronnax and party captives aboard monster submarine boat based Lon. 36 degrees 19 min. South, Lat. 164 degrees 27 minutes West."

From inside his shirt, Conseil took six specimen bottles and set them on the desk. "These hold everything from sea slugs to oysters," he said.

"Good!" grinned Ned. "Dump them down the sink. All I want are the bottles."

"What!" Conseil gasped. He glanced at the messages. "You—you are not planning to put messages in bottles and release them into the sea?"

Ned nodded. "It'll be dangerous," he said, "but it may work. And if it does, Captain Nemo won't be giving any *more* orders—ever!"

A Cannibal Island

Dᴜʀɪɴɢ the next few days, Ned managed to release all six of the bottles containing the messages. He did this so easily he decided to send out some more. As Conseil was not around, he went to the salon to get the bottles himself.

The salon appeared to be empty. But as Ned opened the big glass case, Snoopy the seal flopped out from behind a couch. As usual, Snoopy barked happily at sight of Ned.

"Blow me down!" Ned exploded. "Have you taken to spying on me, too?"

Snoopy barked again. He did not bark a third time because Ned found some seaweed cigars and tossed him a couple. While Snoopy was munching these, Ned thrust several specimen bottles under his jacket. He was reaching for another when Professor Aronnax unexpectedly entered.

"What are you planning to do with that?" Aronnax asked, pointing to the bottle in Ned's hand.

"Nothing," replied Ned, replacing the bottle in the case. "I was only looking at the specimens." He backed toward the chartroom door. Suddenly he felt the hidden bottles slipping and grabbed his stomach.

"Are you ill?" asked Aronnax.

Ned nodded. "The food doesn't agree with me." He staggered out, and down the little passage to the chartroom, as if he were in great pain.

Conseil was entering the chartroom from the corridor. "Ned!" he exclaimed. "Is something wrong?"

"I hope not," said Ned. "The Professor just caught me with a bottle in my hand. But I don't think he suspects anything."

241

Conseil frowned worriedly. "Ned will get us into trouble yet," he thought. "If the Professor finds out about those messages—"

The loud ringing of an alarm bell cut off his thinking. A light flashed on the bulkhead. Nemo's cabin door flew open and the Captain came through it on a halfrun. He paid no attention to Conseil but hurried up the staircase to the wheelhouse.

A moment later, the "Nautilus" went into reverse. There was a loud crunching noise, and the submarine jolted to a stop. The chartroom floor tipped, almost throwing Conseil off balance.

Aronnax rushed into the room. As he did, Nemo and the Mate clattered down from the wheelhouse. The Mate kept on going . . . across the room and up the steps to the main hatch. Nemo paused to eye Ned, who had just returned.

"Wh-what happened, Captain?"

"Our faulty rudder has caused us to run aground on a reef," Nemo replied. "We will have to wait for the evening tide to float us free." He turned to Aronnax. "We are just off the south coast of New Guinea Island, Professor. Would you like to go ashore for some specimens?"

"No!" snapped Aronnax. "I still remember what happened after I went ashore at Rorapandi." He stalked from the room.

A scowl crossed Nemo's face. Then he hurried up to the main hatch, which the Mate had

opened. Ned and Conseil followed him up to the deck.

The "Nautilus" was aground not too far from a bright beach, backed up by jungle growth.

"Look, matey!" cried Ned. "Dry land! I'd give anything to touch one of those palm trees."

Conseil sighed. "So would I, and so would the Professor. But he will not accept any more favors from Nemo—not now, anyway." He sighed again.

"It is too bad. I know he would have liked to collect some specimens."

A sly look came into Ned's eyes. "Maybe Nemo would let you go in his place," he suggested. "And maybe he'd let me row the boat."

Conseil pursed his lips thoughtfully. "It will do no harm to ask," he said.

Captain Nemo gave them permission to go in the little metal boat. "But stay on the beach," he warned. "The natives on that island are cannibals."

Conseil shivered but, with a grin, Ned said, "After that tiger shark, I'm not afraid of anything."

After five minutes of hard rowing on Ned's part, the little boat grated to a stop on the beach. Ned and Conseil leaped out.

"Ah!" said Conseil, stopping to pat the hot white sand. "I had begun to think I would never touch land again."

"Me, too," laughed Ned. He dragged the boat a few feet out of the water so it could not drift away. "Let's have a look around."

"In a minute," said Conseil. He squatted to dig some odd-looking shells from the sand. When he stood up again, Ned was at the edge of the jungle.

"Ned!" Conseil cried in alarm. "Come back!"

"You come here," yelled Ned. "I've found something."

Conseil ran across the sand. "I do not see anything," he said when he reached Ned.

"There!" pointed Ned.

Conseil frowned. "It is only a path."

"But it could lead to freedom," said Ned. "Come on. Let's see."

Conseil shook his head. "I cannot leave the Professor. But that need not stop you. Only—" he shuddered—"watch out for the cannibals."

"Hang the cannibals!" laughed Ned.

Conseil glanced toward the off-shore submarine. "You had better go quickly," he said. "Nemo may be watching us through a telescope." He held out his hand. "Good luck!"

Ned shook Conseil's hand vigorously, turned on his heel and strode off down the path.

The jungle was dense with undergrowth and trailing vines. However, the path was clearly marked. Ned had little trouble keeping to it.

Suddenly he rounded a huge tree and found himself in a clearing centered by a crystal-clear pool.

Running forward, Ned threw himself flat on the ground at the pool's edge. He dipped his cupped hands into the water. Then he froze in horror. Next to his own image, mirrored in the pool, was the reflection of a human skull!

Ned pushed himself up on his elbows to look back over his shoulder. Above and just behind him were many more skulls, each one grinning from the top of a bamboo pole.

In an instant, Ned was on his feet and running back through the jungle. Above the chattering of startled monkeys and the shrill cries of tropical birds came a new sound. It filled Ned with terror. For it was the thundering sound of savage drums!

The Monster in Trouble

Conseil heard the thundering drums, too, and raced for the boat. As he started to row for the "Nautilus," he saw Ned burst out of the jungle.

"Wait for me!" screamed Ned above the drums, which were louder now.

Ned came down the beach at top speed. Behind him arrows showered from the jungle, and a mob of painted, yelling savages raced out onto the beach.

Ducking the flying arrows, Ned plunged into the surf while Conseil awkwardly turned the boat around.

The savages paused to fire another volley of arrows. Some of these whistled about Conseil's head; others fell into the boat. But Conseil did not flinch. He kept rowing toward Ned and, in another moment or so, drew alongside the harpooner. Ned wasted no time climbing aboard and grabbing the oars.

The savages wasted no time either. They launched a fleet of outrigger canoes and came in pursuit.

Volley after volley of arrows whistled through the air. Luckily, none of them hit Ned or Con-

seil. Neither did the spears which some of the cannibals flung.

Sweat poured down Ned's face as he strained at the oars.

Finally the little boat bumped against the submarine.

Ned and Conseil leaped onto the deck. Hurriedly, Ned tied up the boat and raced after Conseil, who was disappearing into the hatch.

A shower of arrows followed them as they crashed down the stairs into the chartroom.

Nemo was standing in his cabin doorway. He wore a strange half-smile.

"Cannibals!" yelled Conseil.

"They're attacking us!" shouted Ned.

Nemo came on into the chartroom. "What else did you expect?" he said.

Arrows poured down the hatch. Wild shouts rang out on the deck above.

"They're coming aboard!" Ned yelled. Snatching up an iron bar, he leaped to the foot of the stairs. "Do something! Close the hatch!"

Nemo's face darkened with anger. "I give the orders here, Mr. Land!" he barked. "Stand aside!" He stepped to the control panel and stood there, waiting.

More arrows rained down the stairs and into

the steel bulkheads. Spine-chilling howls echoed through the air. Dark figures swarmed down the stairs.

Then Nemo moved, slamming a switch. Sparks crackled across the control panel. More sparks zipped, lightning-like, up the steps.

Shrieking wildly, the savages on the stairs turned and dashed for the deck. Here other savages were leaping about, screaming as the electricity Nemo had released crackled along the deck and hand rails. Sparks flickered from the mast and the control tower, whirling about the cannibals' bare feet and legs.

The terror-stricken natives swarmed overboard, swam swiftly to their canoes and tumbling aboard, took off for shore in panic.

"Well, that's one way to get rid of unwelcome guests," said Ned.

"I wish I could get rid of you as easily," snapped Nemo. "Take him in charge, Mate."

The Mate and two crewmen pinioned Ned's arms behind his back.

"What's this all about?" growled Ned.

"You disobeyed my orders," said Nemo. "You left the beach, intending to escape. The natives forced you to come back." His eyes grew cold. "You will regret that, Mr. Land." He gestured at the crewmen holding Ned. "Take him below and put him under guard."

The crewmen were hustling Ned down the stairs when the helmsman cried, "Captain! Smoke beyond the headland!"

The smoke proved to be coming from the stacks of a warship.

"We must break off this reef," Nemo said. "Blow all tanks! Full speed astern!"

The engines roared into action, shaking the "Nautilus" from stem to stern.

Below, Ned went sprawling into his cabin, and the crewmen slammed the door behind him.

"It's a warship!" cried Conseil.

In alarm, Aronnax hurried to the salon, Conseil at his heels. The viewports were open. Through the one on the port side, they could see the warship steaming toward them. Suddenly she turned to bring her guns broadside.

Up in the wheelhouse, Nemo gripped the helm tightly. The engines thundered, straining to back the "Nautilus" off the reef.

Above the roar of the machinery rose the screams of shells. The warship's guns had gone into action!

Nemo pressed his body hard against the wheel and ordered more power fed to the engines. It was done. And as the huge propeller pounded the water, the submarine lifted, inch by inch. Then, with a great scraping noise, she shot free of the reef.

Swiftly her engines were reversed and she headed for the open sea. The warship steamed in pursuit, firing her guns as fast as the gun crews could load them.

Crash! A shell tore a jagged hole in the "Nautilus" below the water line. The submarine tilted crazily. Bits of its hull whirled up into the air.

"Man the watertight doors!" shouted Nemo, struggling to control the helm.

Professor Aronnax and Conseil were trapped in the salon when the watertight doors at each end were closed.

"We are sinking!" cried Aronnax.

At that moment a dull boom echoed through the ship. The salon floor rocked like a seesaw. The viewport shutters closed. The lights dimmed. Then they blinked off, leaving only the light of the blue emergency lamps along the floor.

A New Danger

Like a gigantic stone, the "Nautilus" sank slowly down into the inky blackness.

Ned Land yanked open his cabin door. The crewman on guard pushed him back.

"This bucket's going down!" shouted Ned. "You can't leave me in here!"

For reply, the crewman slammed the door and locked it by fastening an iron bar across it.

In the salon, Aronnax and Conseil stared at one another in horror.

"Unless Nemo can bring this ship under control, we are doomed," said Conseil.

Aronnax nodded. "He will fight hard to save it," he said.

Nemo was fighting with all the skill he possessed. However, at the moment, it looked as if he would lose the battle.

When one watertight door after another gave way before the terrific pressure of the sea, Nemo ordered the emergency pumps turned on. The pumps' clattering and thumping, added to the rumble of the motors, almost deafened the crewmen fighting to keep the water from reaching the engines.

But the water pressed hard against the door of the engine room. Not even a hastily erected steel scaffold could keep the door from buckling. Water shot into the room from the door edges, quickly covering the floor and rising about the men's ankles.

Suddenly a crossbeam snapped and crashed into the main shaft of the engines. The shaft froze, stopping the engines and the pumps. Water poured over the power unit. Electricity crackled through the air. Smoke and fumes filled the room.

A moment later, Nemo raced into the engine

room. One glance was enough to tell him what was wrong.

"Clear that shaft!" he shouted. He strode over to the spare shaft, snug against the starboard side. "Disconnect the hoist!" he ordered. "We will use this spare shaft as a lever to pry the crossbeam out of the main shaft."

The crewmen worked feverishly, although streamers of blue smoke partially blinded them and fumes half-choked them. But at last the main shaft was cleared and braced.

Nemo yanked back a lever. One motor roared, then another. The pumps hammered. The exhaust fans whirred, sucking the smoke and fumes up through the ventilators.

And the "Nautilus" stopped sinking. Briefly, she hung suspended in the water. Then very, very slowly she began to rise.

Crewmen hurried through the ship, opening the watertight doors, checking the damage.

Nemo went directly to the salon where he found Conseil and Aronnax. The Professor had collapsed on a couch. At Nemo's entrance, he pushed himself to his feet.

"Are you all right?" Nemo asked.

Conseil nodded.

"I—I guess so," said Aronnax. "At least, I can breathe more easily."

"The fans are operating again," said Nemo. He glanced at the overhead dials. "We stopped sinking just in time. As it is, we have gone deeper than man has ever gone before." Snapping the viewport control switch, he added, "What we shall see out here now should prove most interesting."

The creatures beyond the viewport were weird beyond description. They were glowing with phosphorescent light. Some formed electric chains. Others flashed in all directions to burst into tiny bits of flame. And others were marked with shining patterns.

Conseil shuddered. "They are horrible."

Meantime Nemo had gone up to the wheelhouse and was watching the weird, glowing

creatures through the rear porthole. All at once, he saw a giant squid swimming in the submarine's wake.

"Emergency speed, all engines!" Nemo shouted into the speaking tube.

The "Nautilus" fairly leaped ahead but it did not lose the squid. The monster rushed for the stern—only to tangle with the racing propeller. The bow of the "Nautilus" reared up sharply.

"We're fouled!" yelled Nemo. "Full speed astern!"

In a flash the engines were reversed. The badly injured squid relaxed its hold and drifted downward. The "Nautilus" leveled . . . but only for a moment. A second giant squid zoomed from the darkness and lunged forward to wrap its tentacles around the hull.

The "Nautilus" sagged under the monster's weight. Then as the squid struggled to secure its hold, the submarine tilted from side to side.

Conseil and Aronnax were tumbled to the salon floor. The former stumbled to his feet, grabbing at a chain-guard for support. He was helping Aronnax up when his eyes grew wide with horror.

An enormous tentacle, bristling with suction cups, was coiling along the outside of the viewport.

"Look!" Conseil cried. "What is that?"

Horror spread across the professor's face, too. "A giant squid! The most ferocious of all the beasts of the sea!"

The squid pulled on the stern and the "Nautilus" dipped at a steep angle.

Up in the wheelhouse, Nemo shouted, "Call all hands to the chartroom! We must fight this thing on the surface."

The crew gathered rapidly. Each man armed himself with an axe, a harpoon or an iron bar.

"Stay clear of the tentacles," Nemo told the crewmen. "And remember the beast's only vital spot is between the eyes. You must hit him there to kill him."

"Surfacing!" yelled the helmsman from above.

The "Nautilus" broke the surface into the red afterglow of the sunset. Clinging to its stern was the ugly body of the giant squid.

"Come!" yelled Nemo, seizing an axe and snapping the switch to open the main hatch. "And remember! If the squid does not die, *we do!*"

A Rescue—And Fresh Peril

Before the crewmen and Nemo had taken more than a few steps, a long tentacle shot through the hatch and down into the chartroom. The men fell back and flattened themselves against a bulkhead. The tentacle lashed about the room, trying to get a grip on something.

"A grating! Quick!" barked Nemo.

Ducking under the sweeping tentacle, two crewmen ripped up a deck grating. They hurled it at the tentacle, which folded about it like a glove and whipped it up against the hatch doorway. Angered because the grating kept the tentacle inside, the squid lashed out again.

Attracted by the noise, Aronnax and Conseil came from the salon. They shrank back in horror when they saw what was going on.

"This way!" shouted Nemo, leaping into the passageway that led forward.

Two minutes later, Nemo and the crew swarmed out onto the deck.

Instantly the squid's second long tentacle uncoiled, knocking two men overboard. Nemo and the others headed aft, keeping close to the wheelhouse and chopping at the tentacle with their axes.

Down in the chartroom, Aronnax and Conseil ducked under the weaving tentacle to drag an injured crewman into the corridor. Here they heard Ned shouting.

"Open the door!" Ned cried. "Let me out!"

Conseil left the Professor to see to the injured man and hurried to unbar Ned's door.

"A giant squid's attacking us," panted Conseil.

Ned pushed the smaller man aside and raced down the corridor. As he reached the chartroom, the tentacle dropped the grating, writhed back up the steps and curled out through the hatch. Ned grabbed up a harpoon and raced after it.

On deck the Mate screamed, "Look out!"

The warning was too late. The long tentacle coiled around Nemo and lifted him up.

At this moment, Ned leaped out of the hatch. He glanced up, saw Nemo in the squid's grip, jumped to the top of the wheelhouse . . . and hurled his harpoon.

It was a perfect throw. The harpoon buried itself squarely between the monster's eyes.

The squid slid away from the "Nautilus" but it did not release its hold on Nemo. Slowly, surely, it pulled him under the water.

Snatching up a knife from the deck, Ned raced for the side and dove overboard.

Underwater, Ned opened his eyes. He was not

far from the squid and its victim. He could see that Nemo was unconscious and tightly held in the squid's death grip.

A few swift strokes brought Ned to the tentacle. Clutching it, he pried it away from the drowning Captain. Then he slashed out with the knife. The tentacle went limp. And Ned, one arm about Nemo, kicked his way up toward the surface. Breaking it, he yelled, "Throw me a line!"

Aboard the submarine, several anxious moments later, Nemo glanced blankly at the faces bent over him. When he saw Ned's, his memory returned. He sat up and said, in a puzzled tone, "Why did you save my life, Mr. Land?"

"Hanged if I know!" replied Ned. He strode away down the deck.

The Mate saluted Nemo. "Do you want Land put under guard again?"

Nemo shook his head. "Give him the run of the ship. It is the least I can do," he said.

The next day Professor Aronnax discovered his journal was missing. When he learned from Conseil that Nemo had taken it, he went to the Captain's cabin.

Nemo was standing at his desk, reading the journal.

"Why did you take that?" demanded Aronnax, pointing to the book.

Nemo smiled. "I was curious." He flipped the journal's pages. "What you have written is very interesting. Especially the part about Mr. Land saving my life. You seem to think he is a hero."

"He is," declared Aronnax.

Nemo shrugged. He stepped to the large chart on the wall. "Enough of talk about him. We are nearing Vulcania. Soon you will see the secret power I have discovered. The power that is all mine!"

"Have you ever thought of sharing this power with the world?" Aronnax asked the question a little fearfully.

However, the Professor need not have been fearful. The question did not anger Nemo. Instead, he said quietly:

"Yes. That is why you are alive today. I told you I might have use for you."

Aronnax's eyes were bright with excitement. "You mean you want me to tell the world about this power?" he exclaimed.

Nemo sighed. "I do not know. I would let you shout it from the housetops if I thought it would make men stop warring on one another. But—" He was interrupted by the sudden ringing of an alarm bell and the entrance of the Mate.

At the same moment the engines fell silent; the "Nautilus" slowed to a stop.

"We have reached the island, Captain," said the Mate.

Nemo turned to Aronnax. His face was dark.

"There are warships ahead, sir," the Mate replied. "They fly no flags." He left the cabin as abruptly as he had entered it.

Nemo returned to Aronnax. His face was dark with anger. His eyes flashed. "Warships!" he exploded. "Sent to destroy me! To capture my secret!" He seized the Professor by the arm. "Come! You shall see how I deal with them!"

Aronnax jerked his arm free. "I will come without force," he said.

"Very well!" snapped Nemo, striding from the cabin.

Slowly, and a little sadly, Aronnax followed Captain Nemo.

Vulcania

Tᴴʀᴏᴜɢʜ the lifting fog, Professor Aronnax peered through the telescope at Vulcania.

It was a rugged, rocky island, sided by steep cliffs. At one end a volcanic cone jutted into the misty sky. Between the "Nautilus" and the island lay a fleet of warships. Aronnax trained the telescope on a cliffside and saw armed men climbing it.

"Those men are the landing parties from the warships," said Nemo, who stood beside the Professor at the rear porthole of the wheelhouse.

Aronnax lowered the telescope. "It is too bad we did not arrive sooner," he said.

"It would have done no good," said Nemo. He turned to the Mate. "We must destroy everything before they reach the lagoon. Prepare to dive."

The Mate issued the order. Captain Nemo took the helm. The engines thundered, and the "Nautilus" plunged under the water.

Aronnax stayed by the porthole, staring out into the depths. Whatever was about to happen, he felt he must see it.

The submarine glided swiftly below the keels of the anchored warships and swooped close to the ocean floor. Suddenly, the searchlight flashed on. And the "Nautilus" zoomed into an underwater tunnel.

Barely two minutes later, the submarine rocketed out of the tunnel, rose vertically and broke the surface of a shimmering lagoon.

Aronnax could hardly believe his eyes. The lagoon was wholly landlocked by towering walls of rock. Along its shore were strange-looking buildings and machines, a half-finished submarine and a giant solar reflector.

The engines were silenced, and the anchor chain clanked loudly.

Nemo clattered down from the wheelhouse, brushed past Conseil and Ned in the chartroom below, and hurried up to the main hatch.

A moment later, Aronnax came down the circular staircase.

"What's all the excitement?" Ned asked the Professor.

"We are at Vulcania—Nemo's base," Aronnax replied. "The island is surrounded by warships. Their fighting men have already landed."

With a whoop, Ned bounded up the steps. At the open main hatch, he paused to look shoreward. Conseil and Aronnax crowded in beside him in time to see Nemo and two oarsmen push off in the little metal boat.

"Look up there!" pointed Ned.

Over the rim of the volcanic cone, tiny figures were pouring. Their weapons glinted in the sun. As they slid down the inner slope, they opened fire on the buildings, the little boat—and the "Nautilus."

Nemo brought the little boat alongside a small pier, leaped to the wharf and—through a rain of bullets—ran for a large building close by. Hastily, the crewmen tied up the boat and ran after him.

As bullets zinged across the deck of the submarine, the crew sought shelter behind the wheelhouse. Aronnax and Conseil and Ned ducked under the hatch.

Suddenly Ned tore off his shirt and bounded out of the hatch. "Hey, you, up there!" he bellowed, waving the shirt over his head. "Don't shoot! We're friends! We sent the messages in the bottles!"

A hail of bullets sent him flying back into the hatch.

He raised himself up, when the fire died down, to look shoreward again.

Nemo and the two oarsmen were returning to the "Nautilus" in a criss-cross of bullets. But, miraculously, none of them were hit. And soon they were safely back aboard the submarine.

"Every man to his station," snapped Nemo. "There is no time to waste."

Suddenly he winced, clutching at his side. Then he straightened and stepped down into the hatch, closing it behind him. Stiffly he made his way to the wheelhouse and took over the helm.

Only the Mate saw the splotch of blood on

Nemo's tunic. He said nothing, but his face grew sad. He had served with Nemo for many years.

Again the "Nautilus" dove, shot through the tunnel and out into the sea, gliding far beneath the warships' keels.

Nemo looked up from the wheel. His eyes were glassy but his voice was fairly strong. "Slow on engines . . . eight degrees down," he said. "Lash the wheel."

The faces of the crewmen paled. That order spelled their doom.

Nemo staggered toward the circular staircase. At the top of it, he collapsed. The men picked him up and carried him below.

Aronnax, Conseil and Ned, who were in the chartroom, stared in open-mouthed alarm when Nemo was carried past them into the salon.

"He has been injured!" gasped Aronnax, rushing out. Conseil and Ned hurried after him.

Nemo had been placed on a couch in front of the starboard viewport. His crew was gathering around him.

"Mate," said Nemo, "we are taking the 'Nautilus' down for the last time."

"We understand, sir," the Mate replied.

Ned started forward, crying, "You can't take us with you!" Two crewmen seized him.

"I am dying and the 'Nautilus' is dying with me," Nemo said. "Take them away, Mate. Lock them in their quarters."

The Mate reached for the Professor's arm but Aronnax stepped to one side. "Wait," he said. Then he turned to Nemo. "Captain, please listen to me. You cannot do this! This submarine is a dream of the future. You made it come true. Do not destroy it."

"If I do not do so, the warships will," said Nemo calmly. "And do not despair, Professor. There is hope for the future. When the world is ready for a new and better life, all this will some day come to pass . . ." His voice faded to a whisper. "All in God's good time . . ." He let his head fall back against the couch and watched the bubbles trailing beyond the viewport.

And the Mate and Professor Aronnax walked softly from the salon.

Hope for the Future

CONSEIL was in the Professor's cabin when the Mate ushered Aronnax into it. The little assistant was pale but calm, even when the Mate closed the door and bolted it.

Ned Land was not calm, however. He was struggling with two crewmen. "You're not going to lock me up to die!" he yelled.

The crewmen forced him through the door.

Suddenly Ned lunged forward, throwing his captors off-balance. As they crashed into the deck, Ned whirled, leaped back into the corridor and smashed the Mate back against the wall with a terrific punch.

Again Ned whirled. One of the crewmen was leaping toward him. Ned's fist shot out. It caught the crewman on the jaw and sent him reeling back into the second crewman. Slamming the door, Ned dropped the iron bar into place. As he did so, the Mate grabbed his arm, spinning him around.

This time Ned hit the Mate so hard, he fell to the floor, unconscious.

Ned raced for the wheelhouse. In frantic haste, he ripped the rope from the wheel and whipped back the control levers. Bells clanged. Motors roared. And the "Nautilus" nosed upward.

Ned lashed the wheel into position and vaulted down the staircase—just as the "Nautilus" struck an overhanging shelf of reef.

The crash sent Ned to his knees and jackknifed the forward passageway. Water poured through the broken hull. It gushed over the Mate, bringing him back to consciousness. He stumbled to his feet, fighting the rushing water.

Ned came staggering down the corridor. The Mate snatched a harpoon from the rack but before he could hurl it at Ned, the harpooner kicked out savagely. The harpoon flew from the Mate's hand. Ned's fist smashed against his jaw. And he fell backward into the swirling flood.

Ned shot back the bolt on the Professor's cabin door. "I've taken over the ship!" he bellowed, flinging open the door. "Let's get out of here!"

Aronnax had only time enough to snatch up his journal before Ned grabbed him and Conseil—each by an arm—and started to lead them down the corridor through knee-deep water.

By the time they reached the chartroom, the water was up to their waists.

"Get up under the hatch!" gasped Ned, pushing them toward the steps. Then he shinnied up the circular staircase to peer into the wheelhouse, from which water was pouring in a solid sheet.

"We're on the surface!" yelled Ned as he dropped back into the chartroom. He sploshed to the main hatch control and yanked at the lever. The hatch slid open. Water—and bright sunlight—streamed down into the chartroom.

Conseil started to crawl up the flooded steps but Aronnax turned back toward Nemo's cabin.

"Professor!" yelled Ned. "Come back here! That island's due to blow up any second!"

Aronnax did not stop. "I must get Nemo's records," he said.

Through the rapidly rising water, Ned waded in pursuit. "Hang the records!" he shouted, reaching for the Professor's arm.

Dodging Ned's grasp, Aronnax tried to push the harpooner away. "Go on," he panted. "Leave me alone."

"No!" yelled Ned. He followed the yell with a hard right to Aronnax's jaw. Then, as the Professor went limp, he dragged him across the room and up the hatch stairs.

On the deck, awash and rocking, Conseil was clinging to one of the lines that held the little metal boat to the "Nautilus." "Is the Professor hurt?" he cried when Ned came out of the hatch, carrying Aronnax.

"Not badly," said Ned. "Hurry! Get into the boat!"

Conseil scrambled into the boat. Ned boosted Aronnax over the side, then slashed at the lines with his knife.

At that moment, Snoopy the seal flopped out of the hatch and, barking wildly, began swimming along the deck.

Ned grabbed the side of the boat, holding it close to the "Nautilus." "We can't leave him!" he shouted. "Here, Snoopy!"

When Snoopy was safely in the boat, Ned shoved clear of the submarine, leaped aboard himself, seized the oars and began rowing.

Conseil bathed the Professor's face with sea water. And Aronnax quickly returned to consciousness.

Suddenly a dull boom thundered across the waters.

Ned looked back toward the island. "There she blows!" he yelled.

And Vulcania exploded!

Great chunks of earth whirled into the sky to burst into huge white puffs and scatter sparks. Flaming rocks hissed into the water.

Now a mammoth fireball spun up into the darkening sky. And a wall of foaming water rushed over the sea . . . over the warships . . . on toward the "Nautilus."

The submarine reared up, its bow toward the sky. For a long moment it hung there—black against the glare of the red-hot island slowly sinking behind it. Then the "Nautilus," for the last time, plunged into the ocean depths.

The little boat rocked dangerously in the great waves. But Ned's skillful handling prevented it from overturning.

Against the horizon, an enormous mushroom-shaped cloud billowed up into the sky.

"Perhaps that is just as well," said Aronnax slowly. "Perhaps the world is not yet ready to learn and understand Nemo's secrets."

The horrifying mushroom-shaped cloud was spreading now, almost filling the sky. The three men stared at it, and thought of the strange man whose genius had caused it.

But, of course, only Professor Aronnax thought of that man's last words: "There is hope for the future. . . . In God's good time."

As Aronnax whispered these words to himself, the sun broke through behind the hideous cloud.

"It is the golden glow of the dawn of a new day," said Aronnax almost as if he were saying a prayer.

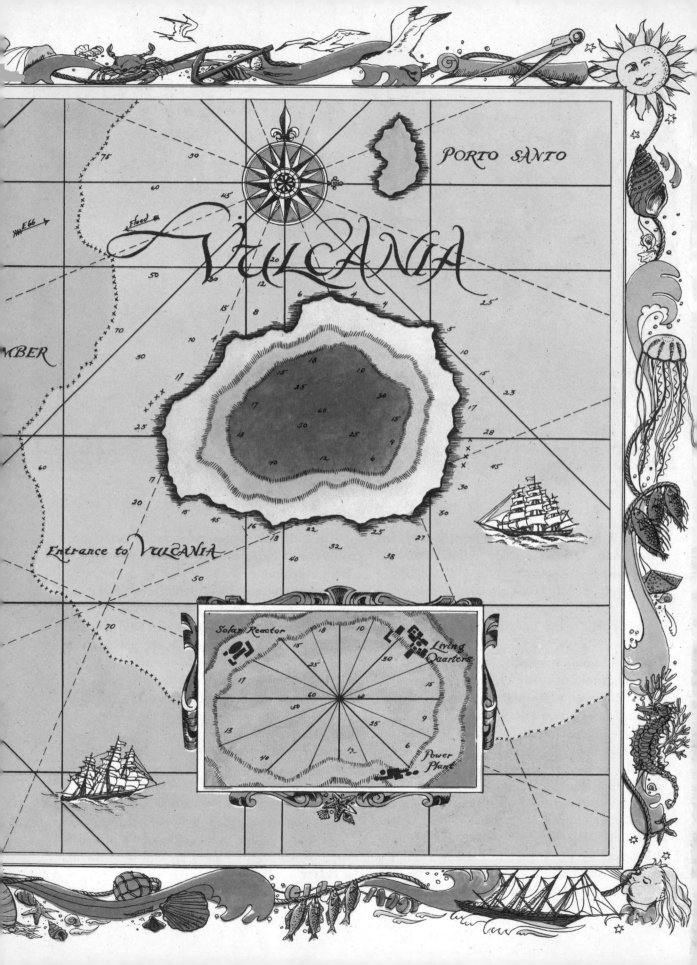

PORTO SANTO

VULCANIA

Entrance to VULCANIA

Solar Reactor

Living Quarters

Power Plant